Loose Ends

Fifteenth of the Prairie Preacher Series

PJ Hoge

iUniverse LLC
Bloomington

LOOSE ENDS
FIFTEENTH OF THE PRAIRIE PREACHER SERIES

iUniverse books may be ordered through booksellers or by contacting:

iUniverse
1663 Liberty Drive
Bloomington, IN 47403
www.iuniverse.com
1-800-Authors (1-800-288-4677)

Because of the dynamic nature of the Internet, any web addresses or links contained in this book may have changed since publication and may no longer be valid. The views expressed in this work are solely those of the author and do not necessarily reflect the views of the publisher, and the publisher hereby disclaims any responsibility for them.

Any people depicted in stock imagery provided by Thinkstock are models, and such images are being used for illustrative purposes only.

Certain stock imagery © Thinkstock.

ISBN: 978-1-4917-0060-0 (sc)
ISBN: 978-1-4917-0061-7 (e)

Library of Congress Control Number: 2013913173

Printed in the United States of America.

iUniverse rev. date: 7/29/2013

Special thanks to Melissa, Terrie and Mike H.

OTHER BOOKS

1967
Fort Point,
Massachusetts

Work was feverish inside the large chop shop on Farnsworth Avenue, in Boston's Warehouse District. There were nervous glances as the group inside worked frantically to get their semi-trailers loaded and on the road before detection.

They only needed a couple hours longer to get the semi-trailers filled with the stolen auto parts and on their way to Albany, Newark and Atlanta. The big bosses were there to oversee their biggest shipment yet. The ring had been working for months; stealing cars, stripping them and shipping the parts off to other large population centers in the state. They had begun moving merchandise interstate a few months earlier and this would be their first inclusion of a city as far away as Atlanta.

The ringleaders had been very careful. They kept the visible traffic in and out of the warehouse low. It wasn't easy to get thirty car thieves, mechanics of dubious reputation, and cocky thugs to ride the bus or car pool, but they did. Only the big bosses were allowed to drive and park near the warehouse.

The trucks were driven inside the warehouse into an anteroom. If anyone came into the warehouse from the street; all they would see is the front office, a secretary and a few trucks. The actual business of the building was concealed. The front was a middle man shipping business and had the paperwork to prove it.

Once the massive doors closed, another set of doors opened to reveal a huge chop shop behind it. The trucks were moved inside and filled with their stolen merchandise before they were sent out the same way.

Great attention was paid to keep off law enforcement's radar. The ringleaders only hired folks who had low-level criminal records; break-ins, car theft, petty theft and their histories were checked. On this morning, there was a full staff. Even the car thieves, who usually only worked on the streets and loaded the cars immediately inside the semi-trailers for shipment to the warehouse; were called in to the chop shop to help load the trucks.

O'Hara, a petty crook and mechanic nervously kept checking the time. Taylor, a skinny street girl who was handy at diverting the attention of an unsuspecting victim while her partner swiped their car keys, noticed O'Hara. She always noticed O'Hara. Truth to be known, she had a thing for the young good-looking fellow. If he was around, she was always within inches of him. He usually appreciated the attention, but that was not apparent this morning.

At ten o'clock, there was a loud pounding on the front truck door. The workers in the chop shop froze and shot panicked glances at each other. O'Hara moved surreptitiously toward the electric lever that opened the huge shop doors. As he reached up to pull the lever, Taylor yelled, "Cop! He's a cop!"

She flung herself at him, but the lever was already pulled. She swung at his face and screamed, "You miserable bastard! How could you? I trusted you! You'll pay for this!"

All hell broke loose as the huge doors opened displaying the entire operation to the fifty or so gathered law enforcement on the other side, all standing with their guns drawn. Not to mention the Feds who had surrounded the building from behind and now entered the back warehouse door. As law enforcement proclaimed their identity and informed them they were all under arrest, a few of the culprits chose to fight back. There was some gunfire, a lot of profanity and several punches thrown; but for the most part, it was over in a matter of minutes. O'Hara moved back toward the police and disappeared out the back of the building.

The news that night reported that at least thirty-nine members of the car theft ring were arrested after a five-month undercover operation by the Boston Police Department in conjunction with state and federal authorities.

There were charges ranging from petty theft and pick pocketing to grand theft auto and attempted murder.

Most pleaded guilty to their charges. After the remaining trials, the raid was deemed a success. The ring was squashed and the ringleaders got stiff sentences while the others all got shorter sentences. However, no one managed to escape jail time.

May, 1972
Merton, North Dakota

The young man felt good that morning. He turned off his shower and reached for a large, fluffy towel from the rack. Ian Harrington dried off and wrapped the towel around his waist. After brushing his teeth, shaving and combing his dark auburn hair, he slapped on some aftershave. Then he wandered out of the bathroom to his bedroom.

He passed through the master bedroom to the small alcove on the other side of the fireplace. It was a small room with huge windows and held only a couple chairs. There, his wife was just finishing her morning prayers. She looked up at him and smiled.

"I'm sorry. I didn't mean to disturb you," he said politely.

"You didn't. I just finished. Were you looking for me?"

"I was wondering if you had anything special you wanted me to wear today? I don't want to have to change again before we get to the airport."

The tiny, dark-haired, brown-eyed young woman giggled, "Your Mom was right! Men can't do much by themselves!"

"Watch it!" Ian laughed. "We'd do just fine, if we didn't care if we got yelled at!"

Ruthie kissed her husband, "You clean up good. Too bad we don't have more time this morning. I could think of something that would require no clothes."

Ian put his arm around her, "We can make time."

The phone rang and Ian reached across his wife's pillow to answer it. "Figures it would be you! Can't a guy have any privacy? What do you want?"

His brother chuckled, "Sorry I interrupted something. You two do realize that Dad will be picking you up, don't you?"

"Yah. Is that why you called?"

"He'll be there in about an hour. Hope you'll be decent by then."

"Stifle it, Matthew."

Ian hung up and Ruthie giggled, "How soon will they be here?"

"An hour," Ian grinned as he sat up in bed. "I suppose we had better hustle. Dad will be chomping at the bit to get moving, too. What do you need me to do?"

Ruthie climbed out of bed, "Your clothes are on that chair. Could you look through your suitcase quickly and see if I missed anything?"

"Yes ma'am. I'm glad I have something casual to wear. That trip to Boston will be a foot-sweller, and that's a blasted fact."

Ruthie shook her head and giggled, "That's why I am wearing these stretchy shoes. I hope it won't be cold out there."

"Likely warmer than here, although it is supposed to get nice here, too. Did you talk to the folks about plowing the area for our garden?"

"I did and someone will do it. What would we have done without the clan?"

"I know," Ian said as he finished pulling his shirt over his head. "What better friends could a guy have? We are very lucky."

"We are," Ruthie agreed as she started to make the bed.

Ian took the edge of the sheet on the other side and they had their bed made in no time. He quickly checked through his suitcase and closed it. "Looks good."

"I could have packed mukluks and a Speedo! You wouldn't know!"

"What do you think I married you for?" he teased.

"Honey," Ruthie became serious. "I know that your arm woke you again last night. Was it in spasm again?"

"Yah," Ian tried to brush it off. "Are these all the bags?"

The petite lady took his arm and looked at him, "No way. You need to tell me."

He stopped and put his arms around her, "I know. I was hoping that I could worm out of it. It hasn't been only waking me at night, but I get the spasms sometimes during the day. It is like having a huge Charlie horse in my whole arm, but feels like I hit my crazy bone. Sometimes, I get spasms in just my fingers or thumb. I thought maybe they'd just go away, but instead they're getting worse."

5

"You need to tell your doctor."

"I know. I will. Okay?" With his arms around her, he leaned his chin on her head, "Ruthie, it really worries me. What if those nerves are misfiring again like after I was shot? Will it always be this way? It seemed to me like I was getting more strength back in that arm, and now this. I'll wait and ask my neurologist. I promise. I have the appointment." Harrington commented, "I'm not traveling all the way out to Boston to not tell him the truth."

"Okay," Ruthie's dark eyes expressed her worry. "I hope it's a sign the nerves are recovering. Is there anything else up here we need to take?"

"No, after I take the bags down, this should be it. Hey, where's my coffee anyway?"

"Should be perking as we speak."

Harrington was putting the last bag in the entry as his brother, Matt, got out of his car. Matt smiled, "All ready? We still have time, so no need to hurry."

"Want some coffee?" Harrington asked. "I thought Dad was coming?"

"Dad got side-tracked." Matt explained as they went into the house. There he kissed his sister-in-law, "Hi, Ruthie. You really going away with this lunatic?"

"I thought I would. Don't want him to get lost or anything." Ruthie poured his coffee. "I'm going to put on another layer of makeup, so you boys visit."

After she left the room, Matt looked at Ian. "How is her morning sickness?"

"Pretty good. It was tough for a bit, but she seems to be getting past that. Marriage is funny. You marry a beautiful girl and think of champagne and strawberries. A year or so later, you are looking at dry soda crackers and an upchuck basket by the bed." Harrington grinned. "Just think! I'm going to be a daddy."

"You'll be a good one. Any child would be lucky to have you and Ruthie for parents."

Harrington froze and studied Matt, "Thanks. That means a lot."

"So, how's the old arm?"

"It's been giving me fits this last month. It goes into spasm at least five or six times a day," Harrington related. "I sure hope that doesn't mean anything bad."

"Like what?"

"Oh, I don't know. Whatever." Harrington shrugged. "I was just starting to get my strength back after the shooting, and now this."

"How long ago was that, anyway?"

"It's been about two years ago. Amazing what a small piece of flying metal can do."

"It was a bullet! Harrington, do you ever wish you were back in law enforcement?"

"At first I did; but now, I don't. I'm getting more clients for taxes and doing the books for a few businesses. Besides this way, I know I'll be home at night. I know our Dad tried, but with his job as a cop, he couldn't be with us kids much. I really don't want to miss my kid's growing up." Ian took their empty cups, rinsed them out and then the coffee pot. "I know Carl doesn't miss law enforcement, even though he grumps about it."

Matt looked like his older brother, but was taller and more slender. Matt dried the dishes and put them away, "We really lucked out. He is a great step-dad. And more importantly, he has been a good husband to Mom. She is happier than she's been since Dad died."

"Just think, she was left with eight kids! I didn't appreciate it then, but I don't know how she did it," Harrington smiled. "I still think it's good that we tormented her constantly because we wouldn't want her to let her guard down."

Matt agreed, "Yah, we had to keep her on her toes!"

Ruthie came in the kitchen and overheard the last of the conversation, "Just wait until I tell her what you guys said!"

Both men in their early thirties jumped about six feet, and tiny Ruthie giggled. "You're such babies! Well, let's go."

"So, Mom is taking care of the house plants and your cat?" Matt asked.

"Yes."

"We would have done it."

"You guys are busy enough," Ruthie grinned. "Things are cool."

As the airplane taxied down the runway, Ruthie took Ian's hand and asked with a smile, "Remember the first time we flew together?"

"I was just thinking about that!" Ian kissed her cheek, "That seems like a long time ago and yet, it seems like yesterday. I still love you. In fact, even more."

Ruthie's eyes filled with tears, "That's the nicest thing to say, but I didn't think that you loved me then."

Ian winked at her, "Well, maybe I wasn't quite up front about it; but I did. I think I fell in love with you the first time I met you."

"I was a novice nun then."

"So? I was a detective," Ian grinned. "I would've never acted on it, if things hadn't turned out like they did. But I wanted to marry you the second I saw you. Didn't you want to marry me then?"

"Oh brother!" Ruthie shook her head, "I can't say I did. I was so messed up about my dad dying and all that. I did think you were cute and a flirt."

Ian frowned at her, "You did? I wasn't a flirt."

"You always called teased and brought me caramels."

"You teased me steady! You were flirting with me!" Ian pointed out. "You were the only one besides Mom that ever called me Ian. Now look! Almost everybody does! You've been my ruination!"

She giggled, "And to think, you've never been happier!"

Ian put the seat arm up between them and they cuddled together, even though they had their seat belts on.

After a couple minutes, Ruthie asked quietly, "What do you honestly think is going on with your arm?"

"I don't know. I think it is either getting a lot better, or a lot worse," he answered seriously.

"I guess that about covers it," she kissed his cheek. "I want to think it's a good sign."

"Are you ever pessimistic?"

"Sometimes, about some things, but I feel positive about this. When you were shot, the neurologist said that it could take a while, but more movement and feeling could come back. You are getting more movement and your arm is stronger. So, I want to believe the nerves are coming back, too."

"I love you." Ian squeezed his wife's hand, "I wonder if Uncle Egan will be there to pick us up."

"Of course, you screwball. He was so excited we were coming out. I hope that he doesn't have too much planned. I reminded him that you aren't going to be feeling all that well. He sounded like he was organizing a North Atlantic fishing expedition!"

"That's Uncle Egan!"

Several hours later, the couple was engulfed in a huge embrace by a tall, burly Irishman with wild eyebrows that shielded his bright blue eyes. His unruly salt and pepper hair swirled around his jolly face with a reddish complexion and humungous smile. He was Ian's father's brother and a crazy man. He had been the surrogate father to Ian and his siblings all the years after their father who was shot to death in the line of duty.

Ian was the shortest of the Harrington boys, about five-foot seven. His wife was only four-eleven, and the couple had recently learned they were expecting their first child in October. He had the signature bright azure blue eyes, tanned complexion and huge Harrington dimples. Ruthie had short, bouncy black hair, while her dark brown eyes were round, sparkling with her beautiful smile. She reminded one for all the world of a pixie.

Egan Harrington proudly ushered the young people through the busy airport to his bright red, brand new 1971 Cadillac Coupe de Ville, "Isn't she a beauty of a thing? I had to buy it for my Vanessa, even though she said she didn't care." Then he winked, "I think she really was wanting it!"

Ruthie giggled, "I'm sure she did, Uncle Egan."

Ian chuckled, "Does she ever get to drive it?"

Egan straightened tall, "Why she was riding in it just this morning, but she harbors a fear of driving such a fine piece of machinery!"

"You are so full of it," Ian laughed. "What does she drive?"

"She is saying she's proud and happy to be driving the '69 Chevrolet. You know, it is an Impala, so it is a good vehicle. She can bounce around the city and weave in and out with it like a pro," Egan explained, "She's more comfortable with it than this fancy thing. This is much more complicated to drive."

Ian shook his head with a frown, "Yah, it has- like a brake, gas pedal and steering wheel. It would be difficult for her to handle."

"That was my thought on the subject, to be sure!" Egan burst into a belly laugh. "So, what day is that appointment with your nerve doctor? I've been lighting my prayer candles that the guy knows what he's talking about, so he can be repairing the damage caused by the lunatic shooter."

Then he opened his eyes with horror, "Begging your forgiveness, my dear Ruthie. I forget that was your kin."

"Don't worry about it. Zach and I have long since decided that Naomi was probably just as crazy as our father. Her husband was a homicidal maniac, for which we will accept no responsibility. We still don't know how to break it to my niece Miriam someday, but we know that she is too little now."

"The poor little tyke is certainly a lot better than when I first set eyes on her! She was so wee and frightened. But now, she is full of the old nick! I think she is a little darlin'."

Ian nodded, "Yes, she is doing well and even has made some friends."

"I was noticing that at Matt's wedding. What is it that Miriam calls herself? Squirrel?" Egan asked.

"No, Gopher," Ian answered.

"Leaping Leprechauns, how could I be forgetting that? Is it true that your stepfather Carl is a bit short on the brain cells? That man is a wacky one!" Egan laughed, "But his heart seems grand and he does love my Maureen. She is deserving of that!"

Ruthie sighed, "Yes, he loves her. But Uncle Egan, you have to know that she is a nutty as he is."

"I do," he nodded seriously and then his face lit up, "I feel extreme pride in that! I didn't want her to be a mopey one after Sean passed over... and she isn't."

Ian laughed, "I know, but I don't think that Mom was ever mopey."

"Not by the standards of the grumps, but she was slipping away. I think it was the fault of you children driving her to utter distraction!" Egan teased.

"I hope you know how much it means to all us kids that you stood by Mom and us kids. You were always there for us."

"Ah, now don't be collecting for a monument on my behalf! Your Mom, herself, was always there with a warm hug and a chilled mug for this old soul. She was my rock when my wife went to join her Maker!" Egan smirked, "If it had been up to me, I would have would've sent you all over the rapids in a cardboard box!"

"Nice, Uncle Egan. Real nice!"

Aunt Vanessa and Uncle Egan had invited Ian's grandparents over for dinner the following night, but it was only the four of them for that first evening. After the couple got settled in their room, Ruthie went down to help Van set the table. Ian poured a beer for Uncle Egan and himself. He took it out to the patio of the cozy Cape Cod home, where Egan was reading the newspaper. "I thought you might be ready for this."

"Aye!" Egan replied with a grin, "And you'd be thinking correctly."

"I don't want to interrupt you. I can bug the ladies."

"Ah, I was just pretending to read the paper so Vanessa wouldn't be dragging me about by the string in my nose!"

"The way you talk! It seems like she treats you pretty well."

"Never let it pass from between us, but she is better to me than I deserve!" Egan said to his nephew. "After my blessed wife died, I thought I was to become the weird old man on the block that pelted apples at wee ones on their way to school. When I started dating Van a couple years ago, I was confounded that someone like her could even think of looking at an old geezer like me. Did you ever be thinking I'd get a fine lady like her?"

"I never thought about it. After my dad and my aunt died, I just sorta thought that everybody only got one spouse and it lasted until it was over. Then, I don't know what was supposed to happen." Ian chuckled, "Of course, I was never a brightest bulb in the pack."

"None of us Harringtons are, but our glow is steady," Egan said. "So, tell your old uncle about this arm thing. What's going on?"

"Well, as you know, I lost movement and a lot of feeling after the gunshot. Ruthie has been an angel helping me do therapy every day, and I have regained a lot of my muscle tone and movement. Now the feeling is weird. It itches, a lot. It hurts sometimes when there is nothing wrong and sometimes it feels hot. Although, a couple areas always feel ice cold. Mostly, it just feels dull… if that makes sense. Lately, I've been getting spasms. I've always had little ones but maybe like once every couple weeks or so. Now, I get them several times a day and they're much longer lasting and severe. I've almost screamed in pain a couple times. I've dropped stuff, or twitched so bad I couldn't hold a piece of paper. I don't know what's going on, but I can hardly stand it. It even wakes me up at night."

"So you're of a mind the doc can repair you?"

"I don't know. If he can't, he needs to figure out a way so I don't feel it at all! I can't do this, and that's a blasted fact! During Matt's wedding, I had a spasm that about brought me to my knees. I had everything I could do to keep standing up front as best man. Everyone saw the tears, but I think they just thought I was emotional."

"And you were! Just not about the wedding, huh?" Uncle Egan patted him on the back. "Well, I'll be your chauffer and drive you two to that nerve guy tomorrow. I am secure that Van will want me to drive you in splendor, so we are taking the Cadillac."

"You're awful!" Ian chortled.

"Come and eat, you two," Ruthie said as she slid the patio door open.

"Yes, my little forest sprite," Egan grinned. "It'll be a grand pleasure to join you!"

"Oh brother!" Ruthie smiled. "The blarney's deep out here!"

That night as the young couple cuddled in the soft, big bed, Ian whispered to his wife, "Ruthie, thank you."

"For what?"

"Being my wife. You have made me so happy. I know I was a butt head when I realized that I had to leave law enforcement. You and Mom helped me get my head on straight."

Ruthie kissed his neck and caressed his chest, "You know Carl really helped you, too."

"That's true," Ian started kissing her neck.

Soon the couple was making love and then fell asleep in each other's arms. A couple hours later, Ruthie heard Ian, "Are you okay?"

He sat up sweating profusely with tears rolling down his cheeks, "No. My arm!"

Ruthie turned on the light and saw that his arm and hand from the elbow down was in a distorted spasm. She looked at him in panic, "Is there something I can do?"

He shook his head no and gasped, "Just wait."

She put her robe on and by the time she sat down next to him, it was beginning to calm. It took another fifteen minutes or so, before it relaxed. She hugged her husband, "Better?"

"Now it just hurts, but it's better. Thanks. Could you reach me some water?"

"I'll get some fresh," Ruthie said as she took the water glass to the adjoining bathroom to refresh it.

When she returned, she handed it to her husband, who was still glistening from the sweat, shook his head weakly, "I don't know how much more I can take of this. Sometimes, it just about kills me."

"You should have told me about it sooner."

"It didn't always happen at home."

"Oh, my mistake. I thought you could've just told me no matter where it happened."

Ian took her hand, "I know. I didn't want, .. I mean… you know."

She hugged him, "Yes, I do. Think you can rest now?"

He nodded, "I think so."

She helped him get settled and then turned off the lights. She slipped into bed next to him and put her head on his chest. "Does this bother you?"

"No, I love it."

The morning was fresh and brilliant. They had breakfast in Egan's flower garden. Vanessa had made a quiche, fresh strawberries and croissants. Two pudgy robins were squabbling over a nest in the big oak by the gate and a squirrel was chattering to its mate over a pile of seeds he had found. It was a glorious morning.

Ian was rather quiet and tired, but nervous. Vanessa poured him more coffee, "We heard you last night. Is there anything that can be done when it hurts like that?"

"Just wait for it to stop. I hope the doctor can fix it. It tires me out. I would rather not have my arm at all than to have it do this," Ian shrugged. "I guess we will find out today."

"I can be imagining that! What time is the appointment? Nine? Do you want me to go in with you? I can testify to the agony!" Uncle Egan offered.

Harrington chuckled, "Thanks, so much, but I think I handle it. If I run into trouble, I'll give you a holler."

Egan grinned, "How you talk, Laddie! 'Give a holler' is not something your Mom taught you!"

"So true!" Harrington laughed, "But you get the point."

At twenty to nine, Harrington was filling out the papers at the neurologist's office. He turned the pages on the clipboard to three, "Good grief, he should have my records from when I saw him before and I know the guys from Bismarck sent him copies of my stuff. What did they do with all that?"

Ruthie consoled him, "Now you know why Sheriff Bernard has such a fit about paperwork!"

"What if I make a mistake filling it out?"

Egan laughed, "Don't worry your head, Laddie! They'll not be reading it in any manner. Of that, you can have assured confidence!"

Ian wrinkled his eyebrows at his uncle, "How is that supposed to make me feel better?"

"Simply the facts, Laddie…"

Soon, Ian was called in and sitting in the exam room. The exam was extensive and the doctor, whether or not he had read anything, asked him a myriad of questions and genuinely showed interest but gave no inkling of what he was thinking. Then he told Ian to get dressed and he would have the nurse bring him to his office so they could talk. Ian shot him a worried glance when he asked if he had a family member in the waiting room.

By the time Harrington was dressed, he had worked himself into a controlled frenzy, worrying to himself, 'What if he really had to have his arm amputated? What if it would never get better and there was nothing that could be done? What if–? How could–?'

When he entered the doctor's office, he was having trouble keeping Aunt Vanessa's good quiche down and his head was spinning with anxiety. He physically relaxed when he saw Ruthie sitting there. She reached out and took his good hand. He leaned down and kissed her cheek before he sat down.

Dr. Turner was a middle-aged man, who was very neat and professional. He was very businesslike, but friendly. Uncle Egan was also in the office , scrutinizing the man. Turner smiled as Ian sat down. "Okay?"

"First things being necessary to get out of the way," Uncle Egan blurted. "You are a trained nerve man. Is that the case? You've been doing this long?"

Turner grinned broadly, "Yes, I have been. Would you like to see my diploma and certificates? I could get my statistics from the two hospitals where I have privileges."

"Are you making light of my concerns, young man?"

"Not at all. I realize that it is important and Ian means a lot to you. I rather like him myself."

"I just don't want him to be chopped by someone who received a diploma from a Chinese cereal box," Egan answered with dead seriousness.

"I assure you, I didn't. By the way, I'm Japanese-American. Mom is Japanese and Dad is from Delaware, where I was born." Turner chuckled and winked, "My name is Taiki Turner. I studied medicine here in Boston, so my diplomas are from America. For the record, I don't like cereal."

"I was sure that'd be the case, but you can never be too careful." Egan continued, "So, you have a drawer full of pills for my Laddie? If he needs the money, you can put it on my bill."

"I wish it would be that easy." Dr. Turner shook his head, seriously, "Ian, it looks like we're going to have to do another surgery. I'd like you to check into St. Luke's as soon as you can and I'll have some tests lined up for you. Tomorrow morning would be the best. You'll be there overnight. At that time, we should be able to choose our plan of action."

"Will you be able to repair the nerve damage?" Ruthie asked.

"Not all of it, I'm sure," Turner explained, "But we should be able to repair some of it, and at least make the final results more tolerable."

"Will I get these horrible spasms?" Ian asked.

"Not as much," Dr. Turner answered, "However, we won't know until we get the tests back. I can tell you, that recuperation will take some time. Will you be able to stay in the area for at least three weeks post-surgery? I know you live in the mid-west, but we want to watch the follow-up and you won't feel like traveling right away."

"Yes," Ruthie answered. "Ian's bosses know that he might be out of commission for a while. Not a problem. We want him to get well."

Harrington raised his eyebrow in objection, but Ruthie interrupted his thought, "We already talked about it, Ian. My boss has help in the office, so I can be here with you. So, don't even start."

Turner laughed, "I see your little lady doesn't mess around. Good for you, Mrs. Harrington. From what I've seen of this young man, he can be a bit determined."

Uncle Egan sighed, "That's the case, of course, but it's coming from the Finn side of the family. The Harringtons don't have a hard-headed bone in their bodies!"

"I could guess that!" Dr. Turner laughed, "Do you have any other questions?"

Ian shook his head no and then they got up to leave. Dr. Turner said, "The nurse will have your instructions at the front desk. Be sure to pick them up on your way out. Have a nice afternoon and enjoy the beautiful day."

"Thank you, Dr. Turner."

As they were driving home, they passed a street that was preparing for a craft fair. Ruth craned her neck to check the tables to see if there was anything interesting in the booths. Ian grinned and Egan blustered, "I'm of a mind that my Van will want to be checking this out. Look for the sign that tells when it opens. We must be making a run, or my Van will take the bus on her own. Lordie only knows the purchases she will make! She'll be having to rent a truck to bring it home."

Ruthie teased, "Or she and I could just take the Cadillac."

Egan instantly frowned, "No. Harrington and I decided we need to be shopping ourselves. You know, presents for our ladies, and such."

Ruthie giggled, "You are so full of it."

Before dinner, Ruthie and Ian went for a long walk. It was a while before they spoke, "When did you talk to our bosses?"

Ruthie smiled, "Before Matt's wedding. We talked it over and made arrangements. You know how the clan works."

Ian shrugged, "I guess I'm not surprised. I thought I kept it covered up pretty well."

"Why?"

"What do you mean?"

"Why did you think you needed to cover it up? It isn't a shameful thing. You certainly must know the clan better than that. We never back away from helping each other."

"I know that and I wasn't ashamed. First off, I was just hoping it would go away. Like if I didn't acknowledge it, it would disappear. I didn't want anyone to think I was a whiner. Then we found out we were expecting our baby and I didn't want to dampen your joy. Then it was Matt's wedding."

"You are such a sap sometimes," Ruthie nestled under his good arm while they walked. "Most of us knew some of it. We want you to feel as good as possible."

"I know, I just-,"

"I understand," Ruthie smiled. "I guess I should have told you about what I did, too?"

"Yah! What about that?" Ian acted offended. "I mean, conniving behind my back without a word to me!"

Ruthie stopped walking and looked at him quizzically, "Now just tell me, how could I connive behind your back– if I told you?"

He frowned, "You are so confounding, and that's a blasted fact!"

"I suppose we need to head back. Boy, Egan sure won't let anyone get their mitts on his Caddy, will he?"

"Nope." Ian laughed, "You mean Van's car, right?"

The next morning, Ian checked into the hospital. Ruthie and Egan walked him to his room and then Egan disappeared to find a candy machine. Ruthie helped Ian get into his hospital jammies and put his few things away. They visited quietly and she tried to dispel his nerves.

"It will be okay, honey. No matter what." Ruthie kissed his cheek, "We will work it out. We always have. Right?"

"I know, but for some reason I'm very nervous."

"About the surgery?" she frowned.

"Not really, it is like something is nagging me. I can't for the life of me think of what it is." Then he took her hand, "Maybe it is just that I don't like sleeping in a bed without my wife."

"That's it, for sure!" Ruthie smiled, "It's probably a lot of things. Honey, the best thing to do is pray about it and then put it away. There is not much you can do about it."

"I know. I don't suppose you could stay here with me?" he teased.

"Of course, if you want to go through labor and delivery with me."

He glared, "Be that way. I'll just suffer here alone and you can do your thing alone."

She giggled, "Chicken."

Just then, a kind looking male nurse came in, "Mr. Harrington? I'm here with your chariot to wheel you off to your grand adventures!" Then the dark-haired man winked at Ruthie, "Don't tell me you're married to this guy! He must be your brother."

"No, I married him. It's a long story, but now I've crossed to the Rubicon."

"You seem very brave. My heart goes out to you." The nurse shook his head in despair, "The best I can do is take him off your hands for most of the day. My name is Greg. I will try to keep him occupied, so you can get some fresh air, shop and have lunch with a friend. He'll be busy until about four-thirty. I'm assigned to him, so here is my card. Just call this number and they can get a message to me. Okay?"

"Okay, do you have my phone number?"

"Of course! Mr. Harrington goofed up and wrote it on his chart. So, I have it. As soon as I stick him on one of my big machines, I'll call you!" he laughed.

"You're quite the comedian," Ian groaned, as he moved to the wheel chair.

"It's a pre-requisite of this job! If a person wasn't a little nuts, he would never do it. It sure ain't for the pay. I can float my yacht in the bathroom sink!"

Harrington teased, "Probably meets your skill level."

"I could be offended, but I won't be. Before the day is over, you'll be at my mercy."

"That's what I'm afraid of." Harrington took Ruthie's hand.

"Seriously," Greg said, "Come back about four-thirty or so. All you will be able to do here is sit in this empty room. While I'm sure the décor is fascinating, it may not hold your interest all day."

Ruthie smiled, "Thanks, Greg. Take care of my Ian. He sort of grows on you."

"Like moss?" Greg laughed. "Well, get your smooching out of the way. I'll keep an eye on him for you. Anything amiss, I'll call."

Ruthie kissed her husband goodbye and then left to find Uncle Egan.

On their way home, Egan and Ruthie drove by the location of the street fair. It wouldn't start for a couple days, so Ian would be able to go with them. When they told Vanessa all about the fair, the three poured over the newspaper ad about it. They discussed what booths they would want to visit and what looked interesting.

The rest of the day, Ruthie helped around the house and even helped Egan clean out his car. Vanessa shook her head, "Ruthie, don't encourage him. He washes and waxes it every day the weather allows. He will wear the finish right off the stupid thing."

"He asked me to vacuum the rugs and seats," Ruthie giggled. "He told me I probably didn't have the knack for polishing correctly."

"Oh yes! And he got this new stuff—some sort of slippery wax that 'sheets' and doesn't leave spots, or something. He let me touch it– once. It must have a silicone polymer in it. It is a very cool product, but he accidently spilled some in the back porch on the linoleum floor. It was so slippery for about a week, it was a death trap!" Vanessa laughed. "But thanks for helping him. He loves the attention."

Ruthie shook her head, "He's a lot like Carl. Vanessa, I've been wondering about something and thought maybe you could help me."

Vanessa Harrington was a middle-aged lady about five foot six with nearly white-blonde hair. She was a classic beauty and topped it off with a great smile. She raised her eyebrows, "What is it?"

"Well, Mo and Egan are Irish, right?"

"Yes, very much so," A flicker of questioning crossed Van's face, "But you couldn't have missed that."

"Not hardly." Ruthie nodded, "But when they talk, it almost sounds Scottish. I'm no expert in either lingo, but is it?"

"Ruthie, those crazy people talk like they talk. Some of it is Scottish dialect, some is Irish, some is English and some is from the planet Zernom! Who knows? Most the time, I just nod!" She laughed. "I have listened to Mo and Egan talk sometimes, and didn't understand a single thing they said."

"Me, either. I wondered it if was just me."

"No, it's just them. Thank God their children speak some semblance of English." Then she looked at Ruthie, "Do you have any idea where Ian got that 'and that's a blasted fact'?"

"No, and he's the only one who says it. I think he says it less now than when we first met, but he still says it all the time."

Van laughed, "And that's a blasted fact!"

Late that afternoon, all three went to visit Ian at the hospital. He was very tired out. "I believe they have poked and prodded every inch of my body. Believe me, if I have anything, they should be able to find it. I'm worn out!"

"Did you have many spasms?" Ruthie asked.

"Yah, a lot. That one test they did, really got it going. I was about out of my mind but then they gave me a shot and knocked me out for a bit. When I woke up, the spasms had stopped."

"But did they feed you good? If not, I'll bring you something in from the street vendor," Uncle Egan offered. "I saw a pretzel guy out there with some pretzels that would make the Lord's own lips smack!"

Ian smiled, "I'm fine, but thanks."

"It wouldn't be a bit of a problem for me to fetch you one."

Van shook her head, "Maybe you can buy one for yourself when we leave."

Egan furrowed his bushy, wild eyebrows, "I might be just doing that! You can never be too prepared. If it is something that would quell a mighty hunger, I would be of a mind to know where to get it for my boy! Right?"

"That would be very thoughtful of you to check it out for me," Ian assured his uncle.

"If you insist, I will be doing that for you."

Van shook her head at her husband, "So, is Greg going to be your nurse every day?"

"From what I understand," Ian explained. "In this unit, we are all assigned a specific nurse who coordinates our activities, and so on. The contact nurse has between two and four patients. The rest are staffed like most hospitals, and the staff varies."

"I think it is nice to have a person to contact who knows what I'm talking about. When you were in Shreveport, it took forever to find something out. Nobody had a handle on it. Do you like him? He seemed very friendly," Ruthie asked.

"Yah, I really do. He explains what is going on, which is nice," Ian said. "Usually you are just at the mercy of whoever wanders in to take you where ever for whatever. And that's a blasted fact!"

Van and Ruthie shared a smile, then Van said, "Come Egan, let's leave these two alone and head to the car."

"Why?" Egan blustered. "Maybe I want to talk to my nephew!"

"Oh, I'm sorry," Van apologized. "I didn't mean to interrupt."

"What is it, Uncle Egan?" Ian asked.

"Ah, it was nothing, since I'm being rushed by the Devil's own self!"

"What is it? I have time."

"Nothing. Don't be concerning yourself," Egan blustered. "I will not be disturbing the lot of you."

The delicate and beautiful Vanessa rolled her eyes, and said softly, "Oh, Egan. You know you didn't have anything to say but blarney. The kids want to say good night. Let's give them some privacy."

The tall, man made a face, "If you insist, but he would have liked what I had to say! Good night, Laddie. Now Miss Ruthie, don't be getting this guy all stressed. He's had a long day and is in need of his rest."

"I promise, Uncle Egan," Ruthie giggled.

After the older couple left the room, Ian shook his head to his wife, "He's such a—I don't know what he is, but he is definitely one!"

Ruthie leaned on the bed, "Ian, you are beginning to make as much sense as he does!"

"Lord have mercy!" Ian laughed. Then he pulled his wife down toward him and they shared a long kiss.

The next morning, Greg called Ruthie about nine-thirty. "Good morning, Mrs. Harrington. I have an update on the dude you left on our doorstep."

"Good morning, Greg. You can call me Ruthie. Hope you are well today."

"I am, thanks. My wifey-poo said she will keep me another week." Greg replied with a smile, "Dr. Turner was by and looked at Ian's test results. The findings seem to imply that he would be a candidate for further nerve grafting. You understand, he will never have his arm as good as new, but there is a chance we can get him to the point he could scrub the kitchen floor for you."

Ruthie giggled, "Well thank you so much, Greg! I would really like that! What is the schedule for today?"

"We are going to let him play with us on more of our dandy equipment and find out in more detail what's going on. He'll have to sleep over again tonight. He was pouting about it, so I promised to make S'mores and tell campfire stories. If he behaves, he should be able to have company tonight. Then tomorrow, Dr. Turner would like to see if you could meet with him in Ian's room about ten to discuss further plans. Will that work?"

"It will be great. Has he been having a lot of spasms? He has a hard time with them and they really knock him back when they happen."

"Yah, especially since we fired some of them up yesterday. He had a tough night and is weak as a cat today." Then Greg hesitated, "Why do people say that? Cats are pretty strong and nimble to my mind. I really must look into that."

"Did anyone ever suggest that you're one bubble off center?" Ruthie giggled.

Greg laughed, "Not in those words, but I think they have! One bubble off center. I like that. Oh, he asked if you had talked to his folks."

"Yes, they are fine and so is everyone at home. Tell him to not worry, but don't tell him they are doing fine without him. He will be devastated!"

Greg chuckled, "And that's a blasted fact!"

"Oh, you've heard him say that!"

"Only about a thousand times. Is that a North Dakota thing?"

"No, it's an Ian thing. Nobody knows where it came from."

"Well, I better go see our boy. I dropped him off in Electroneurography, so I better go rescue the staff there. They are all nice folks. I don't want him to rewire their department. Any questions?"

"No. Thanks so much Greg."

"Not a problem, talk to you later."

Greg called about five and said that Ian was sleeping. They had to give him some pain medication because his spasms were causing a lot of trouble that afternoon. He thought Ian would sleep a couple hours and suggested they came to visit about seven. "Keep your visit short, if you can. He really needs his rest."

"We will. Thanks and have a nice evening."

"You are such a sweetheart. Most folks just mumble bye."

"Silly rabbits," Ruthie giggled.

That evening, Egan dropped Ruthie at the hospital, but he and Van did not come in to visit. "Just tell Ian hello and you two can smooch. We better get groceries so we can build a grand feast for when he gets home."

"I'll tell him. Meet you out front in an hour and a half."

Ruthie entered the dimly lit room and walked over to the bed where her husband was sleeping soundly. She gently kissed his cheek and then moved away from the bed. She checked the card on a bouquet of flowers on the bedside stand. It was signed 'The Clan', the nickname their group of friends and family back in North Dakota called themselves. She was admiring the bouquet of mixed flowers, when she heard him say, "Hi."

She turned and gave him a big smile, "Hi yourself. I didn't want to wake you. Greg said you had a tough day."

He reached out and took her hand, pulling her closer to him, "Ruthie, he isn't a lot of fun to hang out with. He makes me cry! You better tell him to be good."

She laughed softly, "I know, huh? Should I spank him?"

Ian gave her a hug and kissed her neck, "No. I don't think I want you to get to know him that well."

"Jealous?"

"Just not taking any chances. Did he talk to you?" Ian became serious.

"Yes, he told me that it looks like they are going to try grafting. What do you think?"

"I have to do something, Ruthie. I'm desperate. I can't take the spasms. It is like having your arm stuck in a big vice a few times a day. It just tires me out."

Ruthie caressed his cheek. "It must be horrible."

"I told them, if it has to be like this, I want my arm amputated or something. Honey, I'm not kidding."

"Ian, when I sat with you at the Shreveport hospital, I was so afraid you were going to die. I don't care if you have one arm, or two. I want to be with you. I want you to be as well and as happy as possible. I made you that promise then and I mean it. Hear me?"

"I'm so glad I met you." Ian kissed his wife, "I've never been sorry."

Ruthie giggled, "Even when I was throwing up all the time?"

"You and your brother, Zach, do hold the record on that. Suzy and I handed out more barf bags over your father's insanity than either of us ever want to do again! But it all worked out." He looked into her eyes, "I mean, they are happily married and so are we. I think that Miriam is doing well now. Don't you?"

"Yes," Ruthie sat on the stool by the bed. "I still feel bad that she doesn't live with us. I mean, Zach and I are her only family, her aunt and uncle, and she lives with Ellisons."

"I know, but she fits there and her psychiatrist says it wouldn't be good to move her as long as it isn't necessary. She is recuperating from the neglect and abuse of her family life very well and there's no point to disrupt it." Then he put his hand in hers, "But Ruthie, if that ever changes, you know that I would welcome her into our home. She is my little niece now, too. I love that little kid."

"I know, You are great with her." Ruthie leaned over toward him and then traced his dimple with her finger, "How old do you think she will be before we should tell her about her Mom and Dad? I mean, she knows we are her aunt and uncle, but how do you tell a child their father was a homicidal maniac and her mother a murderess?"

Ian laughed, "Geez girl. I would think that before we do that, we need to talk to Dr. Samuels. You don't just dump it on a four-year-old. We will cross that bridge when Samuels thinks it is time. Okay? Hey Ruthie, do you think the reason she is so definite about wanting to be called Gopher, is because she hates her name? I've heard her say, 'No Memeum'."

"I have, too. I talked to Marly Ellison about it and she thinks so. She also thinks that she likes being 'Gopher', because she associates that with her life since she came to North Dakota. I wonder what all happened to her while Naomi and her lunatic husband drug her all over creation. It makes me sick to even think about it."

"I'm pretty sure we would cringe if we knew. Hell, when we found out she had been left in a crib with her dead brother for a day or so, that about fried me! Any one that would bash a little boy's head in and leave him to bleed to death in a crib with his little sister has to be so far gone, it's unbelievable. Sorta makes me put my problems in perspective. How that little girl survived, I can't imagine, and that's a blasted fact."

"Well, Naomi tried her best to blow you away. Had it not been for the doctors you had, we would have never had a life together."

"Ruthie, if it hadn't been for Naomi's carrying on, Zach would have never called me. We would have never met at all. You know?" Ian pointed out.

"Yes I do, but she didn't do it to be good to us."

"Ruthie, she never thought about us, good or bad. She was demented."

"I know." Then she kissed him, "Thank goodness, we don't have stuff creeping up from our pasts anymore. That's all been sorted out."

The nurse came in to give Ian another shot and then he and Ruthie visited a little. Before long, he could hardly keep awake and Ruthie kissed him goodnight. "I'll see you tomorrow morning. Okay? Then maybe I can bring you home."

"I can't wait. Love you, honey. Sleep well."

6

Ruthie met Dr. Turner in Ian's room the next morning. They discussed the surgery and what the expected results would likely be. "It is going to be a hectic few weeks, but if all goes as expected, we should get things working better. You should regain more control of your arm and have fewer spasms. Nothing is perfect in the nerve game, so don't bet your house on it, but it looks very promising."

"Like what percentage?" Ian asked.

"Like 85+%."

Ian looked down and his face fell, "I was hoping more for like 95%."

Dr. Turner raised his eyebrows, "I would like 100%, but things are what they are. It is a decision you have to make. If you don't have surgery, the spasms will get worse. That misfiring is going to continue and would become nearly constant. I don't think you want that."

"I'd kill myself."

"We don't want all that good surgery to go to waste!" Turner chuckled. Then he turned somber, "I understand. Really I do. You told me up front that if it can't get better to amputate. I know you think that would help. But guess what? The nerves that are messed up are not in your arm, but higher up. It is not possible to amputate your neck. So, it would be better to try to fix them. We will, with your permission, rewire and repair the best we can. Then you will be able to control your arms movements much better. The pain should be almost totally diminished. Now, remember, if you get your electrolytes out of whack, they will go crazy. But you already know about that."

The young woman and the doctor watched Ian as he was lost in deep thought. A few minutes passed without any movement or conversation, when the offending arm started to spasm. Within seconds it was contorted and Ian was struggling, "Do what you have to! I don't care what. Just make it stop! Please!"

"I'll order a shot for you now and then schedule the surgery."

Dr. Turner left the room and Ruthie took Ian's good hand. She only moved when the nurse came in to give him his shot. The nurse told her that Dr. Turner would like to see her in the consult room and that Ian would be sleeping for about an hour. Ruthie kissed Ian's cheek and he was already getting drowsy. She smiled, "I'll be back, Honey. Just relax."

Ruthie entered the tiny consult room. It must have been six foot square and almost half the space was desk. It was painted a weird shade of gold. She was trying to decide if she really liked it or despised is, when Turner came in. He noticed the look on her face, "Isn't that the most God Awful color? It isn't as pure as yellow and not as pretty as tarnished gold. Sometimes I wonder if it is trying to be green. It looks like—," then the man looked at the wall and squinted, "It looks like hell."

"It is grim, huh?" Ruthie shook her head. "I bet it is the end of several paints dumped together."

Turner looked up from sorting out the papers he was carrying, "That's a possibility. At any rate, I know I won't be buying a gallon of it."

"So, when can Ian come home?"

"About one. I want to let this shot work itself out now. I am sending him home with some rather strong pills. They will make him tired and out-of-whack, but make him take them. We don't want to let these spasms break through. If they do, bring him in. We will just have to keep him here until the surgery."

"Okay." Ruthie looked at the prescription, "Will they help a lot?"

"They should. If we quit digging around on him, they should settle down a bit. This is Friday, so by Sunday, he should be feeling a lot better." Turner handed her the admission information. "He needs to be here by six on Sunday night. Surgery will be at 7:30 on Monday morning. It will be all day, so most likely about 8 or 9 hours. Then he will be knocked out for a couple days, before we let him come around. It is only then, we will know how well everything is working out."

"Okay." Ruthie nodded, "Sorta like when he was in Shreveport after the shooting."

"Somewhat, but he is a lot healthier now and didn't lose as much blood as he did there. He should do okay." Then he looked up and smiled at

Ruthie, "I sincerely hope this works. There is a good chance it will. Keep positive and try to keep him positive."

"Ian is very positive, until those spasms get to him. He just can't take it."

"Well, it hurts like hell. That amount of pain is hard to cope with. Between you and me, a lot of folks couldn't have stood it as long as he did."

"He's a tough one," Ruthie nodded. "So, I can pick him up about..?"

"Let's say two, to be sure. He will take his first pill before he leaves, so he will be pretty dopey and tired the rest of the day. Don't give him anything heavy to eat. Cream soups, milk shakes, that sort of thing. He can eat again starting tomorrow afternoon, and then has to go on a clear liquid diet starting Sunday noon." Turner grinned, "He'll love that! He was telling me how he wanted to go to some barbeque ribs place. Not a good idea today! But I think he will be tired enough, he won't care." Turner chuckled, "Otherwise, I'm glad you have to be the one to tell him no."

Ruthie giggled, "I won't. I'll let his Uncle Egan do it!"

Turner laughed, "Good idea! Well, no booze or other pain meds. You know the drill. Any questions, call me at the number on this card. Have a good day."

"Thanks, and you, too."

It was three-thirty when Egan turned into the driveway with his shiny, red Cadillac. He had put the top up on the convertible in deference to Ian's condition. The young man was barely able to keep his eyes open for more than a couple minutes.

It took all three of them, Egan, Van and Ruthie to negotiate the man up the stairs to the bedroom. Once he was there, Van announced she would bring him his meals until he felt better. Egan asked if he wanted a television or something in his room. He just shook his head no and flopped back on the bed.

Egan looked at Ruthie, "You need help getting him undressed?"

"I might," Ruthie looked the situation over.

"I was thinking that might be the case." Then he shook his head nervously, "Van would be loving to help you. I'll be busy fixing a tray for him, otherwise, mind you, I would."

"That's fine," Ruthie said. "Van will be a good helper."

"I was thinking that my own self." Egan pronounced. "We are wanting the best for my boy."

That evening, Ian slept most of the time and only had a bit of milk shake and drank some cream of potato soup that Egan had run through the blender. He had no pain, but was out of it. That night, when Ruthie crawled in bed after her bath, he did put his arm around her and acknowledged that she was there with a small smile. He mumbled, "I love you."

Ruthie cuddled next to him, "I love you, too."

7

Saturday morning, Ian slept until eleven. He got up, took a shower and dressed. Then he took a nap. It wasn't until about three, that he felt well enough to ask for help going downstairs. Uncle Egan helped him out to the patio and they visited while the ladies made an early dinner.

"Man, those pills wipe me out." Ian muttered, "I was hoping to see some of the family this weekend, but all I've seen is my pillow."

"You were doing what you needed to do. That spastic thing in your arm sucks it out of you, so you needed to rest. Your quack said you should be more awake tomorrow," Uncle Egan grinned. "We were thinking that we might wander to the big street fair then. Oh, and your sister Nancy and her husband, John Kelly will be here after dinner tonight."

Ian smiled, "Why do you do that?"

"What?"

"Call him John Kelly? He's been in the family for years and you always call him by both his names. I think we'd all know who Nancy and John are."

Egan watched his ancient Basset Hound, Otis, move about ten feet and plop down again, "I think you may be correct. I like his name! I like the sound and the saying of John Kelly."

Ian shook his head and laughed, "Okay. That makes sense, I guess! It is a nice name."

Egan studied his old dog, "You know Laddie, Otis is almost twelve-years-old. That is pretty old if converted to people age, right?"

"Yah, I guess it's about eighty-four. He looks like he has arthritis or something."

"He does, in true fact. And the whole of his day is moving from a sunny spot to a shady spot, to keep comfortable. That and eating. Remember how he used to be howling at the birds? Now, he never barks or howls. He just watches. The other day, there was a pesky bird within two feet of his nose, where he laid. He didn't make a move until he sneezed. Do you be supposing he is allergic?"

Ian chuckled, "I don't know. I guess he might be."

Van opened the door, "Ian, your Mom is on the phone."

Over their dinner of clam chowder and cheese biscuits, Ian told them all the news from North Dakota. Everything else was perking along as usual. About seven, Nancy and John Kelly came over with their kids. Nancy was the thirty-five-year old sister, fourth from the youngest of Ian's eight siblings. She and John had three kids. The twins were Tony and Tammy, now both ten, and John Jr. who was eight. He was called Turk by the family, since he looked like a Butterball turkey when he was a baby.

Nancy was definitely a Harrington. She had the dark auburn hair, bright blue eyes and the dimples. She was about five-six and had an athletic build, probably because she was very active between her job at the Senior Center and the kids. Tony and Tammy were like regular kids, but Turk… Well see, there are two ways to look at something. The way the entire world does, and Turk's way. He is always investigating, testing and inventing. Nothing should ever be taken as fact, in his mind, until confirmed by strenuous testing. On his visits to North Dakota, he had bonded with Charlie and CJ. The entire clan decided they were either witnessing genius or idiocy, depending on what those three thought of at the time. And they always had some sort thought at any time.

John Kelly was about five-eleven with light brown hair and icy blue eyes. He was very good looking and well-built. He had worked with Boston PD and was a well-respected beat cop for years. He was recently promoted to Lieutenant, but stayed mostly in the field. He liked it there and didn't have any desire to be a desk jockey.

He was an easy-going, non-pretentious guy with a big heart and an unflappable nature. It didn't take a lot to get Nancy bent out of shape, but it took a major catastrophe to shake up John Kelly. He was the family intermediary and could be relied on to negotiate the no man's land between the hot heads and the cool cucumbers. Only Turk had an innate capacity to rattle the man. John Kelly had long since decided that Turk was God's punishment for some heinous sin he most certainly had committed in a previous life. He sure wished he hadn't committed whatever in the hell it was, because it must have been a doozy.

The family came in with hugs and greetings, and then Tony and Tammy went to watch a television show they had been waiting for. It was a full feature cartoon movie from Disney that was being broadcast. Van turned on the television in the den and they sat down with popcorn and Kool Aid.

The minute Turk came in the house, he ran to hug his Aunt Ruthie. Then he started asking questions about Charlie and CJ. He talked non-stop until finally his dad suggested that he let Ruthie sit down. Turk stopped talking and looked around, "Where do you want to sit? I think it should be a soft place, because I have a lot of questions."

"Well thank you for thinking about me, Turk," Ruthie giggled.

"Oh, I didn't," Turk answered nonchalantly. "My dad did. He's pretty good at that, don't you think? It saves me time, because he will tell me. See, otherwise, I would have to waste a lot of time remembering it."

"I can see that," Ruthie agreed and Turk took her hand and walked her to the chair he had decided was soft enough.

John Kelly looked at his wife, "I'm so glad the twins were first. Can you imagine if there were two Turks?"

"It would be sad, no doubt," Nancy teased. "What with you being a widower and all."

"Widower?"

"Yah, after your wife threw herself under that subway train!"

Uncle Egan laughed his big belly laugh, "Ah, and you be lovin' the little Leprechaun at half that!"

"Oh, it's not a matter of love." Nancy explained, "It's more like lack of perseverance. And Ian, when is it in October that you two are going to find out what's in your gene pool?"

Ian laughed, "Mid-October. You know, our friends had their baby right before Christmas and named her Holly. Since our baby will be born right before Halloween, I'm thinking if it is a boy, he should be named Caspar. If it's a girl, Morticia!"

John Kelly cracked up, but Nancy didn't think it was funny. "Ian Harrington! How can you even think of something like that?"

"Must be the heavy medication they have me on," Ian chuckled, as he took the coffee that Van offered him. "I've been sleeping almost all day."

"Really wipes you, huh?" John Kelly frowned slightly. "Don't take your checkbook with you to the hospital."

"Huh?" Nancy frowned at him, "What are you talking about? Good grief, about half the time I don't know what goes through your head."

"We've had some complaints lately. Seems that folks have been having their wallets and pocketbooks lifted while they are zonked out at the local hospitals," John explained.

"What's this world leaning toward?" Egan blustered, "A guy can't even get sick and feel good about it!"

They all looked at him and each other without a word. Then Aunt Vanessa asked how their roses were doing.

Later that night, when they were in bed, Ian cuddled his wife. "It was fun tonight, but I wish I wasn't so tired."

"You don't worry about that. You seem to be a lot better than yesterday. Have you had any spasms at all?"

"No, once I thought my muscle was flinching, you know like when your eyelid blinks all by itself sometimes? It only did it a couple times, but it didn't hurt." He grinned, "I think it was too tired to care."

Ruthie snuggled close to him, "Good. Get some rest. I love you."

The next morning was bright and sunny. Ian felt almost like normal. They all went to church and then had brunch at one of their favorite places. It was a gorgeous day, so they ate outside. It would be perfect weather for the street fair.

"Do you think you want to try to go?" Van asked. "If not, we can go later. It will be going on for four more days. We don't need to go today."

"No, I would like to try it. I want to do something outside, but I may not last very long," Ian nodded. "Didn't you say there was a stand with Civil War memorabilia? I'd like to see that."

"Do you have a collection?"

"No. I just like to look at it." Ian smiled at his wife, "Anything you're interested in?"

"Oh, there were a lot of things, so you and I can go to the Civil War place and then I can wander around the stalls nearby."

"Don't you like Civil War stuff?" Egan asked.

"Never really thought about it." Then Ruthie giggled, "You know, I spent my childhood in the deep South and then Texas. Folks there have a different take on it than you Yankees. Of course, in Texas, they have a whole different take on everything from anyone else. See, Texas is the center of the universe, and the rest just revolves around it, like so much space debris."

Ian frowned at her, "You've hung around Uncle Egan too long. I don't understand you either! I never think of you as being from down south. I think of you as being from Pennsylvania."

"I was living there when we met, but I went there from Texas. I had lived in Arkansas or Louisiana until I was nine or ten."

"I knew that, but you have no accent," Ian chuckled.

"Like you would notice any accent being from Boston!' Ruthie laughed.

"And I'm sure to be proud that none of us Harringtons talk with even a bit of accent! We only speak the Good Lord's Own English." Egan pronounced, "Sure and Begorrah! And we've been at talking like this since the year dot. Then everyone else came about to make a dog's dinner out of it!"

Ruthie and Van laughed so hard, they had to excuse themselves. As the girls walked to the ladies' room, Egan looked at his nephew, "What do you think got their trolleys off the cable?"

Ian laughed lovingly, "I have no idea, Uncle Egan. They are just them."

Egan thought a minute and then had a self-satisfied smile, "And we should both be gratified. They are grand lassies. We did an upstanding job in procuring them."

"Good grief, you make it sound like we ordered them from a mail order catalog."

"Ah, not enough money in both our worlds to purchase either, my boy."

They returned home and the family insisted that Ian take a nap. When he got up, they would have time for a 'clear soup' dinner for Ian before they went to the street fair. Then he had to check in the hospital.

Dressed in comfortable walking shoes, with Ian's hospital bag securely locked in the trunk of the red Cadillac, the four paid their admission to the street fair. It took up several blocks and was a busy, crowded place. There were vendors scattered throughout selling every sort of food imaginable, from cotton candy to foot long hotdogs to gyros, with every sort of drink under the sun.

At first, they split off in couples and before long, Vanessa and Egan split apart. He was spending too much time at each food vendor for her. Ian and Ruthie walked together, only splitting up for brief periods while shopping. They wanted to spend as much time together as possible and Ruthie didn't want him to need someone while she was wandering off.

Since everyone had a different stall or interest, they made an agreement to meet at five o'clock across from the admission gate. It would give them plenty of time to make it to the hospital and yet not be so long that Harrington should get tired out.

The young couple browsed and did a little shopping. Mostly, they just spent time with each other. It was about twenty to five when they found the Civil War stall. Ruthie looked around the store for a few minutes, but a shop across the thoroughfare that had caught her attention. He was captivated reading a print out of some soldier's war diary. She took he hand and whispered, "Is is okay if I go across to that Trinket Place?"

Ian looked up and shrugged, "Sure. I'll meet you there in a bit. If I'm not there by ten to five, better come get me. We will have to head back to the gate to meet Egan. I'm sorry, I didn't mean to ignore you."

"You aren't," Ruthie smiled. "I just saw some beads that I thought looked interesting. I'll be right over there."

She kissed his cheek and he nodded absently as he found his place in the diary. She giggled and crossed the thoroughfare.

The Trinket Place was a cluttered, fun place. It reminded Ruthie of something a hippie would operate. There were necklaces, bracelets and beaded headbands all over and hanging from the roof of the tent on strings. The back of the tent was plastered with tie-dyed tee shirts and tops. The tables were covered with scads of small plastic buckets filled with various beads and shells.

Ruthie was wandering through the crowded tables when a skinny girl approached her. "Can I help you, Ma'am?"

"I am just fascinated by these beads! There are so many! I have a friend who beads and I would like to take some to her. I just can't make up my mind."

"When you decide, just take one of these little scoops and put however many you want in one of these baggies and bring it to the till. We'll weigh it there. They are all sold by the pound."

Ruthie nodded, "I will do that. Thank you."

The girl moved on to help another customer. Ruthie chose about four different kinds of beads and put a small scoop of each in its separate bag. Then she checked her watch and decided she had better hurry since Ian would be done any minute.

She went over to the till and waited in line for a tall man to help the person in front of her. He noticed her standing there and said loudly, "I can use some help here!"

The skinny girl appeared from around the side of the tent, put her cigarette out and came over. "Sorry."

The man snapped, "Honestly Taylor, pay attention. This lady needs to be weighed out."

Taylor gave the man a dirty look and then smiled to Ruthie. "Sorry, I was taking a break."

"No mind." Ruthie handed her the bags, "I have four sets in here."

The girl shook her head, making her dangly earring jingle, "No prices?"

"Oh, I didn't know about that."

"I'll do it," the girl snapped. "I guess I forgot to tell you about marking the prices with that big pen. It will be a minute."

The girl moved away toward the tables with her flip flops slapping the pavement below. Ruthie pointed to the middle row, "I made my choices all from the middle aisle there."

The girl looked at her through her heavily shadowed eyes, "Okay. That will make it quicker."

Ruthie answered, "I would hate to have you look all over. It would take forever to check out."

Just then Ian came up to his wife, "Suppose you bought out the store, and that's a blasted fact!"

Ruthie happened to notice that his comment grabbed the girl's attention and she froze to stare at Ian. He wasn't facing her, so continued to talk. "I will go out and catch Van. I just saw her walk by. Come meet us. We'll be just out there."

Ruthie nodded absently, but was frowning. It seemed the girl had disappeared behind some dangling necklaces and was staring, more like glaring, at Ian. When he walked away, the girl stepped out from behind the necklaces and watched to see where he had gone.

By now, the man had finished with the other customer and was also watching the girl who was totally entranced watching Ian. "Are you waiting for pigeons?" he growled.

"What?" the girl asked as she returned her attention to what she was doing.

"I thought you were a statue, or some damned thing. If you don't get with it, you will be replaced."

The girl shrugged and brought the bags over to him with the scribbled prices on it. She handed them to him and asked Ruthie, "Do you know that guy you were talking to?"

"Yes. He's my husband."

"Really? Ain't that just dandy? So you got old O'Hara to take the leap, huh?" the girl looked her up and down. "Never would have figured you for his type."

"Excuse me?" Ruthie studied the girl, "You must be mistaken. His name is Harrington, not O'Hara."

The girl almost snickered, "At least that's what he told you."

"I've met his family. It is Harrington. You must have him confused with someone else."

"Yah, I guess. What chop shop is he working at now?"

"Now I know you are mixed up. He was a detective when he lived here. Ian is an accountant now." The man handed her the bag of her purchases and she paid him. The girl glared at her the whole time she waited for her change. It made Ruthie very uncomfortable. Once she got her change, she hurried by the girl, "Have a nice day."

39

Ruthie couldn't wait to join Ian and Van. She ran up and grabbed his hand, "Let's get out of here, quick."

"What's wrong, Honey?" Ian asked.

"That girl gives me the creeps."

"Which girl?" Ian said as he looked back toward the shop, "I only see a guy."

"No matter, I still want to get out of here."

"Sure," Van said. "Egan went ahead to get the car, so he will be waiting out front for us."

The three didn't notice the girl had moved surreptitiously to follow them. She stayed back far enough to avoid detection, but followed them to the gate. She stood beside the ticket booth, until the three got into Egan's bright red Cadillac convertible. While they were getting settled, she copied the license number on the back of her hand.

As the car left the street fair, Ian gave Ruthie a worried look. "What happened?"

"That was bizarre." Ruthie shivered, "This skinny girl waited on me and after you came to tell me you were going to catch Van, she started questioning me. Ian, I didn't understand what was going on, but it felt like she hated me. I don't know what that was about, but it gave me the heebie-jeebies."

"Like how? Why would she hate you?"

Ruthie shrugged and related what happened, "While you were talking to me, I could see her over your shoulder. When you said, 'and that's a blasted fact', her head sprung up from what she was doing and she zeroed in on our conversation. As soon as you left, she confronted me and almost demanded to know how I knew you."

As she told Ian what happened, his face began to pale. When she finished, he just stared straight ahead without a word for a full minute. Then he asked, dryly, "Do you know what her name was?"

"No," Ruthie answered and then thought, "Just a minute. That guy who seemed to be the boss called her Tatum or something like that."

Ian turned to his wife and asked, barely above a whisper, "Could it have been Taylor?"

Ruthie's face lit up with recognition, "That's it!" Then a small frown flashed across her face, "You do know her then. She said your name was O'Hara. I told her she was wrong, because your last name was Harrington. What is going on?"

Ian countenance changed, and he was almost confrontational, "You told her our last name? You didn't write a check did you, with our address on it?"

"No, I paid cash."

"Well, thank God for that. Uncle Egan, I need to talk to John Kelly before I go to the hospital!"

"You won't have time, Laddie. He should be on his way home from work and you have to check in soon. What's the matter? Can't it wait?"

"No, it can't. I should put off the surgery. I have to see him," Ian was adamant.

"I'm taking you to the hospital, like we planned," Egan said forcefully. "But if you think it is so important, I will call him from there and ask him to come over."

Ian put his hand on his uncle's shoulder while he drove, "Give me your word?"

"Of course, what is this all about anyway? That street vendor?"

Ruthie reached for Ian, "You are scaring me! What's this all about?"

"I think she is someone I met while I was undercover. It could be trouble. From what I know, she and most of her family got jail time. I need to talk to John."

"I will call him as soon as we get you to the hospital." Egan promised, "But don't be worrying yourself. You know, in the cop business, not everyone appreciates your services."

The rest of the drive to the hospital, everyone was quiet, trying to make sense out of the little information they had. Ruthie watched Harrington, who seemed totally wrapped up in his own thoughts. She had only seen him like this on a few occasions before, mostly right before the showdown with her deranged sister and her criminally insane husband.

The whole situation, first with the girl and now with Ian's reaction, left Ruthie very unsettled. There was something very peculiar about the whole thing. He never looked at her and only held her hand because she was holding his. Yet she somehow knew that this would bring about a major change in her life. And she didn't like it.

At the hospital, she and Ian went to check in while Van and Egan parked the car. Egan said he would call John Kelly and then come up to the room. All the while, Ruthie and Ian signed in and rode up the elevator to his floor, Ian never looked at his wife or said a word. When they got to his room and closed the door, he walked over to the window and stared out over the city. He mumbled some profanity under his breath while Ruthie put his things away.

The nurse came in to give him his pajamas and he barely acknowledged her. Ruthie thanked her and after she left, walked over to the window. She put her arm around him, "Okay now, it's time."

He flinched, and turned to her in question, "Time? Time for what?"

"For you to spill it. We don't keep things from each other. You have shut me out since you learned this girl's name. I need to know what's going on."

Ian went back to looking out the window, but never said a word. She rubbed his back for a minute and then said, "You can play it this way, if you want. But it isn't what we do. Know that."

He continued to stare, unmoving. She squeezed him, "Okay. Remember, when you're ready, I will listen. Until then, just know that you are hurting me by not allowing me to understand."

He turned and looked at her with overwhelming sadness, "Oh my little Ruthie."

He put his arms around her, gave her a tender embrace and kissed her forehead, before resting his chin on her head. "God, I love you. I just don't want this to be happening."

"What's happening?"

Then he looked into her big brown eyes, with tears flowing down his cheeks. "I wanted your life to be perfect."

"You bonehead, no one's life is perfect!" Ruthie shook her head, "There's more to this than you getting her arrested. I just know it. You can either tell me, or let me guess. So far, my guessing isn't making me happy. And I can tell you, it would be better if you told me."

"It isn't simple," he said, uneasily.

"It rarely is," Ruthie said quietly.

They were interrupted by another nurse, who came in with some medications for Ian. After she left, he changed into his pajamas and put on the hospital robe and slippers. Egan and Van knocked and came in. Ian immediately asked if Egan had talked to John Kelly.

"Yes, Laddie. I did. He is on his way, as we speak." Egan answered, "Didn't even get a chance to eat his vittles. Better be of a major concern for you, to pull him away like that."

Ian never answered, but had slipped back into his private world. The other three tried to make conversation, but Ian never partook in any of it. They all noticed and the situation was becoming very uncomfortable.

Finally, Van asked, "Ian, would you rather we left and came back to pick up Ruthie later? Do you simply want to be alone?"

Ian only shrugged. Ruthie sighed, "Maybe I should just leave, too."

Ian never moved. Ruthie glanced at Van and they both grimaced. Something was seriously wrong. Then Egan raised his voice, "Ian Harrington! Whatever the bejesus you are fostering had better see daylight soon!"

Ian looked at him, "I just need to talk to John Kelly. Then, I can tell you. Really, I need you to trust me."

"Trust is a two-lane highway, and don't you be forgetting that. The ladies and I are going downstairs to find some coffee. We'll be back, and when we arrive, you had better have a vindicating tale to feed us! If not, we are not about hovering over your sulking carcass. Come girls."

"But Uncle Eg.." Ruthie started.

He demanded, "Now."

The three left the room. Ian still had barely moved.

The trio returned to the room about an hour later and found the door closed. Egan knocked and popped his head in. "We're back. Hi, John Kelly. Need more private time?"

"Only a few more minutes, if you don't mind," John Kelly answered.

"You got it," Egan pulled the door closed and told the ladies, "We'll be going to the waiting room for a short bit. They are just finishing up. Looked mighty grim and serious in there."

When they sat down, Ruthie shook her head, "What the heck is going on? I feel very strange about this. Now you say John Kelly is all grim, too?"

Egan nodded and Ruthie frowned, "Dog gone it! I have half a notion to barrel right in there and demand to know! After all, I was the one who was accosted by that woman!"

Vanessa took her hand, "I know, but I feel it is best to let them finish their talk. You know how police business can be."

"This isn't just police business! I can feel it. Why isn't he telling me?" Ruthie managed to stop the tears from overflowing her eyes. "I feel sick."

"Don't be getting the wee one all excited and nervous!" Egan said quickly and grabbed a wastebasket to set in front of her. "Don't upchuck. Okay?"

She giggled, "I wasn't going to. I feel a different kind of sick."

"Tell us a little more about this girl," Vanessa suggested. "How old was she, do you think?"

"Oh, probably her early to mid-twenties. Extremely skinny, but she was likely pretty when she was younger. She wore a lot of jewelry, but it seemed to have all come from the Trinket Place, so I thought it was a sales gimmick. She has dishwater-colored hair, shoulder length and with a soft curl. She was about five-foot-six and had nice hands. I noticed them because they were so nice. Her eyes were a dark hazel and she wore a lot of mascara. In her long hair, she had woven in beads and some feathers. Her teeth weren't good. Until she became upset with me, she seemed okay." Ruthie grimaced, "...Until she heard Ian say, 'and that's a blasted fact!' I should have known then that she really did know him. No one else says that."

"Well, being he did work undercover, it is very likely that he was known by a name that isn't his. Before he became detective, he worked undercover on this big bust of some family crime ring that was shipping and selling stolen car parts out of town. He worked as a mechanic in their chop shop for a long time before they got enough information to make the arrests. That is the only time I ever knew he worked undercover," Egan explained. "But then, he wouldn't tell me at any rate. Only reason I knew about it was that the arrests were all over the newspaper, although his personal part was never in the paper. His work in the bust was the reason he got promoted."

Vanessa frowned, "Was it organized crime? Like the mob?"

Egan shrugged, "Never paid any attention. I never consider crime organized!"

Van swatted him, "You know what I mean. If it was mob, I can see why he is worried. They are not the ones to mess with."

Ruthie's eyes flew wide open, "You mean we might end up in Witness Protection?"

"What's that now?" Egan asked.

"It is a new program the government started last year," Van explained. "When someone testifies against dangerous people, the government moves them away, changes their identity and keeps them hidden forever or until the danger passes. The witnesses can have no contact or anything with their own families."

"Good Gawd All Friday!" Egan gasped, "I'd not want to be explaining that to Mighty Mo! She's have my carcass shredded in no time! No wonder he looked worried."

"Now, we have jumped to way too many conclusions," Van said calmly. "Let's not borrow trouble. We will have plenty of time to worry when we know what to worry about."

John Kelly approached them and said quietly, "Can you come in now? Ian is getting pretty drowsy but he wants to talk to you before he conks out."

They all three followed him without a word. When they got in the room, Ian had his eyes closed and didn't seem to hear them come in. Ruthie went over and took his good hand. Van, Egan and John Kelly stood by the bed. "Ian, you better wake up to tell everyone goodnight. You will likely not get to talk to them before surgery tomorrow."

Ruthie touched his cheek, "Ian, try to wake up a minute, okay?"

He opened his eyes and looked around. It was obvious the medication was taking its toll. Van went over to the bed and kissed his cheek. "Good luck tomorrow, Ian. We will be praying for you."

Ian smiled weakly and nodded. Then Egan approached, "You just take care of yourself and don't be worrying. We will take care of everything else. Hear me?"

Ian nodded, "Take care of my Ruthie."

"I'll be doing that for certain."

John Kelly came up to his brother-in-law and said in a reassuring tone, "I will take care of this business and keep it as quiet as possible. You have my word."

"Thanks," Ian looked at him. "Counting on it."

"Now, we will leave you two alone."

The three went out into the hall and Ruthie kissed her husband's cheek, "Everything will be okay."

"Ruthie... I...ah... Promise you will listen to John Kelly. Promise?"

"I promise, but I would rather you tell me."

"I'm too tired. If anything happens, know I love you."

"You're scaring me," Ruthie frowned. "I have to believe that everything will be fine."

Then she kissed him and he returned her kiss weakly and fell asleep.

When she got out to the hall, John Kelly had already left. "Where did he go? I need to talk to him! Ian never told me anything. I'm going nuts."

"Calm down," Van put her arm around her. "John Kelly went to contact Aaron and James. He wants them to all come to our house, so we can talk. We'll meet them there. Did Ian say anything to you?"

"Only to listen to John. I don't know why he couldn't have told me before they gave him those shots. He knew they were going to knock him out. He should have told me right off!" Ruthie was getting very upset, "He makes me mad. He should have told me! He owes it to me!"

Egan stopped walking and stood in front of her, "That's enough. Don't do this. He asked we trust him and I intend that we will. You are with me, right?"

Ruthie slumped and frowned at the floor, "I have no choice, but when he is more awake, I'm going to knock him out!"

Egan burst into laughter, "That won't accomplish much to my mind!"

A bit later, Ruthie was in her room at Uncle Egan's house. She had decided to change into her blue jeans and tee shirt. She was emotionally exhausted and yet angry, hurt, frustrated and anxious at the same time. She ran the brush through her mop of curly hair and stared in the mirror. She washed her face and wore no makeup. Since she had cried most of the way home and needed to freshen up, she looked like the wreck of the Hesperus.

Ruth Jeffries Harrington was a nice looking girl. She had big deep brown eyes and a very infectious smile. Even though her childhood was a tutorial on how not to raise a kid, she had a great respect for family and loved children. She had been so happy when she found that she and Ian were expecting in October. Love of family and each other were two of the main things that she and Ian shared.

Family was precious to Ruthie and her remaining brother, Zach. Most of her family had died, in often violent or hideous manners. Miriam, their four-year-old niece, was the only other family they had. The Harringtons were a huge, close-knit family and Ian was very much a part of it. Most of the family was still in Boston and lived within walking distance of each other. In fact, John Kelly, Aaron and Jamie, two of his brothers, were walking over to Egan's that night.

She had always like Aaron, Ian's oldest brother. He was a mellow guy with a nice way about him. His wife, Terrie, was a fireball. She was very outspoken and never hesitated to wade into a fight with knives flying. But Ruthie usually agreed with her point of view on things. Not so much with Vivian. She was Jamie's wife. While James, another of Ian's brothers, was okay, Vivian could be molten hell-fire.

Most of Ian's family was involved in police work of some kind.

Aaron was a Precinct Captain, while Jamie was a detective. Ian's dad had been a cop, until he was shot in the line of duty. Another brother, Patrick was a forensic accountant for the fraud division. A brother-in-law, Frank, was a public defender. Uncle Egan had been a sheet metal worker and stayed far away from law enforcement, but knew about it because he had lived with it all his life. Now, he had a son-in-law who was a cop. He often complained, "Damnation of it all! Even if I was a mind to, I would have a devil of a time breaking a law! My whole family would swoop all over me!"

Ruthie heard the doorbell ring and decided she had better get downstairs. Hopefully, she would find out what was going on. She said a quick prayer as she headed out of the room.

As she came down the stairs, Jamie had just knocked and Van opened the door for him. He was medium height and sported the dark auburn hair, bright blue eyes and big Harrington dimples. Although a bit taller than Ian, he looked the most like him of all the boys. However, there was little doubt that if you ever saw one Harrington, you could pick another out of a crowd most anywhere.

He looked up at Ruthie and held out his hand as she came down the last few steps. Then he gave her a gentle hug, and said, "This is a jam, but we'll see you through it. On our honor."

Ruthie frowned, "I thought cops weren't supposed to make promises they don't know if they can keep."

Jamie winked, "That's for citizens. For family, we can buffalo them all we want!"

Ruthie raised her eyebrows seriously, "I don't want to hear everything will be okay. I just want someone to tell me what is going on! I have been left in the dark, and I don't like it, one bit!"

"That's what we are here to remedy," Aaron said as he greeted her with a hug. "John Kelly should be here in a minute and then we will fill you in. What time is Ian's surgery scheduled for tomorrow?"

Egan answered, "Starts at seven-thirty, but should go about nine hours, they expect."

"How long will he be laid up?" Jamie asked.

"It'll take a while. He is expected to stay here for three weeks, before he can go home. Then he will finish his rehab therapy back on the prairies," Egan answered. He flashed Ruthie a glance, "Isn't that right, Ruthie?"

She just shrugged and nodded, totally unlike her. She took a glass of iced tea from Van and mumbled a thanks; but otherwise, did not seem interested in anything that was going on.

Finally, John Kelly knocked and Van welcomed him in. She brought him a beer like the other men had and then sat on the sofa beside Ruthie. Van patted her arm and then turned to the men, "Now! We've been put off long enough. What's going on? We need to know the facts. The sooner the better!"

"Yes ma'am," John Kelly nodded, seriously. "I know you've had a long day. When I came to the hospital tonight, Ian told me about Ruthie's encounter with the girl at the fair. Here's what we're thinking. Her name is Taylor Collins. She and her brothers were deeply involved in the Norris-Collins car ring. Taylor's mom was living with Arnold Norris, so almost like family. Ian had worked with them, undercover, back in 1967, not quite five years ago. He was able to find out enough information to sink the ring after about six months of work. In order to do it, he had ingratiated himself to the Norris-Collins family. They thought of him as a good, close friend. When he opened the overhead door for the police that day, Taylor saw him do it. She realized he was a cop. She went ballistic, called him a traitor and said she would make him pay!"

Egan listened and nodded, "That seems about the way it would be. But I thought all of that bunch were in the pen."

Aaron answered, "Most of them had to serve some time, but different amounts. After I talked to John tonight, I did a bit of research. This Taylor was released a couple months ago. She had a record of solicitation and petty theft. She was a known addict, but wasn't in possession when they made the bust. She drew a five-year sentence, but just got out."

Van asked, "But it hasn't been five years."

"No it hasn't. With probation, good behavior, over-crowding of the prison– sentences aren't as long. You know the drill," Jamie answered. "I will contact her parole officer tomorrow morning and see what I find out about her whereabouts. What was the name of the stall you were at where she worked?"

Ruthie answered, "The Trinket Place, but she didn't commit any crime. You can't just go after her because she asked me a question!"

John Kelly said sternly, "Ruthie. We have to check this out. You don't know these people. Revenge and pride are their life blood."

Ruth scrutinized John Kelly's answer, "I can't see anything about this that Ian couldn't have just told us. What is it you are not telling us? Are they mafia?"

"No, but that doesn't mean they are good guys." John Kelly shook his head, "Okay. While most of the Norris bunch is in prison, there were a few who were not caught. They took the whole thing as a personal affront and after the sentencing, went on a bend of retaliation. Before they were done, we had three bodies of folks they figured had something to do with the take down. And they were right. They all were informants. One man took a bullet while walking down the street. Another's body was found floating in the bay, punctuated with stab wounds. The third was the wife of an undercover agent. The man was on assignment elsewhere and so they slit her throat. They left a note on her body, 'Was it worth it?' Norris."

Egan cleared his throat, "Surely you're about to tell us that you put those culprits away."

Jamie shook his head, "I wish we could. Two were arrested and one of them said the Norris ring would not rest until the debt was paid. If they couldn't get the rat, they would go after the rat's family. At any rate, there would be retribution."

"Maybe those were the only two involved," Van asked hopefully.

"No, those guys both alibied out for two of the murders. We know there are more involved."

"But the murders stopped," Van said.

"Yah, only because they couldn't find the others. That's when the department pulled Ian off the streets and put him behind a desk. The other guy was moving to Alabama anyway, so he would have been hard to find. Until yesterday, Norris had no line on Ian." John Kelly explained, "I need to know, how much information did you give Taylor?"

Everyone turned to look at her and Ruthie responded, "Why do I feel like this is my fault? I didn't know anything about any of this and I certainly didn't know we had to be slithering around. Ian should have told me."

"He told me that he had forgotten all about it. He's been away from this business for a long time. We are not blaming you, so please don't feel that way. We know you were sideswiped by this. However, we do need to know how much Taylor knows."

Ruthie repeated the events of the meeting. The only information that Taylor could have discovered was that Ian was an accountant now and his name was Harrington. She may have picked up what his first name was, but Ruthie couldn't remember if she told her. That would have depended on how much she overheard.

Aaron listened and then suggested, "Well, he won't find him listed in the phone book here and she doesn't know about North Dakota. She doesn't know your name or where you are staying, so I think it is likely going to be okay."

"Likely? Likely, you say?" Uncle Egan blustered. "Isn't that as much as saying likely not?"

"I guess, but I think the chances of them finding any of you in the next few weeks is less than half."

Egan went over to the whiskey bottle and poured himself one, "Reassuring. I think I'll get more comfort from my bottle."

Aaron laughed, "Uncle Egan, you may need to keep your wits. Being drunk on your ass won't do it."

Ruthie hardly moved and was lost in her own thoughts. John Kelly sat beside her, when Van went to pour drinks for the boys. "What is it, Ruthie?"

"I still don't understand why he couldn't tell me this. There's got to be more to it. I just know it."

John Kelly put his arm around her, "Look, he's very worried for your safety and he was more than a little embarrassed that he hadn't warned you or protected you."

Ruthie looked at John Kelly without expression and said in a flat tone, "I don't buy it. He could have told me all this. There is something else."

"Can you trust him? Or me? Please?"

"Can you trust me? I will give a pass for now, but don't you *not* tell me something. I mean it. If you don't promise, I won't trust you either. I thought I trusted Ian. And look, he didn't tell me about this. He could have. Why didn't he?" She started to cry.

John Kelly pulled her over to him and embraced her while she cried. "I give you my word, I'll tell you anything you need to know, as soon as I find out."

"No," Ruthie shook her head, "Not what *you think* I need to know. I want to find out anything you do. Hear me? Not knowing is worse than dealing with the facts." She pulled back and stared at him, "Have I got your word?"

He stared back at her, "You do."

"Okay then."

12

That night, Ruthie couldn't sleep. She paced, took a hot bath, prayed and cried. She was very frightened, but not of any bad guys coming after her. She wasn't happy about that, but didn't think that was a real worry.

She was upset that John Kelly and Ian's brothers seemed to think that they could handle the information about her life, better than she could. Maybe she wasn't physically strong or big, but she had faced a lot of things those guys never had. She was rather certain that they had never been forced to pray while watching their brother die, after their father forced him to put his hand in a bag with rattlesnake. Or had the courage to crawl in the back of her uncle's trunk at the funeral, hoping he would take her away from her crazy father. Well, maybe that wasn't courage; maybe it was more fear of her father. But even at the age of nine, she knew if she got caught, or if her uncle that she hardly knew brought her back, she would have the same fate as her brother. No, they didn't need to treat her like she was some fragile crystal doll.

Besides, she had never been one for lying and hated to do it, even with polite pleasantries. These guys didn't know how well she knew Ian. She could read him like a typed page. She knew there was something he still wasn't telling. She went crazy trying to figure out what it could be. Sadly, it really wouldn't matter to her if she found out on her own, or from someone else, she needed to hear it from him. He had always told her everything. Even things that weren't nice or easy. Why not this time?

Sure, maybe he was embarrassed that he had not warned her about this group of crazies, but then he would have just said, "I should have told you. I'm sorry." That would have been it. And why would he have told her? The odds of them meeting up with this girl was astronomical.

Something was nagging her about the meeting. It almost seemed to her that this was some sort of fate thing, or God's will. Whatever, it would no doubt make a huge difference in their lives. She knew that in her heart. What difference? She had no idea.

It was almost a relief when Van called, "It's five, Ruthie. I'm putting the coffee pot on, so we can get to the hospital in time to see Ian before he goes into surgery. Okay?"

Ruthie answered, "I'll be right there."

When she came in to the kitchen, Uncle Egan was just coming in from having fed his old dog. He looked at her and said, without a grin, "You look as bad as Otis this morning. Did you shut your lids for a second?"

"I tried, but I couldn't sleep. I imagine about ten this morning, sitting in those comfortable hospital chairs, I will be snoring."

Egan shook his head, "Do you be a loud snorer? You know, the drooling type? I may have to wait on a different floor."

"Egan Harrington!" Van reprimanded him, "Do you ever think how you talk?"

The tall man chuckled, "As long as folks get my drift, there's no matter."

"It's okay, Aunt Van," Ruthie giggled. "I am a drooler."

"The tests the saints have put before me!" Egan rolled his eyes. "Are you hashing your mind to bits over the news of the murderers?"

"No. I suppose if I had any sense, I would be."

"The boys seemed rattled by it. Likely, Ian was too," Van pointed out. "You have to remember Ruthie, he has been taking the crazy medicine all weekend. His mind wasn't working very well."

Ruthie looked at Van, "Thank you for reminding me. I did forget that. Maybe that's why he didn't tell me."

"Might just be, Lassie," Egan handed her a toasted English muffin. "Jam is on the counter. Could you grab it?"

Ruthie got the jam and set it on the table. She bowed her head and they all said grace. When they were finished, Egan said, "Well, we better get moving. At least, the traffic should be light this early."

About six-fifteen, the three were in the hall outside Ian's room. Greg met them there and said, "They are just prepping him now and should be done in a few minutes. Then you can go in."

"Is he very awake?" Van asked.

"No, he's in Neverland, but he is awake. May I speak freely?"

Ruthie nodded, "Of course."

"He seems very worried about something. He keeps mumbling—telling a Taylor no and something like don't hurt them! Also, he's very worried that you weren't coming up to see him today." Greg shrugged, "Drugs can mess you up like that, but I think something's bothering him. Since he's my patient, I don't like to have things bothering him."

"We had some unsettling news," Ruthie said.

Then the door opened and the nurse came out, "He's all yours."

Ruthie turned to Egan, "Can I ask you and Van to bring Greg up to speed about the situation? I'd really like to talk to Ian."

"Sure," Egan nodded. "You got some place we can talk in private?"

Greg motioned down the hall and Ruthie went in to see her husband.

His eyes were closed and he seemed to be sleeping when she went over to his bed. She kissed his cheek and he opened his eyes. When he saw her, he put his good arm around her and squeezed her tightly. "I was so afraid you wouldn't come to see me."

"Why would you think that? Of course, I'd be here."

He looked at her, "Do you still love me?"

"Yes. I'm not very happy with you right now, but I love you." Ruthie said. "John Kelly talked to Egan, Van and I last night."

"He told you?"

"Yah, he did. But Ian, I know there is something else that I'm not being told. I'm not an idiot."

Ian squeezed her again, weakly and mumbled, "I know you aren't. I wish I had more time and was more together. I just can't now."

"I know," Ruthie rubbed his cheek. "You're pretty zonked. None of this other junk matters right now. I'm here and your job is to get through this surgery. Okay? We have the rest of our lives to work out these other details."

Ian had a big yawn, "I love you. I really do. Just remember that, no matter what."

"We'll be hanging around here today until you get back from surgery. Maybe we will get to see you again. Okay?"

"Okay," he mumbled as he drifted off to sleep. "Love you."

After a few minutes, Van came in. She looked at Ian, "Sleeping, huh? I take it you didn't get to talk to him."

"Not really," Ruthie said. "I guess I shouldn't expect too much now."
"No, likely not."

When Egan came in the room, the orderlies were just taking Ian out of the room. He was awake enough to tell them goodbye and give Ruthie another kiss. They walked with him to the elevator and Greg rode down in the elevator with him. "I want to make sure my guy gets to the right place. I'll be back up to talk to you after he is tucked in."

They went back into the room and sat down, Egan said, "Greg seems like a fine person. He was very interested and helpful. He said that if there is anything that he can do or should know, to remember to keep him in the loop. I said we would."

Ruthie started to say something sarcastic, and then caught herself. "Yes, we need to do that. Greg is a good guy."

They fiddled around for the twenty minutes until Greg returned. "Well, I got him checked into the Ritz. I sniffed good and none of the staff have been hitting the bottle, so he looks to be in good hands. There is a waiting room on second floor, near the OR and a nice diner across the street from the hospital. I would highly recommend it. You might think you want to eat at our dining room, but I'm not even sure it is healthy. I saw a cockroach grabbing for his gas mask in my gruel yesterday." Then he grinned, "If you go across the street, I know that number. If anything happens, I will call you there. What do you say?"

Van smiled, "You are a fine salesman. We will go across the street. How long will it be before we get the first report?"

"About nine," Greg said. "I'll come out to find you in the waiting room on second as soon as I hear anything. You are planning to return after breakfast?"

"Yes, we will do that." Egan said. "Then we will make sure that someone is always in the waiting room or tell you if we have to leave. But we don't plan on it."

"Good." He smiled at Ruthie, "Try to relax. Mr. Harrington explained the situation to me and I know it's hard. Keep positive. If you need to talk, you have my number."

"You are a sweetheart," Ruthie smiled.

"Well, thank you, Ma'am. And you are the same."

The day drug on with a tedious rhythm. Greg popped in and out with reports on how things were going. They rated from 'as expected' to 'better than expected'. About one, the trio walked over to the diner for lunch. By four o'clock, Greg reported that things were looking better than anticipated. They would begin closing him up in about an hour. He should be back in his room by six or seven.

They were all relieved, as they were bone tired. It was seven-thirty when they brought Ian back to his room. Egan and Van told him good night and Ruthie spent a few minutes with him.

"You look tired," he said drowsily.

"I will, Honey." Ruthie smiled, "Greg said things went better than expected and you did well. I hope you can rest tonight."

"Did you talk to Turner?"

"No, I guess we will see him tomorrow. Greg said to be here about ten. We will see him then." Then she took her husband's hand, "Do you want me to stay here tonight with you?"

"No need," Greg said as he came in. "I get to sleepover with Ian. You go home and sleep. I will be right over there on that little cot with my pillow and blankie."

"You don't need to do that," Ruthie objected.

"Yah, I really do or I'll get fired!"

"What about your wife?"

"She can't sleep here. There's only room for one on the cot and I'm not letting her sleep with Ian. Besides, she has hot plans tonight."

Ruthie giggled, "What's that?"

"She's going to a make about three dozen cupcakes for some school thing. Believe me, I'd rather be here." Greg grinned. "Seriously, it is our policy and we found everyone does better this way. You can rest, the patient can rest and I don't have to come in the morning and find out my patient's families painted their fingernails bright purple while they slept! Okay?"

"Okay." Ruthie kissed Ian's cheek. "You're in good hands."

"I love you."

She smiled and then they left for home.

Egan volunteered to call Mo and fill her in on her son's surgery. They had agreed not to say anything about the business with that girl. Ruthie looked around the kitchen, "Should I call John Kelly?"

"No," Egan said vehemently. "I will talk to him after I talk to Mo. The whole family wants to know how the surgery went. I can find out what they learned then. I want you to go to bed and get some sleep. If anything happens, you'll need to have your wits about you."

"What about if John Kelly found out anything?"

"If it is worthy of the fuss, I will tell you right off. Elsewise, morning will be soon enough. Now, off with you."

Ruthie shrugged, "If I wasn't so tired; I would put up a fight, but I won't. I'm going to take a hot bath and go to bed. Besides, we should be very grateful. The surgery went well and it looks like they had good luck with the grafting. So that is a blessing."

"It certainly is.

13

Ruthie slept like a rock that night. The first sound she heard was the telephone ringing and she looked at the clock. It was only five-thirty. Her first thought was something happened to Ian. She sat straight up in bed and tried to get her bearings. Then there was a knock at her bedroom door. "Ruthie, John Kelly is on his way over. I'm going to put the coffee pot on. He wants to talk to you," Aunt Van said.

"Be right there," Ruthie said and jumped out of bed.

It was only about twenty minutes later, when Uncle Egan opened the door for the young man. "You must have got up before breakfast," Egan chuckled.

John Kelly laughed, "Yah, I did. I have to be to work at eight and I promised Ruthie I would keep her updated."

"I take it you learned some tidbits, then?" Egan asked as they headed toward the kitchen.

"I did. How's Ian?" He asked as he nodded a thanks to Van for the coffee mug and sat at the table.

"Haven't heard anything since last night, so I guess he is doing as expected." Ruthie answered. "We'll meet with his doctor at ten this morning to find out more."

"Want an egg or something?" Egan asked.

"No thanks. Nancy made me an omelet this morning. It was good. She put this cheese sauce over the top of it. I liked that." John Kelly set his cup down, "I talked to Jamie and Aaron last night and we compiled our notes. Ready?"

"Shoot." Egan nodded, "We are dying of curiosity."

"Well, Taylor had four brothers. Her mom, herself and three of the brothers got prison sentences. The youngest brother hanged himself in prison about a year into it. The Norris-Collins ring went ballistic about that. The other boys are still on the inside and are looking at a couple more years. One of them has managed to add time to his sentence because of fighting in there."

"Sounds like a fun group."

"Most certainly. Well, Miss Taylor was recently out on parole. Jamie talked to her parole officer on the phone. She said she had skipped the last two meetings. She had taken up with this guy. Streak is his nickname. He has a record longer than my arm and is a sleazy character. She was going to move in with him and her PO advised against it. So, she quit going back to the PO. The officer thought she was probably using again, too."

"What is her addiction?" Van asked.

"Heroin," John Kelly answered. "The PO ordered a drug test, but of course, she didn't do that either. Streak seems to be involved in everything from petty theft to drug sales. He has never had a job, nor does he seem devoted to a single type of crime."

Ruthie frowned, "Was Streak part of the Norris ring?"

"Yah, he was, but wasn't there when the bust went down." John Kelly continued. "I'm planning to go talk to him today, if I can dredge him up. I talked to the man from the Trinket Place. He said he'd just hired Taylor for the day on the suggestion of another vendor. He said after you left, so did she. She came back a bit later, got her things and disappeared, without even asking for her pay. He was glad because he said she was worthless as help. We have no idea if the Norris ring was told about her finding Ian, or anything like that. Aaron has an informant that hangs with the Norris' and he is going to keep his ear to the ground. That's it."

Ruthie studied his face, "What else?"

"I said, that's it. When will you be able to talk to Ian? I mean, really talk?" John Kelly asked.

"He will be pretty much out of it a couple days, at least. That was how it was in Shreveport. Maybe it will be better this time," Ruthie explained. "Why?"

John Kelly frowned and started to say something. Then he drank his coffee and never put voice to what he was going to say. Ruthie reached his hand, "John, what is it? We had a deal, remember?"

"Look, Ian asked me to... well... I don't..." John Kelly stopped.

Van interrupted, "Egan and I like to take our last cup of coffee on the patio in the morning sun. You guys need to talk and so we will just scoot out there. Okay?"

Egan grumped, "I want to know, too."

"Come on, Mr. Busybody," Van said as she refilled his coffee cup. "If these folks want to tell us, they will. Now, move it. Otis is lonesome."

"Damn it all," Egan groaned. "I want to know the scoop."

After the couple went out to the patio, Ruthie said, "What did Ian ask you to do?"

"When we talked, he wanted me to promise to keep this under my hat until he could tell you himself. I don't know if I should break his confidence."

"Fine. Don't. Break our deal, instead," Ruthie growled. "I think I'll just get my airline ticket changed and go home. If I cannot know what's going on, I might as well just wait at home."

"Ruthie."

"Don't Ruthie me." Ruthie snapped, "I knew there was more to this than the 'story'. How many other people were trusted with this information that I'm not trusted with? The whole crowd?"

"No, just me." John Kelly cleared his throat, "Look, if it was up to me, I would've told you the other day, but I did promise him. He said you would want him to tell you."

"He's right about that, but he told you instead. Didn't he? That boat has already sailed and when he's well, he is going to have to do some fancy explaining to worm out of it. I know it and he knows it. I'll give him one chance when he's well, but you are healthy. If you don't tell me, I'll just wring your neck!"

"Nice!" John Kelly grimaced. "Okay. It isn't really that big of a deal. I think not telling you is making it a bigger deal. When Ian comes after me for spilling the beans, you better have my back."

"You got it."

"When he first started working with the Norris' crew, Taylor took a shine to him. The boys were all very suspicious of everyone who wasn't somehow kin to them. So…"

"Ian played up to her. I figured that."

"Well, yes. By the second month, they were together a lot. They started to mess around. Ian said he didn't sleep with her until one night on a big drunk. After that, it was a lot."

Ruthie nodded, "That's why she thought he was a traitor. He was, you know."

"I guess from her point of view, but he would've never given her the time of day had it not been for the assignment."

"You mean he was like a prostitute then?" Ruthie shook her head. "I love how men can make screwing around as being a somehow noble cause! Makes me sick."

"I'm sorry to have to tell you. Ian said he wanted to tell you, but knew that you'd have a lot of questions and his mind wasn't working very well with those meds."

"Like it slowed him down enough so he couldn't give me a slick smooth-it-over line? Look, I knew he wasn't a virgin when we met. That's life. I can't understand why he didn't tell me about this deal, right off. I mean, not before the day at the fair, but he should have then. That is the betrayal. He did not trust me."

"Yah, I can see that. The only reason that he told me about it was because he figures Taylor won't let go. She wanted a permanent relationship with him and she will pursue this situation. Either out of the hope they can rekindle their relationship or vengeance because he had married someone else. Ian felt that he had made things worse for you because of what he did. Do you understand?"

"I do. What I don't understand is why he didn't think I would. Never mind, we can go around and around about this. It is between him and me, and you shouldn't have to be the middle man. I'm sorry."

"He said she never meant anything to him."

"That's baloney! I know him that well. He may not have ever thought it would amount to anything, but he had feelings for her. Otherwise, he would've told me right off! You men! You think you can pull the wool over our eyes; all the while you forget we probably spun the yarn." She patted his hand, "I figured this was the deal. I want to thank you for telling me and you have my word that before I knock Ian out with a heavy brick, I'll make certain that he doesn't blame you."

"I'm glad you're taking it so well." John Kelly laughed as he noticed Egan's face pressed against the sliding glass door. "Now, what are we going to do about him?"

"If we don't tell him, we'll have to smother him!" Ruthie giggled. "We might as well tell them. I would prefer that it goes no further, unless we have to. I know that Ian values his reputation, but probably wouldn't like the whole family to know it."

"Yah, he's that way." Then he looked at the door, "Shall we let him in before he steams up the glass?"

"I guess."

John Kelly slid the door open, "Come in, we know it is killing you."

"I just bumped that glass," Egan mumbled. "Checking the caulking, you know."

"Yes, we know." Ruthie giggled, "Sit down and I'll tell you. John Kelly can't because he is bound to keep it under wraps. However, I'm not."

"But he told you," Egan blustered.

"A medical emergency," Ruthie answered. "If he hadn't come clean, he'd have needed a medic!"

Over the next few minutes, Ruthie told the couple. They asked few questions and Van nodded, "I thought as much. I figured you did too, Ruthie."

"Well, he was just trying to do his job and..." Egan started.

"Don't bother, Uncle Egan," John Kelly shook his head. "Ruthie isn't buying it. She isn't mad that he was messing around, she is mad that he didn't tell her a couple days ago when this first came up. Between you and me, I agree with her."

Egan stirred his coffee vigorously, even though it contained no milk or sugar. Then he looked up and stated, "I agree, too. But don't hold it against him."

"I won't, but he still has to tell me, himself." Ruthie said, "John Kelly and I decided not to spread the information any further unless the need arises. Agree?"

"Of course, that's what I would do," Van said. "Jamie and Aaron don't know, do they?"

"They haven't been told, but my guess is that they figured it. I mean, it's not that uncommon to use someone to get information."

"Well, I'm just glad the mystery is solved. Now we can deal with getting Ian well."

John Kelly chuckled, "Twice. Once from the surgery and once after Ruthie gets a hold of him."

"I may have to take a swing at him myself," Egan stated. "He had me worried beyond sense."

Van got up and kissed his cheek, "You are such an old busybody."

After a quick cleanup of the house and a change of clothes, the three headed off to the hospital. By quarter to ten, Greg met them in the hall. "He had a good night, but this morning, his arm started to give him hell. Dr. Turner is with him now and should be ready to call you in soon." Greg noticed Ruthie, "Looks like you got some needed rest. Good."

They all gathered in Ian's room a bit later. He was awake, but in and out of consciousness. Ruthie went over and kissed him gently. He smiled before he closed his eyes again.

"Yesterday, I was very optimistic," Dr. Turner began. "Today, I am still optimistic, but it is tempered. He is beginning to exhibit the same issues that he had in Shreveport after that surgery. We are going to try to catch it before it gets ahead of us and he has convulsions like down there. We are going to keep him heavily sedated for a few days to let the healing start."

"Like how long?" Ruthie asked, still holding his hand.

"Maybe three. We will then lighten it up and see how he's doing. You will be able to see him, but he won't be able to visit more than he is now. However, the surgery went well and the grafting seemed good. I think he will have a good recovery, once we get past this. Any questions?"

"Will he be in the hospital a lot longer then?"

"No." Turner said, "Once he gets past this misfiring, he should do very well. Greg will be here with him, so if you have other things to do, I would suggest that you do them. Sitting here for three days can be tiring and will serve no purpose. Greg will let you know if he is going to be awake."

"Then the only face he will see is Greg's?" Egan blustered. "Gawd All Friday! He will probably think he is his soul mate!"

Greg jumped into the conversation, "No. I promise. He's seems the nice sort, but I prefer my wife."

After a few more questions and conversation, Ruthie kissed him goodbye and they left Ian to sleep.

14

When they got back to the house, the phone was ringing while they unlocked the door. Van ran to answer it, "Hello?"

"I was just about to hang up," John Kelly said. "How's Ian?"

"They are going to keep him heavily sedated for a few days," Van answered. "Here's Ruthie."

Ruthie took the phone and they talked a bit about Ian's condition. Then John Kelly said, "Have some worrisome news."

"About Taylor?"

"No, haven't been able to locate her or Streak yet. Aaron's informant reported that the Norris ring knows Ian is in Boston. They are in mission-mode, again." John Kelly said. "Now, that doesn't mean that they know where he is or anything, so don't freak out on us."

"John, we talked to Greg, Ian's nurse coordinator or whatever they call him. We told him about what's going on yesterday morning. He is very reliable and said he would be glad to help in any way. He also asked that he be kept in the loop, especially if it has something to do with Ian's welfare. I will give you his phone number, okay?"

"Might be a good idea to have it. Thanks, Ruthie." Then he hesitated, "Ruthie, I want you to know that you are a real trooper. I can see why Ian loves you."

"Thanks. I can see why Nancy loves you, too." Ruthie answered, "Is there anything we should be doing?"

"Not yet. We will let you know if you need to take any precautions. Just don't go on television or do any sky writing. Okay?"

"You have my word."

Ruthie called Mo, Ian's mother, and updated her and then Carl, Ian's stepfather and retired FBI agent, wanted to talk to her. First, Carl gave her an update on their garden and then asked about Ian. Before the conversation was over, she had told him about the situation, minus the affair, with the Norris ring. "Do you need me to come out there? I can be on the next plane."

"I know, but since half the police force is Harrington, I think we will be okay. Thank you anyway. It is more important you keep Mo under control. You know how our Mighty Mo gets. Okay?"

"I'd rather be out there fighting crime!" he chuckled. "Well, keep me informed and be careful. Let John know you told me. Okay? Be careful."

"Thank you, Carl. Did I ever tell you how much you mean to me?"

"Not yet. I'll clear a day off my calendar for it. Need more than eight hours?" he laughed.

"No, I should be able to cram it in," Ruthie laughed.

They spent the day doing household chores and getting the laundry done. Of course, Egan washed his car in the front drive and polished it to a brilliant sheen with that silicone oil stuff. Van bawled him out when he got some on the driveway. "This spot is so slippery, it is going to cause broken bones! You better figure out how to get this stuff off here. I'm warning you, I'm going to throw that junk away."

"You can't! I need it. And it would be too expensive to throw out three full cans of it!"

"Three full cans? How many did you buy?"

"Four came in a case. I got a discount for buying a case." He explained. "No point in having a beautiful car without a vivid shine! Keep your mitts off my silicone!"

"Look Buddy, if I slip one more time on these spills, it will be history! And you might be, as well! What kind of stuff is it that even makes concrete slippery?" Van growled with authority, "This is your last warning, Mister!"

"Yes, Ma'am."

As he went back to buffing his car, he talked soothingly to his Cadillac, comforting it so it wouldn't be hurt by Van's insensitivity toward it. Van walked back to the house shaking her head, "Ruthie, I have no idea what possessed me to marry that goof ball."

Ruthie watched as he almost slipped himself on the slippery concrete. "I think it was a service to the community. Someone has to keep an eye on him." She patted her shoulder, "Is there something that will take that stuff off?"

"When he had it on the linoleum, we had to use this strong stripping solution. It was a horrible and caustic."

Mid-afternoon, Greg called and said that Ian should be more awake about five, if they wanted to see him. "Okay," Ruthie said. "How's he doing?"

"Sleeping like a baby, since you left this morning."

"Have you been with him all day and night?"

"No, I slept in his room last night, but today I was mostly working with my two other folks. I may go home tonight if he gets back to sleep after dinner."

"You should," Ruthie answered. "One of us can sit with him."

"Nope, not Dr. Turner's policy. But even if I sleep here tonight, I will go home to see my family for a couple hours this evening. Don't worry."

"Do you ever get time off?"

"Sometimes I'm off a few days in a row, at a time."

"Oh Greg, I gave my brother-in-law John Kelly your phone number and I told him we had filled you in on the situation with these criminals. Today, he told me they got word that ring is actively looking for him."

"I'll go out now and tell the nurses' station that he is to have no visitors except you three and this John Kelly; without permission from me or you. Okay?"

"That would be wise. I doubt they know he's there, but he would be a sitting duck when he is unconscious," Ruthie thought aloud.

"I might call and talk to your brother-in-law. Think that would be useful?"

"Likely." Ruthie answered, "Thanks, Greg."

The three piled into the shimmering red Cadillac and headed down the street. A few houses down and across from Egan's house were some old junker cars parked, with some hoody-type teens hanging around. Egan scowled, "As soon as their folks leave, these punks invite their friends over. The place looks like the apocalypse! How can the folks be so nice, and these kids be such a loss?"

"They aren't bad kids, Egan," Van cajoled him. "They are just acting like teenagers. You know, 'against the man'. They are only making their mark."

"If Otis makes a mark like that, the city says I need to be using my pooper-scooper!"

"Calm down, their folks will be home in a few days and all of the junkers will disappear."

"Sure hope so," Egan complained. "I don't want their rust to rub off on my Caddy."

Van crossed her eyes and Ruthie giggled, "You are certifiable."

When they arrived at the hospital, Greg was just getting Ian set up in bed for his supper. Ian was groggy, but somewhat awake. Greg smiled, "Look who's here? Your family came to help you eat this gourmet meal."

Ian looked at him with drug-induced wonder and then smiled as Ruthie gave him a kiss. He tried to say hi to Van and Egan, but closed his eyes to sleep some more. Greg explained, "He will be in and out. Could you feed him his dinner? Wait until he is awake and then give him just little teaspoons of this stuff. Let's see, he has puree of steamed chicken, puree of steamed rice and puree of some indistinguishable vegetable. For dessert, he has a portion of puree of puree. Looks nummy. Try to get him to eat it, even though it isn't much more than a cup, total. We want to get his body used to working again. Okay?"

Ruthie nodded, "Are you going home now?"

"Are you trying to get rid of me?" Greg put his hands to his chest, feigning indignancy. Then he laughed, "Actually I am. I have to see my daughter's ribbon that she won at the library for reading a whole book by herself."

Ruthie broke into a broad grin, "That's wonderful! How old is she? What did she read?"

"She's four and this is her first book, *The Little Train That Could*." Greg laughed, "I really think she won the ribbon for remembering to turn the page!"

Egan frowned, "How would that be the case?"

"She read it to me over the phone this morning. She didn't even have the book with her! Marcy, the wife, said she had read it over so often, she knew it by heart. Since she was supposed to read it, I told her to be sure to turn the pages," Greg related proudly. "My little girl pulled it off without a hitch!"

Van laughed warmly, "Well, tell her that it is a wonderful achievement."

"I will," Greg smiled. "I'm out of here and I'll be back at seven. Are you going to be here, or should I tell the nurses' station to have someone watch over him?"

"We will be here," Ruthie assured him. "Don't rush back. Your family is important, too!"

Greg smiled, appreciatively, "Not a problem. See you in a few."

Feeding Ian his dinner took the better part of an hour. He was so dopey; he hardly could remember to swallow. The family managed to get him to eat most of it, but Egan tasted it. "Leapin' Leprechauns! I think these guys need a salt shaker! It is like eating flour with water."

"How would you know how that tastes?" Van crinkled up her face. "Never mind, I don't want to know."

"I know stuff," Egan blustered. "You just don't realize how much I know. I'm not as dumb as I act."

Van just laughed, "I hope not!"

About quarter to seven, John Kelly knocked at the door. "Can I come in?"

"Sure," Egan grinned. "It's a pleasure to see you."

John Kelly's was somber, "You might not think so when I tell you what's going on."

Ruthie went around the bed to him, "Before you tell us, do you want to say hi to Ian? He is really out of it, but he can wake up a bit. Okay?"

John went over and after a couple tries, got Ian to open his eyes and recognize him. "Hi, I came to check up on you? Are you behaving?"

Ian shrugged slightly, "Care of Ruth."

"I'm doing that," John Kelly assured him. "You go back to sleep and don't worry about a thing."

Ian studied him a second and then went back to sleep. John Kelly stepped back from the bed, "He's pretty out, huh?"

"Yah." Egan said. "Do you want to talk here, or in the hall?"

"I thought I'd wait until Greg is here. They told me at the nurses' station, he is on his way back in."

"No, I'm not," Greg grinned as he came in. "I'm already here! Did you take care of my guy?"

Ruthie filled him in on how things went and then said that John Kelly wanted to talk to them. Greg's eyes darkened with worry and he said very softly, "Let's just step out into the hall. I don't want my boy to overhear something and get his blood pressure torqued."

In the hall, John Kelly explained. "Aaron heard back from his informant about half hour ago. He said that Ian has been located. Seems Taylor followed you at the fair and jotted down your license number. She saw you get into the vibrant red Caddy! Yesterday, they had one of their 'people' inside the DMV run the plates. Taylor knew his last name was Harrington but wasn't sure about the first name. When she heard Egan, she thought that might have been it. They followed you up to the hospital yesterday, but didn't see Ian. Today, they were keeping watch on the house for him, but by noon decided that maybe he was in the hospital. So, they had someone up here check it out. The informant said this one guy goes with a gal that works on sixth floor and she called him with his room number about an hour ago."

Egan's mouth fell open, "My car? My car did it?"

"Don't be silly. If you guys got in an old Ford, she would've still written down the license number." John Kelly assured him. "We're sending up a man in street clothes to sit in the waiting room and watch his door."

"Why not post them out front?" Egan asked. "Like they do in the flicks?"

"Because then we might as well paint a dotted red line right to his room. The only one of the hospital staff that will know there's someone out there, is you, Greg. Since we are still scoping out who this girlfriend is who works here, we would like to keep quiet about it."

Greg nodded, "So, you are expecting big trouble?"

"Don't know. We know they'll make a move, but how or when, we don't know. If you want, we can put a cop inside his room."

"I'd rather you didn't. He should get as much rest as he can and not be disturbed."

"I can sit here with him," Egan announced.

"So can I," John Kelly offered.

"If this girl works here, she would know Dr. Turner's policy. That would be a major tip off that we are on to her. I was an MP in the military. I've had some hand-to-hand training. I'll watch out for him. If I need help, how would I get the guy in the waiting room?"

"If someone is in here already, just yell or push a buzzer. Any ruckus, the guy will rush in. Hopefully, you won't know who he is. There always seems to be folks sitting around in these waiting rooms, fidgeting. So, hopefully, no one would notice. He will be armed." John Kelly explained. "If they make any attempt and they'll know we know, so we will just post some men outside. Then it won't matter. Tomorrow, we will probably have a couple folks in the waiting room."

"Tomorrow is going to be tricky," Greg said thoughtfully. "I have two other patients and won't be with Ian all day."

"I will be here then," Egan stated. "It's settled. How will I know who is a real nurse and should be in here, and who shouldn't?"

"I will give him his bath and stuff. If you are here, you can help me lift him. There should be no one else."

John Kelly said, "Aaron will come to relieve Egan about two."

Egan nodded, "You got it. I'll be here at what time?"

"Six too early?"

"Not a mite. I'll not be sleeping a wink. I have to hone my skills tonight."

John Kelly wrinkled his forehead, "Which skills would those be?"

"Turning my body into a lethal weapon."

15

Everyone was very quiet on the way home, and barely said a word to each other before going off to try to sleep. They had decided not to call Carl and Mo because it was late there, and there was nothing they could do but worry anyway.

Ruthie said her prayers and took a hot bath. Then she went to bed and lay there. Her mind was a blur of 'what ifs' and 'I shoulda said' until she cried. Then she cried herself to sleep.

##

Greg got his patient settled for the night and then moved his cot over by the door. It wasn't blocking the doorway, but would make it difficult for anyone to come in without him being aware. Then he washed up and spread out on his cot. After tossing and turning, he was finally able to get to sleep.

##

Officer Dorman was trying to keep his leg from falling asleep in the waiting room chair he was sitting in. It was right across from the entry to the hallway, with a perfect view of the door to Ian's room. He had arrived about nine-thirty at the waiting room, which was between the nurses' station and the elevators. After he sat down, another man came in, talked to the nurse on duty for a minute, made a phone call and then sat down. He read a magazine and tried to keep awake, like everyone else. There were three other people in the waiting room. A middle-aged woman, who had her feet up on her humungous handbag and was knitting, and a couple.

The couple consisted of an elderly man, and a young woman who seemed to be his granddaughter. The young woman was watching the old man, while he was staring down the opposite hall.

The only one that Dorman was suspicious of was the man who came in the same time that he did. Not for any specific reason or thing he did, but simply because he sat almost next to him, affording him the same view of Ian's door as his own. Most folks tend to spread out in a large room, to have their own space. However, Dorman could think of a thousand justifiable reasons why the man wanted to sit there.

About one-thirty, the man got up and made a phone call from the pay phone by the elevators. He only spoke a few minutes and then went into the men's room, before coming back to his seat. The old man had stumbled over to the water fountain to get a drink of water and fell. The young lady rushed to help him up and the nurse and Dorman helped her. When they got him sorted out, Dorman checked the waiting room. The man was gone. He looked down the hall and just caught a glimpse of the door closing to Ian's room. He took off down the hall. The nurse yelled, "Sir, you can't go down there!" and ran to call security.

##

Greg's wristwatch alarm had gone off and he got up to check Ian's vitals and give him his medication. He was standing, facing away from the door, between the door and Ian. He was taking his blood pressure when out of the corner of his eye, he noticed the hallway light shine into the room as the door opened.

He was beginning to turn when he felt a strong arm around his neck and a wet cloth over his mouth and nose. It was chloroform. Greg kicked backwards as hard as he could and broke loose of the man just before he passed out from the chloroform.

Dorman dashed in as Greg's head hit the side of the bedframe on his way down to the floor. The officer lunged at the man and they pushed Ian's bed toward the window. Dorman saw the knife the man was holding and tried to grab it. The man was in a rage and leapt toward Ian, lunging he knife into his chest once.

When he tried for another stab, Dorman wrestled it from him. At that point, the hospital security guards came in. One turned on the overhead lights, while Dorman yelled, "Boston PD!"

The guards took him at his word and helped cuff the man with the knife. About then, Greg was crawling his way back up from the floor. He saw that Ian was bleeding and rang the buzzer for help and worked to stop the bleeding.

Within seconds, more staff arrived and they were able to get Ian stabilized so they could take him down to OR. One attendant put a bandage on Greg's forehead. Dorman took the man out of the room as the security guards stood guard at the door.

##

It was a few minutes after two when Egan called Ruthie. "Come girl. Throw on your clothes. We have to get to the hospital, right away!"

The three were at the hospital in minutes, with Egan explaining the phone call he had received from Jamie, explaining the situation. "John Kelly is going to meet us there."

Ruthie was crying silently when they got to the door of Ian's hospital room. Greg was there and said, "Come with me. We can go down to the OR on second, where we waited before."

"How bad is it?" Ruthie asked.

"Bleeding like crazy, but it didn't hit anything vital. He didn't need to lose blood like this, but the ER doc says he should do alright." Greg put his arm around Ruthie. "I'm so sorry. I didn't do a very good job caring for him."

"Nonsense, young man. You saved his life and took a beating besides. That isn't in your job description." Egan said, "If you were in a real war zone, you would've earned a medal of valor, no doubt."

"Well, thanks, but I don't feel like it. I was supposed to protect him." Val smiled, "You need a break. You should be able to rest."

"I couldn't now anyway. I am going to check my other patients and then go down to OR. I will talk to you when I hear something. Okay?"

"Okay." Ruthie smiled, "Thank you for all you've done for Ian."

About two hours later, after John Kelly had joined them in the OR waiting room, Greg came out to announce that Ian was being moved into Recovery. "He's doing fine and should be shipshape in a week or so. The doc will be out in a minute. I'm going to sit with him in recovery. He should be back up in his new room in about an hour. But, he'll be okay."

"How are you, Greg?"

"Got a major chloroform headache, but other than that, alright."

Grey had just left, when a young doctor came up and introduced himself. "Hello. I'm Dr. Beeson. I just stitched Mr. Harrington up. Except for a nasty nick of his lung, the knife missed all the vital organs. He is all stitched up and should be on the mend in a week to ten days. Of course, he was lucky, if you can call it that. He was only a couple floors from OR and almost sedated when it happened. I can honestly say, I don't think he felt a thing, or even knew what was going on. He should do fine."

"Will he have any permanent damage or problems with this?" Ruthie asked.

"He shouldn't. After he is out of recovery, we are going to move him back to the neurology floor, but in a different room. The police want to tape his old one off to fingerprint or whatever. He will be in 4152 this time. I will look in on him in a bit and then check on him later tomorrow. Okay?"

"Thanks, Doctor." Van said.

"You folks look worn out. I hope you can get some rest once we get him back into his room. Take care," the doctor shook their hands and left.

Without asking, Egan went over to the desk and told the attendant to let Greg know they were going across the street to the diner. They would be back in a bit. No one argued with his decision.

As they sat down with their coffee and oven fresh muffins, they all shared a big sigh. "Gawd all Friday!" Egan groaned, "Well, this should settle it now, huh? Only good I can see of it."

John Kelly methodically buttered his blueberry muffin, "I wish. They failed. That's all. They'll try again. The more failures they have, the more they will try."

"You mean forever?"

"No, but until we get the lion's share of them. We should have posted men by his door. That was a mistake."

"Now don't start that. You had reasons why you did what you did. They seemed reasonable. Don't go second guessing yourself." Van said, "Everything is okay. You were diligent. Are you certain they will be back?"

"Yah," John Kelly nodded. "Jamie is going down to interrogate this slime. I still want to talk to Streak and see what he knows. You guys okay?"

"Just tired." Ruthie answered, "Should Egan sit with Ian today?"

"No, we are posting men outside his door. I think Greg should go home to get some rest, too. You guys need to go home and get some sleep."

Egan's eyes became huge. Ruthie asked, "What is it?"

"Who is going to tell Maureen? Miss Mo will have my hide!"

John Kelly laughed, "Aaron said he'd call her. Actually, I think he is planning on talking to Carl and letting him tell her."

"When I get home, I'm unplugging my phones! She'll have her dial finger a-spinning in no time!"

16

After stopping to see Ian in his room, the three went home. As they drove up the street to Egan's home, they passed the teenagers congregating again at the end of the block. Egan had a fit, "If they hadn't drug all their trashy cars up here, I might have noticed those Norris people! I'll be having a grand talk with their parents when they get home. That is a pronouncement you can build on!"

"Oh now Egan, don't jump to conclusions. They aren't bad kids," Van said. "I don't want you causing a ruckus with their folks. Hear?"

"Because of them, our boy almost met his Maker."

"Uncle Egan," Ruthie said sternly, "That's ridiculous. And for all you know, that Norris might have been driving a Mercedes. These kids had nothing to do with what happened."

"Mind my words," Egan continued, "You get this stuff in the neighborhood and next thing you know, you are selling heroin at your lemonade stand!"

Ruthie raised her eyebrows, "I think someone needs a nap!"

No one got a nap, however. The phone started ringing before they got the coffee pot on. They did take turns cleaning up, doing the household chores and fielding phone calls. Carl called, having talked to Aaron. He had not told Mo yet and was going to talk to Matt before he did. He thought it would be wise to have back-up. He said, "You know, she is going to want to come out. She about went goofy on us when Matt was in the hospital in Maine. She doesn't like anyone messing with her Leprechauns."

"I know that to be a fact," Egan agreed. "But what point would there be to putting herself in the midst of it. The hospital doesn't want family up there all the time. Turner has strict rules about that with his patients."

"Why? I would think that would be easier on the staff," Carl asked.

"Greg said Turner had two cases back to back where some helpful, well-meaning family members moved a limb that tore the grafting or in the other case, fed a sedated patient and the man aspirated. He nearly died. The doc just decided never again. So, this is how he does it. He has a great reputation."

"Makes sense. Well, I'm going to talk to Mattie." Carl said. "We will talk to Zach, too. He is already worried about his sister."

"She is holding up as well as the rest of us," Egan said. "She was going to call the clan when she can find a minute. Did you tell them yet?"

"I filled in them a little last night. Well, seems we have a small revolution arising in the playroom. Mary and Martha! These kids will turn my locks to pure white!"

Things had just begun to quiet down and Egan had dozed off on the living room sofa. Ruthie was heading upstairs for a nap, when Van answered the phone. After she said hello, her tone became very hushed and focused. Ruthie stopped on the stairs and came back to the kitchen to hear better. Van was nodding and said, "Certainly, I will tell her. Thanks, John Kelly."

She hung up and gave Ruthie a big hug. "We need more coffee. Sit and I will fill you in on what John Kelly just told me."

Apprehensively, Ruthie took two mugs from the cupboard as Egan came in, yawning. "Best make it three."

They all sat down and Van said, "Aaron got a call early this morning. There was a drug overdose brought in and the patient was DOA. It was Taylor Collins."

Both Ruthie and Egan stopped in mid-motion and their mouths dropped open. John Kelly is on his way to see this Streak. They had moved into a flophouse, where her death was reported. Streak was arrested at the scene for possession of narcotics and stolen property. John Kelly will see what he can find out. Taylor overdosed in the early hours of the morning. Aaron's informant hasn't checked-in, so he hasn't heard about the fallout from last night. The man can't call very often. The guy that came after Ian last night clammed up and is not saying a word. They did uncover the girl who worked at the hospital and she no longer has a job there. What else? Oh, John Kelly has an appointment with Taylor's parole officer about eleven. Although it isn't as important now, John thought he should still talk to her."

Egan sat shaking his head, "A fine-upstanding group, these Collins-Norris folks."

"Makes me sick," Ruthie shrugged. "In that environment, who has a chance?"

A little after noon, they were just sitting down to their toasted cheese sandwiches and tomato soup, when John Kelly knocked at the door. Egan answered and grinned as he opened the door, "Come on in. You look like you need a bit of hot soup. Van, put another bowl out."

John Kelly smiled, "I won't argue. That sounds good."

After he got settled with his soup and sandwich, he began to fill them in. "I talked to Jamie, and they've found no more than a few hours ago. Ian's assailant got himself a lawyer. I talked to Streak. He's a piece of work."

John took the last bite of his toasted cheese sandwich, "He just sat there with a belligerent sneer on his face until I mentioned Taylor."

"I imagine he was pretty upset that his girlfriend died," Van suggested.

"I've seen folks more upset when the fly they swatted quit kicking. He was only furious. He was irate that she OD'd. He said she started to whine after she heard the ring was going after Ian. Next thing, she injected herself. The landlord happened by and saw she was dead. The landlord is the one that called it in."

Egan frowned, "What was Streak planning on doing with her body, for Heaven's sake?"

"Guess he wanted to dump her. He didn't want the cops 'rooting around' his place. Of course, they did and he got arrested for all his contraband. So, he was mad as hell. When I asked him about his girlfriend, he said she was just an easy lay and he didn't give a damn what happened to her or her bastard. He went into a rant about how she ruined his life and so on and so on." John shrugged, "Can't see how anyone could ruin what he had, but I guess."

Ruthie shook her head, "It doesn't seem like the girl had a chance."

"Well, I went to her parole officer." John Kelly took Ruthie's hand. "Do you want the straight of it? In private or what?"

She studied his face, "What would be good. Just tell the whole thing. It saves a lot of time. I'm tired of all the intrigue. What could you possibly have to tell?"

John Kelly grimaced, "Taylor started hooking and luring drivers away from the car keys at an early age. She was likely about thirteen or fourteen. Dropped out of school and was into drugs by then. At the time of the big bust on the Norris car ring, she was twenty. Seems she wanted a real life, but by then, her course had been set. Then she met O'Hara, or Ian. He was nice to her and treated her like a real person. She liked that. Of course, we know that they became involved a few months before the bust. After the arrests, she never saw or heard from him again. She knew he had opened the door for the cops, so at first, she was angry, but she missed him. She had hoped she had made a mistake and that he was in jail, too. However, she had no way of knowing or wasn't clever enough to find out.

"Her court-appointed attorney suggested she plead guilty and just start serving her sentence right away. She would be free sooner and with less trouble. So, she was in the Women's Prison before Christmas. The bust was in mid-November. It was there they discovered that she was about two months pregnant."

Egan dropped his spoon into his soup bowl, "All the Angels on High!"

Ruthie didn't move and just continued to watch John talk, but Van reached over and took her hand. John Kelly cleared his throat and continued, "She had the baby in June in 1968. Of course, the little boy was taken from her and placed in the Child Service system. She refused to sign a release on the child for adoption and vowed that when she got out of jail, she would get him back."

Van looked puzzled, "Did she have him with her when she died?"

"No. He is still in the system. She didn't have a job or a home for him to go to. Besides, the PO thought she was using again. She would have to prove to Child Services that she could take care of him, and she couldn't do that."

"So, where is this boy?" Egan frowned.

"Jamie is on his way over to Child Services as we speak. He'll find out. This we do know, he wasn't adopted because she never signed away her parental rights. That's all we know. So far, no one has claimed her body and her autopsy is scheduled for tomorrow morning."

Then the young man looked at Ruthie, "Say something."

"I don't know what to say. Do you think Ian knew she was pregnant?"

"Highly doubtful. I don't think she knew and he had no contact with her at all after the bust. If he would have known, he would've told me the other day. So, no. I don't think he has a clue. And just because she was pregnant, doesn't mean a thing about who was the boy's father. The only one I know wasn't, is Streak."

Numbly, Ruthie picked up her dishes without a word and put them in the sink. The rest of the folks sat in silence at the table and watched as she went upstairs and heard the door close. Then they looked at each other. After a few very long minutes, John Kelly mumbled, "I shouldn't have told her."

"You had to. She said she wanted to know and if she found out later and you hadn't said anything, you would be in deep trouble." Van reassured him. "I will give her a bit to absorb this and then I'll go talk to her. What do you think, John Kelly? Do you think that boy is Ian's?"

John Kelly shook his head slowly, "Timings right, but your guess is as good as mine. I am certain that Ian knew nothing about any pregnancy. That I know. I guess we will know more after Jamie goes to Child Services." Then he looked up the stairway, "I shouldn't have told her."

"Yes, you had to. We will let Van talk to her." Egan said. "What do Aaron and Jamie think?"

"Neither of them think Ian knew a thing about it. They said I should find out more about it before we jump off a ledge."

"That ledge is looking better every minute," Van nodded.

17

It was one-thirty when Dr. Turner called. He said that he had met with Beeson. The nick on the lining of Ian's lung seemed to be responding to treatment well and the surgery was successful. However, Greg was not doing so well. Turner wanted to send him home to get some sleep and wondered if someone from the family wanted to come up to sit with Ian. Egan said that he had had a good nap and would be right there. Greg was expected to be back later that day, but his headache was really giving him grief.

Van checked on Ruthie who was sleeping. "I didn't wake her. She is all curled up clutching Ian's sweatshirt. I think it would be best if you just go, quietly and let her get caught up on her sleep."

"Turner said Ian is not awake at all and he won't know if anyone is there. But he thought maybe, because of all this trouble, someone might want to be with him, just until Greg gets back. I should be home late, so you guys go ahead and eat dinner. I was going to clean that silicone off the drive. Just leave the stuff here on the counter. I guess it will have to wait until tomorrow." Egan kissed his wife, "You may be right. That stuff is treacherous."

"I love you, Egan Harrington." Van hugged him.

"And I'm so proud that you do. You are my life, you know?"

"I do."

The phone rang about two and Van answered. It was Ruthie's brother, Zach, and he asked how things were going. He said that it was his half-day off, so he had a chance to talk to Matt. Together, they talked to Mo, who went ballistic.

"I imagine she wanted to commandeer an airliner to come out," Van guessed.

Zach chuckled, "Something like that! We got her to settle down, but she packed her bag anyway. She said next thing that goes awry, she's coming out. Seriously, Van, do you want someone there? How is Ruthie doing?"

"Right now, we are all tired, but she has been sleeping for almost two hours now. Egan went to the hospital to sit with Ian this afternoon. The doctors say he is doing okay, but he is heavily sedated now. Ian's brothers are working very hard on this case and trying to piece things together to keep us all safe."

"Matt told me about that girl that they ran into at the street fair. How's Ruthie handling that?"

"Okay. She was upset that she and Ian didn't have time to talk about it," Van said. "There has been a lot going on and he was just barely awake again when this last bit happened. They have a strong relationship. I feel it will weather this."

"I'm glad you are there for her. Just let her know I love her and I will be there as soon as I can– the minute she needs me."

"I will let her know. You take care of your wife and the little babies."

She had no more than hung up, when she thought she heard Ruthie. She up went the shiny, hardwood steps to her room and knocked, "Ruthie? It's Van."

Ruthie opened the door and gave her a big hug, "Oh Aunt Van. This is such a mess!"

"I know, but maybe if we bake some cookies, it will help."

Ruthie giggled, "You sound like Grandma! How will baking cookies help this?"

Van shrugged and laughed, "It can't make it any worse! And then we can have some with hot coffee."

"I'll be right there. I suppose Uncle Egan is polishing his car."

"No, he went to the hospital."

Ruthie froze, "Did something else happen?"

Van told her that Dr. Turner just wanted to send Greg home for a rest.

"That poor guy really needs it." Ruthie said as they went down the stairs to the kitchen. "I'm glad you didn't wake me. I don't know if I want to see Ian right now. Does that sound mean?"

"No," Van said as she set her recipe box on the counter. "You need some time to absorb all this. I put a corned beef in the oven for dinner tonight. Could you thumb through this and find the recipe for Root Beer Cookies? They are Egan's favorite."

"That does sound good." Ruthie pulled the box over to herself, "I was lying up there trying to hate Ian, but all I could do is cry."

Van giggled softly, "I'm glad you didn't succeed. I know this is hard for you to handle, but let's be practical. You know how men are. They love with their hearts, true enough; but that has little to do with the rest of their bodies. Ian is a kind, good man, but he is after all, just a human. He never would have done anything like this if he knew the hurt it would cause you. I want you to remember that."

"I know that. I just wish…"

"That he would have talked to you? You must realize that you are probably more willing to forgive him than he is to forgive himself. And he doesn't even know all of this about Taylor. Don't be expecting him to talk to you about feelings he hasn't had time to form yet."

Ruthie listened intently, "I know you're right. I guess I need to quit being a baby about all this. Oh, here is the recipe."

They both jumped when the sound of a couple loud motorcycles roaring up the street. Van picked up the box of silicone cans, "Glad Egan isn't here. He would be throwing a tantrum to those kids."

Otis went crazy in the backyard. They looked out the patio window and saw two thugs coming over the fence. They looked at each other in horror and took off for the front door. Through the corner glass by the living room. Ruthie saw that three more men were coming toward the front door.

"Quick, upstairs! We have no way out!" Van said in a panicked whisper. "Maybe they'll go away if they don't see us!"

Ruthie shook her head, "Don't think so. Van, give me a can of that silicone."

Van and Ruthie each grabbed a can and moved quickly up the landing and stairs, spraying the steps behind them all the way up. At the top, they could hear the men pounding on the front door. Ruthie asked, "Will those steps get slippery?"

"They should, if concrete will. Let's go call the cops."

The women ran to the phone in the master bedroom, but the line was dead. Van's eyes darted around the room and then she went to their bedroom window. "Grab me that throw blanket!"

While Ruthie did that, Van pushed the window open. It faced up the street when the teenagers were hanging out. She and Ruthie waved the blanket out the window, until it caught the attention of the boys. Once they knew they saw them, they waved frantically for them to come.

Downstairs, they heard the patio door crash in and the men come into the house. Then they heard the front door open and the other men come in. "See 'em?" Someone growled.

"No. Look around. They gotta be here. Nobody left here but the old man."

One of the men crossed the landing at the bottom of the steps and slid. Ruthie heard him fall. One man yelled, "What the hell! Can't you stand up? Big help you are!"

A second later, the women heard another man fall, "What's going on? Son of a ..." then another fall and a lot of profanity.

The women had now moved to get some weapons. Van found a metal statue of a some Roman goddess and stood in the hall at the top of the stairs. Ruthie still had a spray can in her hand. They heard scrambling, another fall and a gunshot. Then there was another fall, followed by another gunshot and more cussing. A gruff voice screamed and yelled, "You stupid ass! You shot me in the damned leg! Son of a ...!"

The women could not see, so they moved to the edge of the stairs. At the bottom of the stairs, it looked like a bunch of clowns crawling out of a Volkswagen! Men were falling and flailing about. One had apparently accidentally shot one of his compatriots in the leg.

One man made it about three-quarters the way up the steps by holding on to the railing, until he lost his balance. He slid belly-first down the steps, banging his bottom jaw on every step of his descent. He crumbled into a heap at the bottom.

Finally, one man managed to put his feet in between the railings and hoisted himself almost to the top of the steps. He almost fell and dropped his handgun. Van ran out from behind the door and clomped him with the statue. He pushed her back and she fell against the wall. Ruthie ran up to him and sprayed him in the face with the can. He grabbed at her and caught her wrist. He pulled her over with him, as he fell backwards the seven feet toward the floor as the stair railing gave way under their weight.

Seven young teenagers, between fifteen and seventeen, had come in the house by this time and had easily subdued the intruders. Jeremy yelled up the steps, "Mrs. Harrington, Gloria called the cops! I think they're here now. You okay?"

"I just twisted my ankle. Can you see to Ruthie?"

The teens had the culprits tied up with their headbands when the police arrived just seconds later.

Jeremy looked around and pointed to her, "Is this Ruthie?"

"Yes, is she okay?"

The boy looked her over, "She isn't bleeding, but she isn't awake either."

As they were speaking, four policemen came through the door, "Hold it, freeze in place with your hands where we can see them."

The teenagers all raised their hands and grimaced. Van told the police from the top of the stairs, "Not the kids! They saved us! They're our heroes! It's these guys. Could you check the young lady? She was pulled off the stairs from the top. Jeremy said she isn't awake."

Jeremy directed the cop over to where Ruthie lay, "She isn't bleeding."

The policeman yelled to another cop, "Call an ambulance."

"Is she okay?" Van asked, frantically, "She is pregnant, due in October."

"Why don't you come down here?"

"We sprayed silicone on the steps. It is too slippery!"

Jason, one the teenagers, said, "My dad made me clean up that stuff when I got it on the garage floor. I got some remover in my car. I can run get it."

Another cop said, "Good idea, kid. Do that."

They had a time getting the battered men on their feet when no one could get their footing. The boys helped the police and Jeremy stayed by Ruthie until the ambulance attendants arrived. Jason sprayed a path to the top of the steps and helped Van come down.

Almost everyone; cop, paramedic, teen or criminal, had slipped on the steps or landing at least once before they got everyone out in the front yard. John Kelly and Aaron drove up. John Kelly rode to the hospital with Ruthie, who was still not awake.

Aaron called the station and got a couple cops out to post at the house. Then he thanked the boys for saving Ruthie and Van. The boys were pleased and volunteered to clean the steps and landing so no one would break a leg. Aaron smiled, "I'd be glad to pay you."

Jeremy said, "We'll do it for nothing. We were just hanging around anyway and Mrs. Harrington is always cool. Maybe she can bake us some cookies one time.

Van hugged him, "I might even do it twice. Thank you so much."

18

The first sensation of movement and then nausea caused Ruthie to stir. She opened her eyes and could just make out that John Kelly was cramped next to her. She made a face and then started to gag. The ambulance attendant helped her. John asked, "She okay?"

The attendant nodded, "We won't know until we get her checked over. She's awake and that's good."

The attendant wiped her face and then John Kelly took her hand, "Hi Ruthie. We've had quite the adventure, huh?"

She looked at him with question and then asked, "Where?"

"We're on our way to Mercy Medical to get you checked out, Ma'am. You took a nasty fall," the attendant explained.

"Mercy?" she looked at John Kelly.

"Ruthie, it's closer than the hospital that Ian is in. Okay?"

She frowned and got sick again.

John Kelly paced the waiting room floor until the doctor came out. The doctor explained, "Your sister-in-law seems to be doing fine. She has a slight concussion and will have a full-blown headache but nothing is broken or anything."

"The baby?"

"Seems fine. We want to keep her here overnight to monitor things. In the early months of pregnancy, the babies are protected by the pelvic bones. She landed on her hip, so the little one probably just felt a jolt. Rest assured, we'll keep a close eye on things. Her head will give her the devil for a day or so, but she's awake. You can see her now, if you'd like."

The young policeman nodded, "Yes, please. I will be staying with her tonight."

"Not necess…"

"Yes, it is." John Kelly explained the situation to the doctor as they walked down the hall to her room. "Since she will be here overnight, I'll just stay. Or have my brother come in."

The doctor nodded, "I understand. Life is hard enough without some creeps running around making things worse. I will alert security and let the charge nurse know there will be a policeman around."

"Thanks."

John went in to the small room where Ruthie was resting. "Hi."

She smiled faintly, "What you must think."

He grinned, "You must not think we do a very good job protecting you! Aaron's informant had just called and we were on our way over when we heard about the break-in over the radio. Good thinking with that damned spray stuff!"

Ruthie shook her head and said weakly, "Don't tell Uncle Egan. He'll probably buy another case."

"I don't think Van will let him in the house with it. I called them and told them that the doc says that both your head and your baby seem okay. The doctors just want to watch over things tonight, before they send you home."

"I know," she looked at him. "This is like the worst hangover you can imagine."

John Kelly chuckled, "I've had some beauts! Doesn't sound fun."

"Is Egan home?"

"Yes, he just got home. Jamie said he came in all spouting about the neighbor kids, until he realized those boys were fixing his stairs!"

"Oh brother!" Ruthie smiled, "I bet he about choked!"

"Jamie said he had just called in an order for pizza for them!"

Ruthie nodded, "Does Ian know what happened?"

John Kelly became serious, "No. Greg was called, but Ian is out yet. Jamie was going to call Matt. I don't know what they are going to say to Mo. I know how she feels, but it wouldn't be good for her to be here. She can't do anything."

"I know, but she is worried."

"I understand, but if she had been here, she might have been wound up with those thugs at the house!"

Ruthie giggled, "My money would have been on Mo."

John Kelly chuckled, "Yah. They don't know how lucky they were.

Oh, in case you wondered, the man that slid down the steps is in surgery, having his jaw wired. One guy is having a bullet removed from his leg and the guy that pulled you down the steps not only has a concussion, but had to be intubated. That silicone really messed him up. The other two are bruised all over. Intake asked if it was a case of police brutality and one bad guy said, 'Hell no! That would have been better!'"

"Oh, I'm sorry," Ruthie mumbled.

"They deserved a hell of a lot worse." John Kelly straightened her blanket, "You go to sleep and I'm going to read that magazine. If you need anything, I will be sitting right over here."

"You don't need to…"

"Yes, I do."

The doctor came in to see Ruthie early in the morning. "Things seem to be A-OK with you, so you can go as soon as you have a ride."

"I will take her home," John Kelly said. "She is my sister-in-law."

The doctor smiled, "Nice to have your own security service, Mrs. Harrington. Looks like you need one! You will have a heck of a headache for a day or so. I have a prescription for you and that should help."

"Is everything okay with the baby?" Ruthie asked.

"It is fine. However, if you get any cramping or spotting, have someone bring you in right away. And Mr. Kelly," He turned to John, "If she drowses off in the middle of a conversation, becomes extremely dizzy, disorientated or confused, bring her back in, immediately."

"I'll see to it," John shook the man's hand, "Thank you so much."

Ruthie looked at him, "Yes, thank you."

"You're very welcome. Take care."

It was almost ten by the time John Kelly and Ruthie arrived at Egan and Van's home. It was a bustle of activity. There were men putting in a new patio door and some other workmen replacing the banister. Egan was out on the front lawn talking to some of the teenagers from up the street.

Ruthie looked at John, "I sure hope he isn't giving them the business about something."

"Doesn't look like it," John Kelly shrugged. "Let's go."

He helped her out of the car and they walked over to where the teens and Egan were talking. Egan was saying, "So, once we get things sorted around here, you bring that old junk heap up here. If you're of a mind,

I can show you how to fix it so it doesn't rattle and clang. I won't do the work, but I can show you how to handle a wrench. And that bike of yours, Jason, that thing smokes worse than Mt. Vesuvius! You bring it up here and I'll show you how to make it hum like a baby without polluting the planet!"

"You'd do that for us?" Jeremy asked.

"I said I would, didn't I? I'm a man of my word." He looked the boys over, "Now, don't be taking this that I approve of all your carrying-ons, but I think you got the makings of upstanding men...with proper training. Since I owe you more than I can ever repay, I think that I could help point you down the right path."

"You gonna lecture us?" Jason asked with a grimace.

Egan nodded, "Most likely, I will."

John Kelly started to laugh and they all turned, "Boys, you can count on it. But I have to say, you'll get used to it! I know, we all did."

Egan snarled, "And I'm thinking you need more."

Ruthie went over and hugged each of the boys, "Thank you all so very much for helping us."

Jeremy blushed, "You okay? You were out like a cucumber!"

"That I was. But the doctor says I'm fine, just a little headache."

"That's good," the boy said. "Well, the guys and I are going back to our house now. We need to clean up the joint. Mom and Dad will be back tonight."

Egan stepped forward sternly, "And I want to have a talk with them!"

"Why?" Jason's eyes sprang open. "You gonna tell them we had cigarettes?"

"Didn't know that," Egan frowned. "You gonna keep smoking?"

"No, sir," Jason mumbled.

"Then there's no reason bringing it up. Just stop before you get too started. Hear?" Egan's look riveted the boy.

"Yes, sir."

"I was thinking on telling them what a fine lot of heroes you were! I will wander down tomorrow. Now, you best go clean up your mess or your folks will have your hide."

"We will," the boys promised, "Bye."

"Bye boys, and thank you again."

Egan watched them walk toward the house and said, matter-of-factly, "Fine young men. I always said that."

Ruthie and John Kelly exchange a grin and headed toward the house.

The day was rather quiet, except for the workmen. Egan went up to the hospital to see Ian after lunch and planned to come home to make an early night of it. The patio door was replaced and in working condition before Egan left. The carpenters had the banister replaced by four; however, the resanding of the steps, staining and finishing would not be done until a later time.

Van and Ruthie sat on the patio and visited while keeping Otis company. The old dog had been quite excited that the neighbor boys came up to see him in the morning.

"I think it was good for him," Van smiled. "He probably thinks were are as old and boring as we think he is."

"Maybe he just likes the attention. I almost fell over when I heard Egan talking to those boys. One would think that he had always been their champion."

"He likes to talk a big act, but he really is a softie. You know, a lot like Carl."

"I've thought that before." Ruthie said thoughtfully, "Van, did you ever know Sean? Was he like Egan, or was he quiet like his boys?"

"I did know him. My husband used to play billiards on the same team as him. In fact, he and Sean died the same year. I was on first name terms with Maureen, but we didn't see each other very much. You know, most of my time was taken up with school."

"What happened to your husband, if I'm not prying?"

"Not at all. He had gall bladder surgery and it all seemed routine. He came home from the hospital and seemed fine. I woke up the next morning to find he had passed over while I slept."

"Oh Van."

"The autopsy found a blood clot had formed and hit his heart. At least, he wasn't sick and struggling a long time, like has happened to so many. But I had an awful time sleeping for a while after that. I still wake frequently and check to see if Egan is breathing. He breathes heavy while he sleeps. Sometimes I listen to him and find it comforting to know he is okay." Van admitted, "But back to Sean. He was more like his boys. Those young men are all rather quiet and thoughtful. They like to have a good time, but they aren't outspoken like Egan. Mo was always more outgoing than Sean; but after Egan took her under his wing, he put the vinegar in her. He told her she couldn't be shy because she had a big job to do. He would help her, but he wasn't going to carry the load and her, too."

Ruthie nodded, "That sounds like him. Well, she sure doesn't take a back seat. I'm actually surprised she isn't out here already."

"While you took your nap, Matt called. He said that she wanted to come, but Carl told her that it would just be more work for everyone and more folks to protect. He talked her down from the ceiling."

"I feel badly. I would call her but my head hurts and I just don't feel up to it today."

"She knows, Ruthie," Van assured her. "They all do. They send their love and ask that you call them when you feel better. The whole clan is praying for you."

Ruthie looked out across the yard, "Do the guys think that Norris' are about finished now?"

"The guys didn't know. But now they are actively searching them out, and so they will make no bones about giving us protection," Van shuddered. "People amaze me."

"Sometimes, Aunt Van," Ruthie confided, "I'm more amazed when folks are good than when they are bad. I don't want to be that way, but it's hard not to feel that way."

"I know, but if you give in to it; it is just feeding the tiger."

"Van, why do you think Ian didn't tell me? Didn't he trust that I would understand?"

"No. I think he was embarrassed. And Ruthie, you can expect that he will be even more so now after what happened last night. You can about bet on it."

19

The next morning, Jamie called while they were eating breakfast. "How're things going?"

"Good," Aunt Van replied. "How are things with you?"

"Okay," he hesitated. "Ah, is Ruthie handy? You know, forget it. It'd be better if John goes over to talk to her. You going to be around?"

"We can plan on it. Is there something new with the Norris crew?"

"No. They're busy pouting and licking their wounds. They won't talk except to tell us how maligned they are. Poor babies. But we did learn something else, and it looks like we will need Ruthie's help. I was going to tell her," Jamie hesitated. "On second thought, I think it would be better that John does. They seem pretty close."

"Doesn't sound like good news."

"Neither good nor bad, more like sensitive." Jamie said, "John will be here soon and then he can come over."

"How is he doing with his job? Isn't this taking away from his duties?"

"No. His precinct reassigned him for this. Aaron was given permission to work on it, too. The big shots know they can't keep us out of it anyway, so might as well utilize us."

"Makes sense." Van agreed, "We will make certain that we hang around here. Hope your day goes well."

"You, too."

It was about eleven when John Kelly knocked on the door. Van let him in and he looked around, "Those dudes really made a mess of your stairway. It was always so beautiful."

"Well, as much as I'd like to blame them, I think Ruthie and I messed it up. Between the spray and then removing the silicone, the finish is but a memory!"

"Yah, guess it just didn't have a chance, huh?" John nodded. "How's Ruthie?"

"She's much better. She said her headache is about gone. You look like you are more rested."

"Got some real sleep last night. It felt good, I have to say." John smiled, as Van handed him some coffee. "Turk was all bent out of shape that he didn't get to come over to help you and Aunt Ruthie. He really thinks that he could have wiped those bad guys out without the neighbors help.

"That and some silicone," Egan chuckled as they entered the kitchen. "Tell him thanks. It is good to know he has our back. Well, me and Van are trotting down to tell the Fergusons about their boys saving our backsides. I think Van has some cookies for them. I will carry them for her."

"Nice of you," John Kelly laughed.

"Well, she went through a lot, you know. A guy needs to help out. Miss Ruthie is out in back. She was talking to Otis."

John went out the back door and saw her playing with the ancient dog, "You look chipper today!"

Ruthie looked up, "You do, too. Did Aunt Van give you some of her killer Root Beer cookies?"

"No, I think she took them down to the neighbors."

"She has some more. Let me wash my hands and get you some. Van said you wanted to talk to me." She looked in his eye, "Bet you hate it that Ian asked you to take care of me."

"Not at all. But I have to admit, I always imagined you as a church secretary, not a daredevil crime fighter!" John Kelly laughed. "Nancy asked me last night how we got along. I said, 'I don't know how we'd do on a day trip, but we sure could write a crime series for television'!"

Ruthie handed him a couple cookies on a napkin, and they went back out to the patio. "You've been great. I think we'd do okay on a day trip, but we might get bored. So, what is the grim news you are bearing today?"

"How do you know it's grim?"

"First, they sent you. And second, I can tell you aren't happy." Ruthie touched his arm, "John Kelly, I'm sorry that I gave you such a bad time about Ian not talking to me. This morning, before I got up, I was thinking about it. I really made a mountain out of a molehill. I acted like a selfish brat. Will you forgive me? Ian is a good person, I love him with all my heart, and I need to remember that."

John dropped his eyes, "I'm glad you feel that way. Ruthie. We found out more about Taylor and… Ah, we found out yesterday, but no one wanted to disturb you because of your old head."

"I love how people let you feel better, so they can make you feel worse again!"

John Kelly gave her a surprised look and then laughed, "We do, don't we?"

Ruthie nodded, "You look almost sick. Just spit it out!"

"Taylor's autopsy was finished yesterday and the results are about as we expected. Drug overdose, but the Coroner is still waiting on the tox screen. No one has claimed her body yet, so it is going to be stored for a week or so. Since most of her next of kin is locked up or dead, it looks like she will be buried by the state in Potter's Field."

Ruthie winced, "John, I have a major thing about that, after the business with my dad. Can I ask you a favor? Before they do that, let me know. I will pay for her burial and get her a stone. Promise?"

"Why would you want to do that?"

"Zach and I inherited a lot of blood money from our father, so I can afford it. I also plan on paying Egan and Van for their repairs."

"They have insurance."

"I know, that's what they said. So I thought that maybe I could send them to that Country Inn place they like so much, while their steps are being redone. They can't stay here then and they can take Otis along to the Inn. That is the least I can do." Ruthie smiled, "As far as Taylor, just know that I really hate for anyone to not at least have their own casket and headstone. Can I count on you?"

"What would Ian say?"

"He would completely understand."

"Okay then." Then he shuffled his feet, "You may change your mind. Taylor does have next of kin, not that he can help with her burial."

Ruthie studied his face, "Who?"

"Her son."

"Oh, I forgot she had a baby. A boy, huh? Did I know that? Doesn't matter. The baby can't pay for her burial. Isn't he in a foster home, or something?"

"The little boy is here at the County Family Center. He is not a baby anymore. He is three and will be four the end of this month. He has not been adopted nor is he in a permanent foster care situation."

"What happened?"

"Well, he was with his first placement from the time he was born until he was over two. Those folks wanted to adopt him, but Taylor would not sign a release. She wanted to get out of prison and get her boy back. He went back to the Center and then was placed with another family a while later. He was there about three and a half months. They had to pull him from there because it was a bad situation. The foster parents had two more foster kids and turned out to be quite abusive. They brought the little boy back to the Center, but he hasn't been placed again. He was quite withdrawn after that last family."

"He's only three, you said."

"I know, but the social workers knew Taylor would be out of jail soon, so thought it might be wise to not place him again until they could see how she was. That fizzled, of course, and they were thinking they would place him again. Now, she's gone."

"He will likely do better when he is eligible for adoption, huh? I mean he is still just a little kid."

"They had hoped the first family would still want him, but they lost contact when they moved out West." John explained. "Ruthie, you know how jammed up all the Children's Services are. Right?"

"Of course."

"Well, they really want to find out, if they can, who his father is. Seems that Taylor had let it slip once to her PO that she wished that O'Hara knew about their boy. She was sure they would have a great life together."

Ruthie put her cup in her lap, "So, she thought Ian was the father."

"I guess, but you know Ruth, just because she wanted him to be, doesn't mean that he was. She was 'working' all that while. It could have been any number of men." Then he stared at the floor.

"What is it that you want to say?"

"The state would like to have some blood tests to prove or disprove paternity. They don't want to put the little boy in another situation where he might get a family and then have it pulled back again. Nor do they want to pay for raising a child who has a family. You know."

"So they want to do blood tests. Doesn't Ian have to sign for that?"

"He should, but because of his condition, he can't very well. They would really like to get this sorted out."

"I would think they could wait a few days. Good grief! It isn't like anyone is going anywhere!" Ruthie was adamant. "They can just wait until he comes around."

"Ruth, you can sign now to authorize the blood test. They will do a blood match and DNA."

"I know how it works. That's what they did with me and my father." Then she frowned at John Kelly, "What happens if the child is his?"

"He has a decision to make. Either he signs his rights over to the state and they will proceed to place him; or accept him as his child."

Tears started to fill Ruthie's eyes, "I just knew this was going to happen. I just knew it! Why can't things be easy?"

John Kelly's shoulders bent and he shook his head, "I have to say, I sorta thought this, too. But we need to get the blood tests authorized and done with. No decisions can be made until that is done."

"Why do I have to do it?" She raised her eyebrows, "I don't know what he wants! Or would want! Remember, he never even told me about his affair with her. Now, I'm stuck with this decision!"

"I know, but look—you and I both know that whether or not Ian likes it, the blood tests have to be done. You can simply sign the papers for him and they can take the blood while he is out."

"Simply? You make it sound so easy! It must be nice for him to sleep through all the mess he made!" She stopped and looked at John, "That was horrible for me to say! You must think I'm a monster."

"No, I don't. I have to say, on the way over here this morning, the same exact thought crossed my mind. We're just tired and this is a trying situation. It isn't his choice to be unconscious and I know he would do it for us."

"Yes I know, but I'm still mad about it." She raised one eyebrow, "I don't suppose you just happen to have the authorization papers with you?"

"Yes, just happen to!" He reached in his jacket, "Ruthie, it should be done. You know that."

"What if he wouldn't want to do it?"

"Then, I guess he should have stayed awake!" John Kelly said flatly. "I will take the papers to Jamie and they'll get the tests lined up for today."

"How soon will we know the results?"

"Tomorrow we will have the preliminary blood tests, but the DNA will take a while."

Otis brought his old ball up to the patio and set it by her feet. Ruthie picked it up, tossed it across the yard and watched as the old dog ambled over to it. She smiled, "He doesn't even bother to run."

"No, looks like he isn't concerned someone else wants it."

"John, do you know what the little boy's name is? Or anything like that?"

"His name is Taylor Collins. No middle name. That's all I know."

"Can I go see him?"

"Do you think that is a good idea? You may have no connection to him at all. I think it would only serve to get you upset." John pointed out. "I think that might be a bad idea."

"I think this whole thing is a bad idea. Somehow, I really want to see him. I feel that I need to and don't ask me why."

"Are you sure?"

"No. I'm not sure about anything." Then she looked at him defiantly, "I will only sign the authorization papers if you set it up so I can go see him."

"What are you going to say to the little kid? He's only three. He is likely not even Ian's boy or Ian will just sign his rights away. So, you might be making trouble."

Ruthie pursed her lips, "Yah, and we really don't want trouble. You have my deal."

"Ian will have my hide."

"Him or me, your choice."

"I might be able to outrun him for a while yet," John grumbled. "Okay, but I think you are making a big mistake."

"Thanks."

John had left by the time Van and Egan returned to the house. Ruthie had set the table for their lunch and was acting very mechanical. Uncle Egan watched her a minute and then made a questioning grimace to Van, who just shrugged. "John Kelly left?"

"Yes. He had to go take some papers to Jamie. Lunch is ready."

They sat down and said grace, but Ruthie never offered any conversation. Then Egan said, "I'll be ready to go up to see Ian in about an hour. Does that give you girls enough time to get beautiful?"

"I'm not going," Ruthie answered matter-of-factly.

Van frowned, "I thought you planned to."

"Changed my mind."

"I will stay home with you," Van offered.

"No need."

"What are you covering up, Girl? Out with it!" Egan blustered.

She related what she and John had discussed and that she had signed the papers.

"So, you plan on punishing Ian because he may or may not have a kid?" Egan growled.

"Nope," Ruthie answered, non-pulsed. "I'm waiting for a phone call."

Van took her arm, "Who from?"

"John Kelly. I asked him to set it up so I can go see this child."

Egan pushed his chair back and jumped to his feet, "Why in the Name of Glory would you do something that stupid!"

"I want to." Ruthie answered calmly without raising her voice. "Sit down before you have a stroke. I think I need to and I don't know why. I told John Kelly that I wouldn't sign the authorization unless he did it."

"What did he say?"

"Pretty much the same thing that you did, but without yelling. He said I'm making a mistake." She nodded her head to the side with a small shrug, "It would be hard to know one mistake from another in this mess. I want to see him."

Van took her hand, "Do you think that is wise?"

Ruthie choked a laugh, "What about this is wise? I just feel I should. No reason. Maybe it is God, maybe it is the Devil, and maybe I'm just bored. But I'm not leaving this town until I see him. There you have it. I would love for you to come with me, Aunt Van; but if you won't, I will call a cab. I am determined to see him."

"What in the Royal Hell do you plan to say to this baby?" Egan roared.

"I know how to talk to little kids. I just want to meet him, to see him and to have him be real. I don't like the fact that he has never been any more than a footnote in anyone's life. It is much easier to make a decision for a non-person than for a real one."

"Ian will be furious! If the blood tests do come back that the kid is his, he will just sign him away! I know he wants to have a family with you and your children. You are just messing it up!" Egan bellowed.

"I beg your pardon?" Ruthie smiled, "I don't think that I did. And it isn't just up to him if we have a family together or not. These are his doings, intentional or not. I am the one stuck with making decisions alone. My life has been disrupted, too. I'm not going to argue. I am going to see the little boy. Ian can be furious if he wants. It's his prerogative."

Egan opened his mouth, but Van shot him a warning look. He closed his mouth and sat back down at the table. Van said quietly, "Let me know when John Kelly calls. I will go with you."

Egan never spoke to Ruthie again, but left for the hospital. About one-thirty, Van answered the phone. It was John Kelly. "I set up an appointment for Ruth today at two-thirty at the Family Center. Tell her I will be there to pick her up about two."

"She asked me to go with her," Van explained.

"Thank goodness. I really don't think she should go."

"I know and Egan had a fit, but she is determined. I will take her."

"I don't get it. Is it a woman's thing?"

Van shrugged, "Might be, but remember, her childhood was a nightmare. She probably feels a lot of empathy for the boy."

"I hope she realizes that the kid likely isn't Ian's."

"She does. I don't think that makes a difference to her. She is looking at it from the boy's side of things." Van calmed him, "I will be there with her. It will be okay."

"Thanks, Aunt Van."

The ladies didn't talk except about the directions, all the way to the Center. After they parked and before they got out of the car, Van took Ruthie's hand. "Have you thought about what you want to find out? Or what you are going to say?"

Ruthie shook her head no, "I don't have any idea. I just feel this is something I really have, or need, to do. I promise I would never say anything to the boy or put him on the spot. He is the real victim in all this. I feel terrible that no one seems to appreciate that."

"I think we all know that, but you are right. He is not the center of the concern."

"I just have to do this," the young woman said. "And honestly, if Ian doesn't like it, it is just too damned bad!"

They went in and introduced themselves in the office. A stern, matronly woman who was in charge of the Center, came out and took them to her office. She gave them an uncompromising lecture. "These children are not a curiosity or something you can tell you friends at the charity about. They are real people. I will not allow you to upset them. Most have had more than their share of problems and don't need some do-gooder making brownie points at their expense. Make them no promises that you do not intend or are not able to keep. Do we understand each other?"

"Yes," Ruthie said. "I not only understand, I completely agree with you. Could you tell us a little about the boy, Taylor Collins?"

The woman made a face, "The cop that called said that's who you wanted to see. I don't like to do this. I think it is wrong, but I have to. He is a quiet boy and was deeply hurt at the last placement. It took us about six months to get that sorted out. He doesn't trust anyone and is a loner, but well-behaved."

"Did his mother ever visit him?" Van asked.

"Once, a few months ago, when she got out of prison. She came in here all rainbows and lollipops, made him huge promises and left. I think he really thought she meant what she said. Yesterday, I had to tell him that his mom died. He just shrugged and said, 'She didn't like me, did she? She said my daddy doesn't want me either.' Then he went back to his coloring. I don't know what he was thinking. But if either of you start messing with him, I will boot you out of here in a heartbeat."

"We won't," Van assured her.

The lady took them into a back hall. A few feet down, there was a large playroom on one side with a one-way glass to the hall. The workers could see in, but the children could play without feeling like they were under a microscope. There were about eleven children playing in the brightly colored room.

There were some shelves to the back that were filled with books and toys. To the right there was an open area with some games and toy cars. In front of the shelves were a few short tables with crayons on them and coloring books. To the left, there was a carpeted area with an old sofa and a television tuned to a cartoon channel.

The children were clean and well-groomed, wearing play clothes. Some of the kids were playing together. A couple girls were watching the television and one girl was looking at a picture book. Three boys were playing with plastic cars in the game area, and one was coloring.

Ruthie looked them all over and her eyes were drawn to the little boy who was coloring. She pointed at him, "That's Taylor, isn't it?"

The matronly woman glared at her, "I thought you didn't know him! Are you pulling a scam?"

"Not at all," Ruthie smiled. "It was just a guess. May I go in and talk to him?"

"Against my better judgment." The woman motioned for them to follow and they went into the room.

They entered the room, but none of the kids paid any attention. The woman pulled the chairs out at the table the little boy was sitting at, "Mind if we sit here?"

Ruthie was glad that her tone softened considerably when she spoke to the child. The little boy shrugged, but didn't respond any further. The lady patted the back of his hand, "These ladies came to say hello to you."

He looked at her with his big, deep blue eyes, "Why?"

"Because they just wanted to say hi."

He looked at them and said, "Hi."

Then he went back to his coloring. The women sat there, for a minute, but he paid no attention to them. Then the woman asked the two guests, "Well, you ready to go?"

Ruthie frowned, "Not yet. I would like to visit with him alone, if I may?"

"I warned you, no funny stuff," the woman became stern again.

"Cross my heart."

Van asked the lady if she would show her some of the activities that they had in the room for the children and the woman reluctantly got up to show her. Before she left the table, she warned, "I'm watching."

Ruthie nodded and moved over beside the little boy. "This is a nice place to play, huh? What are you coloring?"

"A page."

"That is a very pretty green," she commented as she noticed the entire paper was colored green, inside and outside of the lines. "Is that your favorite color?"

The little boy studied the paper but never looked up, "Yup."

"So, my name is Ruthie. What was yours?"

"Tater."

Ruthie smiled, "That's a cool name. You are a good colorer."

"I know."

"Do you do it a lot?"

The little boy looked at her for the first time, "I coddor ever day."

"What else do you like to do?"

"Watch Widey."

"Who's that?"

"Widey Coyote on TV! He's good," the little guy almost smiled, revealing a big dimple.

"You mean Wile E.Coyote? He is one of my favorites, too!"

He looked at her, "Do you have a TV?"

"I do. Right now I'm staying with that lady, Aunt Van, and she has a nice TV."

His eyes went over to the lady, "Aunt Van?"

"Yes. She makes the best cookies, too."

"Good," he said and went back to his coloring.

Then the theme song came on for *The Bugs Bunny and Roadrunner Show*. The little boy jumped right up and left his book. He went over and sat on the floor in front of the television.

Ruthie walked over with him, "Can I sit by you?"

He nodded and said, "You have to be quiet."
Ruthie smiled, "I promise."
He gave her a penetrating look, "Is that yes?"
"It is," she giggled. "I will be quiet."

They watched the show and then Taylor went back to his coloring. Ruthie went back with him and Van was already sitting at the table. "Hi," she smiled.

He nodded and picked up his crayon. Ruthie watched him, as he scribbled bright green on the page. "I have to go now, Tater. Would it be okay with you if I come see you again?"

He shrugged, "Yes." Then he looked at Van, "Aunt Van, too?"

Van was pleased, "Yes. I would like to come back."

"Okay." He continued to color.

When they got in the hall, the woman said, "I guess it was okay. Thank you for not upsetting him."

"He seems like a good kid," Ruthie asked, "Does he always watch Wile E.?"

"Tater loves his Widey. That's about the only time he ever gets animated." The woman said as she moved toward the exit, "Well, hope this helped you."

"Thanks," Ruthie shook her hand. "It really did."

In the car, Van never said anything. Ruthie waited for a bit and then said, "You know, too. Right?"

Van just nodded, "The minute I saw him."

"That dark curly hair, bright blue eyes and the big dimple. If he's not the spitting image of Ian, I don't know who could be. Like we say, if you've seen one Harrington, you have seen them all."

Van said, "When I saw him, I thought if he isn't Ian's kid, he is definitely Jamie's!"

"Oh my God! Can you imagine Vivian! She would totally go off the wall!"

Van got serious, "How are you going to be about it? I noticed you said we'd come back."

"I will, even if you don't want to. I don't know what I think about it. He is a cute little guy, small for his age, like Ian was. I don't know Van. I don't know what I think. Good night! Ian doesn't even know he exists."

"What do you think Ian will say or do?"

"I have no idea." Ruthie shook her head. "If he reacts at all like Egan or John Kelly, I guess he'll just sign the release papers."

"What do you think?"

"I want to weep. It would be easier if I knew how I feel about it, but I don't know if I could live with it. Or if Ian could? You know how he is about family. When I saw that little guy, all I could think about was my niece, Miriam, when she was so abused and neglected. But, it isn't my decision. I just need to decide if I can live with Ian's decision."

"What do you mean?"

"I don't know exactly. I really want to know how he is going to react."

"Ruthie, this is not a testing game. It is a 'for keeps' thing. I understand why you might want to know how he will react, but he won't be able to make the decision all on his own. His decision will depend on you. He will need to know your feelings."

"I know. Really, I do. But we haven't been able to talk to him about any of it yet."

"When do you plan to go back to see the little boy?"

"I don't know. Maybe tomorrow."

"Are you going to see Ian tonight?"

"I'm not certain."

21

The ladies had dinner ready when Egan came home. One look at him revealed it had not been a good day. Van gave him a hug and kiss on the cheek and Ruthie said, "Hello, Uncle Egan."

He kissed his wife and without a word went upstairs to wash up. It was unlike him to not say anything. When he didn't come back down in a couple minutes, Van frowned, "Can I ask you to watch the gravy? I'm going to see what's going on."

A couple minutes later, she came back into the kitchen. It was easy to see she was upset. "What is it, Aunt Van?" Ruthie asked with worry. "Is it that he's upset with me? I will just get a room somewhere. I'm so sorry."

"Don't go apologizing," Van stated. "He will be right down. They had a contentious day and he needs to talk to both of us about it."

"He was very unhappy with me this morning. I talked back to him. I had no right to do that. He is Ian's uncle, not mine. I overstepped my bounds. I shouldn't be imposing."

"Girl, you had a right to speak your mind," Egan interrupted as he came in the room. "I was spouting out of frustration. This whole thing is driving us all crazy. Good thing for Ian he is sleeping. I was jealous of him today!"

"How is he doing?" Van asked.

"They are hoping to begin to bring him out of it tomorrow, but slowly. They tried to this morning, but his arm went berzerk. They are worried. Doctor Turner talked to me and said he wants to see us tomorrow. You too, Ruthie. No more hiding from Ian."

"I'm not hiding from him, Uncle Egan. My head was bad and then today... well, you know."

"Yah, I know. Tomorrow at ten. Will you give me your word that you will be there?"

"Yes, I will. I would have anyway. You didn't need to act like I was going to turn my back on him."

"I don't know what anybody is going to do about anything anymore."

"Surely what Dr. Turner had to say isn't the cause for all this. What else happened?" Van asked.

They all sat at the table and after grace, Egan put the mashed potatoes on his plate. "The boys and I met for coffee at the diner this afternoon. The blood had been drawn for the paternity test." Egan shook his head, "It turned into a scene from Sherman's march through Georgia."

"Who was there?"

"Aaron, Jamie, John Kelly and then Frank, Colleen's husband. Well, the discussion came up about the blood test. John Kelly said you had signed for the paternity test on Ian's behalf, and that bent Frank out of shape. He agreed it had to be done, but he didn't think that Ian would have signed for it. Jamie pointed out that the state want to have it all settled before they try to place that kid again."

Ruthie nodded, "That's why I signed it. John Kelly said that was the case."

"I know, he said that. Then Frank settled down. He said, 'Well it probably isn't his kid anyway.' Jamie commented that it wouldn't be much of a matter anyway, because even if the test came back positive, he was sure that Ian would just sign his rights away. Then everyone could go back to normal."

Egan cleared his throat, "Then John Kelly told them that you had requested a visit with the boy. They went ballistic. John Kelly tried his best to calm them down, but to no avail. I even tried, but they were having none of it. Jamie about lost it. 'Why in the hell isn't she up there sitting with her husband instead of running around looking for bastard kids?' Then John Kelly got mad and came to your defense, and Frank jumped all over him. 'What brought all this big defense for her, anyway? Have you no decency? The man is in the hospital and you are getting all cozy with his wife!' Then Aaron defended John Kelly. Frank said, 'I know, but this will affect all of us. You know how our family sticks together."

"Oh my goodness." Van set her fork down, "Did someone tell him that Ian specifically requested John Kelly?"

"I did that." Egan replied, "Then Aaron said, 'I don't know what you're spouting about. John Kelly is as much family as you, Frank. You guys all married into it.' Then Jamie said, "A decision like this should be left to blood family only.'"

Egan shook his head, "I tell you, it was horrible. Before the coffee cups were empty, the whole damned bunch was arguing. Jamie and Frank were going to tell they wives! God help us, that's all we need! So, enjoy this quiet time. They are all converging on us tonight."

"Oh no, Egan!" Van squeaked, "We just got the house put together from the last brawl."

"The thought crossed my mind that we should've held off on getting the patio door replaced."

Ruth was frowning at her place, "I thought we were going to keep this quiet until Ian had a chance to find out. He doesn't even know about the pregnancy yet."

"I know, but it's hard to keep this on the down under when everyone is working in some part of law enforcement. Frank knew all about it because he was assigned one of the creeps who broke in here. He talked to the guy, who thought it was funny that his last name is O'Hara, since the guy they were after they thought was an O'Hara, who turned out to be a Harrington. Then Frank put two and two together and recused himself from the case. He did talk to the other public defender who got the case and that's when he found out that Taylor was pregnant when she went to prison. He talked to Jamie and the rest is now public record."

Ruthie stirred her gravy around in her potatoes, "What a horrible mess! We should have gone to San Francisco for his surgery. None of this would have ever happened. The family has always been close. Now look!"

"Don't be giving your little self all the credit for the squabbling. This outfit can argue over how to tie shoelaces. And I know it to be true because I've seen it happen! None of them are shy nor do they let someone else speak for them."

Van pursed her lips, "What he is trying to say is that they are a headstrong, argumentative bunch. They are not like the clan, Ruthie. But they are close and always hang together to the outside world at least, saving our discord for our private, personal moments."

"Has anyone called Mo?" Ruthie asked.

"Not that I know of."

"I think we should do that before Colleen and Vivian get wind of this."

The remains of a perfectly good dinner was put in the fridge without being eaten. Ruthie went to make some calls, while Van and Egan cleaned up the kitchen and removed any sharp objects from the living room before their guests arrived.

Ruthie didn't get very far with her phone calls. She decided to call Matt, Ian's younger brother, first for advice on how to tell Mo. Besides, they were close and she really needed to talk it all over with him. She was fortunate to catch him before he went to to help milk. She said she could talk to him later, but Diane, his wife, insisted that she would go help milk and then Matt could take his time and talk in private.

Ruthie explained everything that happened to fill him in. He listened to the entire thing, with only a few comments or questions for clarity. When she was all done, she said, "Now, I need to know a few things."

"I can see where you might. Let me first say, I'm so sorry for all that's happened. I will do anything at all to try to help."

"I know you will; but first, I need to know, was it wrong that I went to see Tater? Most of the folks here think so."

"Ruthie, can you tell me why did you go see him?" her brother-in-law asked.

"I just felt I had to. I honestly don't know why I felt I should."

"Then you did the right thing. Had you not, you would've always wondered. What is he like?"

Ruthie explained the visit and then said, "Matt, I know he is Ian's son. Aunt Van thinks so, too."

"Then we just need to wait for the blood tests to confirm. Can you tell me how you feel about it?"

"I don't know. I look at him and I see Miriam. I know that is projecting and not the same, but that's how I feel. It breaks my heart."

"Would you want Ian to raise him?"

"I don't know if I could get past the fact that he is Taylor's son or that maybe someday I would resent it. On the other hand, I don't know what I would think of Ian if he could turn his back on his own child, without a flinch. If he could do that to Tater, why couldn't he do that to our baby?"

"It's different."

"In some ways, it is. But in many ways, it is not. All this talk about the Harrington family—are they the only ones they want to consider Harringtons, or all of them?"

"I don't know and I don't believe they know. I think the boys and Egan just want to hide their heads in the sand a little longer. They are hoping the tests come back that he can't possibly be his son. Then they can just sweep the little embarrassment under the rug. When you went to see him, you made him more real. Right now, they don't want that."

Ruthie laughed slightly, "And that's one of the main reasons I wanted to see him. I didn't want Tater to be 'that kid'. He is a real person. Matt, I think you would like him."

"It sounds to me like he has a great ally. How are you going to handle it if Ian signs him away?"

"I don't know. Matt? I don't even want to see Ian. I love him and care about him, but right now, I have no desire to even see him. What is wrong with me?"

"I think you are just angry with him right now. You have all the mess, decisions and guff. He doesn't. You almost always talk everything over with him and now you can't."

"That is true. You know, when he was in the hospital in Shreveport, I sat there and talked to him for hours. Even though he was asleep."

"Can you do that now?"

"Not really. I could more than I do, but Dr. Turner doesn't like having family lurking around all the time. And then others want to see him, too. Honestly, I wouldn't even know what to say to him. About half the time, I want to knock his block off."

Matt chuckled, "I think that is because you had this all dumped on you and he isn't helping. You know, if he was awake, he wouldn't want them all ganging up on you. That is why he asked you to listen to John. He is the only one of the boys who is level headed. Zach and I can come out."

"No, that might just make more spoons in the broth. I just need to know you are in my court and that I'm not way off base."

"I am and you're not. But Ruthie, be careful. If you let yourself get attached to Tater and Ian doesn't want him, then what?"

"I worry about that. But in that case, I don't know if I would want Ian."

"You already married him. For good and bad. Remember?"

"Yes I do. I only want this all to go away."

"I know, but we both know it won't. Listen, tonight you stand up for yourself. Don't let Viv and Colleen badger you. They can be a fright."

"I'll try."

"I will go over now and talk to Mom. I might ask Zach to join us. It would be better if we told her so she will have a heads up before Viv or Colleen get to her. This way, she can be ready."

"Thanks. I was hoping you would."

"We love you. I'll talk to you later. Okay? Try to be strong."

John Kelly and Nancy arrived first, much to everyone's relief. Nancy greeted Ruthie with a big hug, "My heart goes out to you. I'm so glad you have John to lean on."

Ruthie was relieved, "Even if Frank thinks it is inappropriate?"

"Oh, Frank and Colleen look at life through a distorted lens. I just ignore them most of the time."

"I'm so relieved. That was a worry that I didn't want you to have."

"I know my husband is a good shoulder to lean on," Nancy smiled. "That's why I love him."

Van hugged Nancy, "And I doubt you have to worry about him straying."

"I don't." Nancy said, "When are we expecting the troops?"

"Any time." Egan said, as he brought some iced tea in for everyone. "Let's sit in the living room."

Within minutes, the other boys and their wives appeared. Aaron and his wife, Terrie, came first and brought another brother, Patrick, and his wife, Marge, with them. Aaron explained, "Didn't want them to be left out."

"Good thinking," Egan said. "I thought about it myself, but didn't know if they were up to a brawl tonight."

"I can't understand what there is to brawl about! Good grief, you would think this was the royal family or something," Pat chuckled. "We're just a bunch of middle-class crazy Irish Catholics."

"I know," Terrie replied, "But you know, some of us don't always get that."

Then James and Vivian came in with Frank and Colleen. One look and everyone knew that Viv and Colleen were primed. Neither of those women ever shirked their responsibilities of sharing their pontifical opinions on the rest, whether they were required or not.

They all sat for a minute with their iced teas, waiting for the first person to open the conversation. No one seemed willing to take that first dive until Ruthie did. "Okay, we all know we have a lot to say. So, let's get this over with."

"It's always one of those two youngest ones that are bringing shame on our families! Mom spoiled them after Dad died. She really messed them up," Colleen blurted out.

"Now Colleen," Egan responded, "I don't think that's fair."

"Oh really? It wasn't any of us that pulled this stuff! First Matt gets booted from the priesthood and now we find that Ian was shacking up with some hooker! My goodness, it makes me want to change my name. I'm afraid someone will know I'm a Harrington."

Egan shook his head, "It would be a waste to time, since your last name is already O'Hara."

"That's another thing! Why did Ian pick O'Hara for his undercover name? He didn't ask my permission!"

"It wasn't his choice. The department gave him the name because they had a profile worked up for that name. So, take your gripe to them," Aaron growled.

"And just what in God's name do you think you're doing; looking into this tramp's kid? Have you lost your mind? His mother's a criminal!" Vivian attacked Ruthie. "His whole family is degenerate."

"His mother's side has problems, but he has another side to his family. He is likely a Harrington." Ruthie snapped back, "So back off."

"His father might be any old john that tramp dug up! Don't even begin to tell me he is my nephew!"

"I won't. I don't have to. I don't care whether you like it or not."

"I didn't know the tests were back yet," Pat said.

Van interrupted, "Not yet, but Ruthie and I saw him today. If he isn't a Harrington, it would be a miracle."

"What?!" Colleen ranted. "You actually went to see this product of dubious beginnings! Have you taken leave of your senses?"

"Not at all. And he is not a product. He is a little boy named Taylor. I would appreciate it if you would call him by his name." Ruthie said with determination, "It would be wise for all of you to remember, this situation was not of his making."

Colleen glared at her, "Maybe not, but you don't need to see him. The next thing you will be dragging him into our lives!"

"If he is Ian's son, quite likely," Ruthie responded, matter-of-factly. "So, you might want to prepare yourself for that."

"Aren't you getting the cart before the horse?" Jamie asked. "If the tests are say he is Ian's, then what? Most likely, Ian will sign off on him."

"He is a child, not a piece of merchandise. You don't 'sign off' on your Flesh and blood." Ruthie retorted, "He is a little boy."

Egan stood, "Ruthie is right. We don't turn our back on our own."

"Well, you don't have to, but I will not have my children around him," Vivian said smugly.

"Good for you," John Kelly said. "I don't think the rest of us care."

"Jamie!" Vivian barked, "Talk some sense into these people!"

"I think we are all crossing too many bridges too soon," Jamie answered. "We will get the blood tests back tomorrow, although the DNA will take longer. Tomorrow should tell us most of the story. Then we can decide what to do."

"I don't think that it is a decision that we *all* need to make. It is between Ian and me," Ruthie said. "Once we decide, it is up to you to accept it."

"Do you think you can drag some hooker's bastard in here and expect us to go along with it?" Colleen raged. "You have some nerve!"

"Colleen, settle down. This has been a lot for Ruthie to handle," Nancy answered. "I think she is right. If you don't want to support their decision, that is up to you. But it isn't up to you to make the decision for them. How soon will you be able to talk to Ian?"

Egan answered, "In a couple days. So, just keep a lid on it."

"Well, it is up to the Harringtons to decide to accept another Harrington," Vivian answered, defiantly.

"Yah, well we accepted you, now didn't we?" Nancy snapped. "We didn't hold a family meeting to see how we all felt about that!"

Vivian glared at her and then Colleen started to cry. "What will people say?" Colleen mumbled.

"Hell, they probably won't know and mostly wouldn't care," Terrie said. "You are the only one who thinks your family has a pedigree or something."

"I never! I knew this was a waste of time. Come on, Frank. Let's get out of here!"

Frank never moved, "Now Colleen, you should think about this before you go all nutty. We don't want a rift in the family."

"I'm not making the rift! It is Ruthie," Colleen defended herself. "Mom will be beside herself. What are you people trying to do to her? And Pappy and Nana? It will ruin their lives!"

"I doubt one little boy could ruin anyone's life," Van said calmly. "If a life is ruined, it is because of the reaction to him, not anything he did. I can tell you, beyond a doubt in my mind, that he is Ian's son. I saw him and I talked to him. He is a shy, lonely, little boy. Even you, Colleen, wouldn't be able to treat him like a leper. So, just take it easy."

"You guys make me sick," Colleen grumbled. "And that Ian. I always thought he had some sense. I never would have thought he was philandering with the likes of that woman! Has he no morals! I'll give him a piece of my mind."

"You leave him alone!" Aaron said, "He made a mistake. I remember a few you made, too, Miss Vivian. So don't get all high and mighty around me."

"We all know that you, Mr. Aaron, are no saint! Don't we?" Vivian retaliated.

Egan stood, "That's the whole point we've been trying to get to. This is it. No one is a perfect. We will face this as a loyal family. However, it works out. So, I am telling you now…we will go about our lives like always and make adjustments as the situation requires. But I will not allow one of you to decree who is or isn't allowed into our family. Have I made myself totally clear?"

They all sat quietly and looked at him. Within a couple minutes, they all said they understood, even Viv and Colleen. "Okay, then, you will all keep your traps shut to Nana and Pappy until we have something concrete to tell them. And if you can't be supportive, you better not talk to Mo. She is having a devil of a time with this."

"You can't tell me not to talk to my mother!" Colleen ranted.

"I am not." Egan looked straight at her, "I would prefer that you didn't, but if you are going to, be very careful what you say. If I hear one thing from Carl that you upset her, you will have to deal with me. Matt is going to bring them up to speed tonight. I want you to give her some space and time to digest it all."

"Matt is telling her?" Vivian snorted, sarcastically, "Using all his priestly skills, no doubt."

"Enough!" Egan bellowed. "That is just enough!"

They had a short stare down, but Vivian backed down. "I'm sorry, I guess that was over the top. There is no one else to tell her."

The phone interrupted the conversation. It was the police station and they wanted to talk to Jamie. He took the line. After a few minutes, "I hate to break up this party, but we have to go; Aaron, John. The Norris' are on the move. Can the rest of you see to it that everyone gets home?"

"Is Ian in danger?" Ruthie asked.

"Don't know where they are headed and the informant hasn't called. We are putting a few more cruisers on this street. Let's go."

Before John Kelly left, he gave Ruthie a quick hug and said quietly, "I'll let you know anything we find out. I was proud of how you handled it tonight. We'll talk."

"Thanks, John."

They were picking up the glasses in the living room, when the phone rang. It was Matt. Ruthie took it in the den.

"How did it go with Mo?" Ruthie asked.

"She cried, then she got better and cried again. I think she is doing okay. When she heard that you were in trouble for wanting to see the little boy, she said I should let you know, that is exactly what she would have done." Matt continued, "Zach and Suzy were there. They said to let you know that they love you and Ian. Whatever you decide, they will support. You need anything at all, they will be there for you."

Ruthie started to cry, "What did Carl say?"

"Nothing for a long time, and then he said, "It looks like I might need to rearrange the cubes in the Gopher room to make room for another one.""

"I love him," Ruthie cried. "You guys are the best."

"How did it go there?"

"It was a like an evening in a badger colony. Viv and Colleen told us all what they thought, beyond a doubt."

"How did it end?"

"Well, Uncle Egan told them to settle down and then we got a call. The cops had to take off because the Norris' crew is on the move. So, everyone left."

"Trouble?"

"We don't know yet."

"Try to get some sleep. Remember, if you need us, we will be there."

"I know."

22

That night, Ruthie slept with vivid dreams. They didn't wake her, but the near nightmares wouldn't allow her to rest. She was up before five and had taken a shower before she heard Van go downstairs. She went down to help her prepare breakfast.

While they were making blueberry scones, Van said, "You look tired. Didn't you rest?"

"I slept okay, but had the weirdest dreams." Then Ruthie giggled, "Vivian and Taylor were chasing us, you and me. We were running to catch Wile E.Coyote. It is funny now, but we were really upset in my dream."

"I don't think I'd want Vivian chasing me!" Van smiled, "I know she is a good mother and seems to be a good wife to Jamie, but she is not one bit soft and cuddly. I have never felt close to her. Actually, I can understand Colleen better. She is just an old war horse, knows she is and makes no bones about it. But she does have a sentimental side. If Viv does, I've never seen it."

"Jamie isn't as compassionate as the other boys, though. Of course, I haven't been around them all that much. He's nice enough, but just not easy going."

"No, I guess he isn't." Van said as she measured out the flour, "I wonder what happened last night?"

They heard Egan's steps and then the phone rang. He yelled, "I'll get it."

A few minutes later, he came into the kitchen. "That was John Kelly. He is on his way home. They just got finished with the call from last night. Seems the Norris crew decided they had to attend to some of their regular business. They broke into Pembrook's Warehouse to help themselves to some merchandise. Since they were under surveillance, they got caught red-handed. John Kelly said that took about eight more of them off the street. That only leaves three out there to seek revenge."

"That is good, huh?"

"The downside is that the informant was taken down, too. He was arrested with them. While they don't know he was not really arrested, he is no longer going to be on the inside. He talked to Aaron however, and said that they are tiring of the chase. They have to generate some income in a hurry. There seems to be a lot of resentment that Taylor and her brat brought this all on them. Of course, she really didn't; but she is a handy scape goat. Maybe it will be a good thing for us."

"No one gives that little boy a bit of consideration, do they?" Ruthie asked, not expecting an answer.

"So, tell me about your visit with the little piker. He looks like Ian, you say?" Egan said as he sat down with his coffee. "You and Van both seem pretty certain of that."

"We are, Egan," Van said. "You should come with us to see him when we go back."

"You going back?" Egan asked. "Do you think that is wise? What if he turns out to be someone else's kid? Will you be having your souls shredded?"

Van reached over and took her husband's hand, "Egan, you need to come see him. I insist, and you know, I don't insist on very much."

Egan got up and took the dog dish out of the dishwasher. He was silent while he put the dog food in the bowl and then said, "If you insist. But you know, I am a stern man. Don't expect me to be pandering about him. I've seen plenty of tykes in my time."

"I won't," Van said.

As Egan closed the patio door behind him, she smiled to Ruthie, "He is worse than you and I put together!"

Ruthie laughed, "I know. Look at him, now he is turning his garage over to the neighbor boys to help them work on their junkers."

Van giggled, "Maybe he just wants a stake in that lemonade stand that sells dope or whatever he was harping about!"

About a quarter to ten, the three met Greg in the hall. He greeted them with a smile and teased, "How are my favorite crime fighters?"

"Good, and you?" Ruthie laughed.

"I want to tell you, when I met you folks I thought, now here is a nice young couple I would like to be like. So sweet, loving and have such nice jobs." Then he crossed his eyes, "Boy, was I wrong about that!"

"What do you mean?" Ruthie frowned, "We are."

"Yah, that's why the armed guards, stabbings and what is this about you ladies and a stair case?" Greg shook his head, "Not exactly Ward and June Cleaver."

Egan laughed a big belly laugh, "More like the Meat Cleavers!"

The two man enjoyed their joke while the women remained unimpressed. "How is Ian today?"

"Better. Dr. Turner is with him now. He is going to be a bit more awake, but we are knocking him out again after his exam. His arm is still misfiring. Turner will tell you about that. You should be able to talk to him for a little bit." Then he turned to Ruthie, "This morning when he was coming out of it, he seemed very distressed that you don't want to see him. I hope you can alleviate his concern. That is not helping his recovery."

"There has just been such so much going on, Greg."

"I get that, but I am his advocate. So, just thought I would pass it along to you."

"I know. I'm glad that he has you."

Dr. Turner came to the door and invited them in. "I was just talking to Ian. I am going to put him out again for another day. It is improved, but not enough so we can get things working. One more day, two at the most. Yesterday I was worried we might have to do another surgery, but today I think it just needs a little more time. All this stress isn't helping."

"The cops picked up more of that gang last night, so it looks like that is almost cleared up. We should all be more relaxed," Egan explained. "There isn't anything we can do about it."

"Oh, I realize that. Please don't mistake my comment. I didn't mean it as a reflection on you. I know you have been in a horrendous situation. I am just thankful that some people will put themselves through this kind of thing for the protection of us all. I just meant that stress is definitely playing a factor in his recovery. Try to keep him as calm and stress free as possible. Any questions?"

They visited for a bit and then Dr. Turner shook their hands and left. Egan and Van went over to the bed and told Ian they were going to get coffee. He just nodded and closed his eyes again. On their way out, Van said, "Best you keep the conversation light today."

"I thought that, too."

When they were gone, Ruthie went over to the bed and took her husband's good hand, "Ian? Can you wake up for me?"
He opened his eyes and seemed surprised to see her, "Is it really you?"
She hugged him, "Yes, it is really me. I've missed you."
"I was so worried," he kissed her. "I was afraid you were gone."
"Ian, I'm not leaving you. Don't even think that. I love you."
"I didn't tell... I mean... I'm sor..."
"Ian, shh. Stop worrying."
"I didn't see you."
"I know, I had to stay home with a headache. So I didn't get to see you."
He looked at her with worry, "Okay now?"
"Yes, it's okay now. I'm fine. I can't wait for you to get better so we can talk. I have so many things to tell you."
"Good stuff?"
"Oh, I talked to North Dakota. Schroeder's are back from Pine Ridge. Guess they trip was good."
Ian nodded, "Garden?"
"Yes, our garden is planted and Carl is organizing his little Gophers to be the weed patrol."
"Good," he smiled. Then he pulled her closer to him, "I'm so sorry I didn't tell..."
"It's okay, really. I understand." Ruthie said, "Quit worrying."
"I love you," he said as he kissed her.
They shared a few kisses and a hug, before his arm started to spasm again. Ruthie put on the light and Greg came in. "Okay, let's give you that shot and then you can say good night."

They stopped at a shopping mall and picked up a few things before they went to get a bite of lunch. It was about two when they were finishing up. Van noticed Ruthie looking at her watch, "Can we make it in time for Widey?"
"What time did it come on?"
"I think it was three." Van answered.
"Would it be too much to ask if you would clue me in as to what you are jabbering about?" Egan asked.
Van answered, "We are going to stop over to see Tater and watch Widey with him."

Egan frowned, "What is a Widey?"

Van giggled, "Wile E.Coyote. You like him, yourself, so don't pretend."

"I do and it is a fact. One of the finer cartoons, I think."

"Tater thinks so, too."

Egan shuffled his feet, "I'm not dressed for the occasion."

"What outfit do you think you should wear? You are going to watch a cartoon with a three-year-old. Good grief, we all know you are nervous. Don't you think we were the first time we went?"

"No. You are girls."

"What has that got to do with anything?" Ruthie asked, and then looked at him, "Never mind."

Twenty minutes later, they were in the office of the Family Center. Ruthie introduced Uncle Egan and this time, the woman was much friendlier. "I was wondering if you would show today. I'm glad you did. Tater never said anything, but I noticed that he started watching the door a bit ago. You know the rules? And I trust you filled Mr. Harrington in?"

"You mean did I get the lecture?" Egan made a face, "They yapped at me all the way over. Has me so afraid, I almost decided to sit in the car."

"I'm glad they lectured you," Mrs. Feldman laughed, "Saves me the time. Come on then."

In the hall, Egan took one look through the glass and saw Tater. "My God Above!"

"What is it?" Van asked.

"I know you said it, but I didn't be believing it! Look!" He pointed as the little boy walked over to the bookcase, "He even walks like him!"

The woman turned, "Be very careful to not say anything like that when he can hear! We are waiting for the tests. No false hopes. I need your word."

"I'm sorry, Ma'am. You have my word."

"Wile E.Coyote will be on in about fifteen minutes."

They went in, but the woman didn't follow them. The little boy looked up when the door opened and even though a smile briefly flashed across his face, he quickly concealed it. He sat down with his coloring book until they came over to the table.

Ruthie smiled, "Hello, Tater."

"Hi." Then the little guy looked at Van, "Aunt Van."

"How does he know you are Aunt Van?" Egan asked.

"Ruthie told him. Tater, I would like you to meet Uncle Egan."

Tater studied the tall man for a minute and said, "Hi."

"Mind if I have a sit?" Egan asked.

The little boy giggled, "You won't fit."

Egan looked at the short chair that barely came up to his knee, "No, most likely I won't. If that ain't a fine how do you do!"

Tater got up from his spot and took Ruthie's hand. He led her to an adult-sized chair on the back wall. "He can sit on this."

"Can I move it?"

He shrugged, "I guess."

Ruthie brought it over and then Egan sat down. "That was a fine thing you did, young man."

"Tater," the little boy said.

"That is a fine thing you did, Tater." Egan watched him, "So, I hear you like to color. Do a lot of it, do you?"

"I guess." Tater handed him a crayon, "You want to?"

"I'm not good at it."

"Tater show you." The little boy took his book over to Egan and then put the crayon in his hand and wiggled it. "See? It's easy."

"Well, thank you. I think it just might be. Should I do a picture?"

Tater corrected him, "A page."

"Okay, I'll do a page."

They colored in silence and then Ruthie asked what he did that morning. "I coddored." He turned the pages in his book, "See?"

He showed her two pages, all in green, that he had done.

"Very nice."

He frowned at one page. "Messy."

They talked about the pages until the theme song came on for the cartoon show. Tater stopped what he was doing and dashed over to the television. He sat on the floor and then looked back at Ruthie. He motioned for her to come. The three went over and Van and Egan sat on the sofa with a couple of the little girls, but Ruthie sat on the floor with Tater. Then he turned and warned them all, "You have to be very quiet."

They all nodded.

When the show was over, he got up and looked at Ruthie, "Wasn't that good?"

"It was, Tater."

"I liked it, too," Egan said.

Tater asked Van, "Did you think it was good, Aunt Van?"

"Yes Tater, I really liked it."

"Okay," he said and went back to the table. "I have to coddor some more."

The woman came in and over to the table, "Tater, these folks have to go home now. It is almost time to get ready for your dinner."

His face fell, but he didn't fuss. "Yes, Ma'am."

Egan stood up and shook his little hand, "If it is all the same to you, I might like to come back for another coloring lesson. Could you be helping me?"

He shrugged and then he looked at Van, "Aunt Van, too?"

"Of course."

He nodded and then said, "Bye."

Ruthie said, "We will see you soon, Tater."

He looked at her and patted her hand, "Okay."

They were silent all the way to the car. Then Egan took out his big old handkerchief and blew his nose. "Damnable Allergies!"

"It isn't allergies, Egan." Van took his arm, "What did you think?"

"You'd have to be blind, deaf, dumb and stupid to not know that is Ian's little boy. Almost a carbon copy, but his hands are different. He has exceptionally nice hands for a little kid."

"I noticed that, too. Remember I said that Taylor had such nice hands. They were just like that. I never pay attention to hands, but they both have slender graceful hands."

"When will we hear from the blood tests?" Egan asked.

"Supposed to be today, but we haven't been home to take a call." Van pointed out, "Egan, you know you made that little boy a promise. You said you would come back to color."

"I know what I said. I'm a man of my word. Can't see where I have anything so pressing I can't fit in a bit of coloring." Egan blustered. "I like to color. Always have."

Ruthie and Van share a look and let the man have his own set of facts.

The late afternoon was quiet. The ladies did some household chores and Egan went out to mow the lawn. Within minutes, the women heard talking and looked outside. Jeremy and Jason Ferguson were there helping him. They trimmed, weeded and carried the clippings to the compost heap. Then they moved to the backyard to mow.

Van smiled and then Ruthie noticed that she had tears in her eyes. "Whatever is wrong, Aunt Van?"

"Egan is in his element. He loved having the kids around. Now that they are all grown up, and he doesn't see the grandkids as much, he is alone a lot. Look how much he loves it. I think he was really taken with Tater, today. Don't you?"

"Yes, you know those allergies!" Ruthie laughed. "I think Tater liked him, too. He really likes you."

"Me?" Van asked. "Why do you say that?"

"He calls you Aunt Van. He doesn't call me anything."

"I think he just likes to say Aunt Van. Do you think he can even say your name?"

"Hm, don't know." Ruthie thought, "I felt so dishonest today when I was talking to Ian. I tried to act like everything is okay and it is in turmoil."

"Do you think he believed you?"

Ruthie shook her head no, "Not for a minute. We know each other too well. I don't know what to do. I'm going to have to talk to him about some of these things soon. I can't very well do it, if I can't be honest. Turner wants him to relax. How can he?"

Van put the furniture polish away, "You know Ruthie, I think it might be better to just tell him the truth. You know how pent up you got when you knew he wasn't telling you the whole thing. It made you more nervous than when you found out. I imagine that's the same with him. Arm or no arm, he has these decisions he has to make in a very short time. If he is unable to do it, you will have to in his stead. And you don't know what his wishes would even be. I think it is too bad, but that's the hand you were dealt. You guys have to have an honest talk. Especially, when the blood tests get back. Most of the time, it is better to just put it out there than to dance around it."

"Yes, I feel that way, too. Once we get the test results, I will just tell Turner or Greg what's going on, and tell them we have to have a real, stressful talk. No way around it."

"Good idea." Van agreed, "I'm going to take our yard men some cookies. Want to join us?"

"I think I better go call Matt."

"Aren't you going to wait for the blood tests?"

"Oh why? Even Uncle Egan says he is a Harrington. Did you see the look on Egan's face when he saw him?"

"He looked like he had seen a ghost, a ghost of Ian as a little boy. Now, I don't know how he would take it if the tests came back that his isn't!"

"I don't know how I would take it!" Ruthie pointed out.

"Me either!"

Matt answered the phone. Ruthie and he had a long talk. She told him about Ian's condition, the visit with Tater and Uncle Egan's reaction. Matt chuckled, "Well, that's all the blood test I need. I'm anxious to meet this little guy."

"Matt, Ian's doctor says all this stress is hampering Ian's recovery."

"Don't you believe that? I mean, I would be surprised if it didn't. Not to mention getting stabbed might have thrown a monkey wrench into the works."

"I know, huh?" Ruthie agreed. "I tried today to talk to him, but not talk about anything. I knew he wanted to talk about it, but I veered away. I could tell by the look in his eye that he knows I wasn't being up front. I think he was just as upset when I left as before. He knows there is something going on. What should I do?"

"Gee, Ruthie," Matt pondered. "I hate this kind of thing. You two are so close. You both know when the other guy isn't telling the whole thing. I think you should just tell him. Let's face it, he is going to have to know. But, I don't think it is going to be any more stressful for him to know, than to not know."

"That's what Van said. I thought I should just tell Turner or Greg that we have to have a major talk and let them give him blood pressure medicine or something. I have to talk to him. If he can't tell me what he wants, I'll have to make all these decisions on my own. I can't very well do that for him."

"I think that you and I both know what he will want to do; but then again, you're right. It is not our decision to make. Ruth, how will you feel if he wants to sign Tater away?"

"I don't know how I'd feel. I don't think he would. If he does, I guess then I really don't know him very well."

"Ruthie, I am asking you to make me a big promise. Will you?"

"What is that?"

"Don't take his first reaction as gospel, or even how he really feels. You've had time to let Tater be real. He still doesn't even know Taylor was pregnant. If my guess is right, his first instinct is going to be to protect you and your life together. He is going to be mortified that he brought all this on you guys. And Tater isn't even a real person to him." Matt explained, "He is going to have a bit of a struggle. So, be patient and give him some time to mull."

"I think he has to meet Tater."

"That would be the ideal, but he probably won't want to. It is easier to erase something that isn't real. You know. How is Egan coping?"

"Oh my, Matt," Ruthie giggled. "As we left the Center, he was crying. He said it was allergies. I think he would have brought the little guy home with us!"

"I figured that. He's such a big windbag." Matt said, "Like Carl. Know what he is doing? Today he is measuring the wall in the Gopher room to see where he can add the new cube. He has room on the bottom, but he thinks Tater wouldn't want a baby one. He will want one that is on the next row, so he can reach it. Zach and I just crossed our eyes. He is determined to make a major operation out of it. We tried to convince him to just add more cubes on the top and repaint them, rather than move them. But he thinks the kids want their 'real' cubes. I honestly don't know how Jeff and Rain can stand to live with the lunatic."

"How's your mom handling things?"

"I talked to her again for a while this morning. You know Mom. She said she is planning on boxing Ian's ears for not keeping his pants zipped, but she understands the situation. I think Carl helped her with that. He told her that while it is not 'in the handbook,' for law enforcement to get involved, everyone knows it happens. Like the CIA. If you are living a deep cover, you have to live it. Or if it really becomes obvious that you are pretending, you can earn a bullet."

"I think it is a stupid way to live. They're not a big leap up from prostitution. Same difference, just not paid in greenbacks."

"What about people who marry for money or power? Isn't that the same, too?" Matt asked.

"Yah, I guess it might be. What a terrible subject," Ruthie groaned. "What does Mo think about maybe having another grandchild?"

"What do you think?"

"I don't know about this situation."

"A grandchild is a grandchild. Mom doesn't care if they are legitimate, adopted or part-kangaroo! She and Carl are ready to take this little guy in, even if he isn't Ian's. Which, by the way– Mom said right away, her gut tells her it is. How her gut could know is beyond me!"

"I knew, before I saw him. There are some things a person just knows."

"You're right. " Matt got quiet, "Honestly, I knew, too. Well look, I think that once the blood tests come back, you have to talk to Ian. Stress or no stress. It's up to you if you want to talk to his doctor, but if you don't have this talk with him, your visits are going to stress him anyway."

"I know. Thanks Matt." Ruthie smiled into the phone, "Oh, I almost forgot. How did Zach and Suzy react?"

"Like we thought. Zach thinks you need to give the child a home and Suzy agrees. But they will support whatever decision you make." Then he hesitated, "You need any or all of us out there, and we will be. Know that."

"I know and it gives me confidence. But with all the cops and robbers stuff, I think fewer is better."

They had just put the last dish away from supper, when John Kelly came to the door. Egan invited him in, "Hi, want some coffee?"

"No, I really don't have time. I want to get home and get some sleep. I'm about a zombie. We got the blood tests back. Now these aren't definitive like DNA, but it is extremely likely that Ian is the little boy's father. A few years ago, before DNA was as advanced as it is, these results would have been considered conclusive." John Kelly looked around the room, "Nobody's saying anything?"

"We already knew it," Egan stated. "Saw him today. He is his boy. No doubt about it."

"You saw him, too?"

"I did. Fine young lad, to my notion. He's teaching me to color."

John Kelly laughed, "Then he has his work cut out for him!"

"I don't think it is that funny! I can color very well!" Egan frowned, "So, now what?"

"We have to wait for the DNA, but you might want to tell Ian so he can digest it. He will have to decide what to do in about eight more days." John Kelly added, "On another topic, those boneheads we arrested last night are in the slammer. That leaves three out. Their leader is Taylor's oldest brother, Ted. He is a piece of work and not very bright, but meaner than hell. The other two are his minions. From the little we learned from those we arrested last night, they are desperate to get their hands on some serious money. Ted is bent on making Ian pay for what he did to the Collins' family."

"Gee, I thought that was about settled," Egan frowned.

"It might just be Ted blowing off, but he might try something. He is getting down to his last hurrah now. Remember, cornered is often reckless."

"John Kelly, does the Center know about the blood tests?"

"Yes, they were informed. That boss lady said something about she was glad for that. I thought that was a bit strange for her to say."

"Not really," Van said. "I think she would like Tater to have a good home."

Over breakfast, those at Uncle Egan's home made their plans for the day. They were going to go straighten up the house, see Ian, have lunch and watch Widey with Tater. It sounded like a good plan.

Then the phone rang. It was John Kelly. He had just talked to Greg and set up an appointment for Jamie and him to talk to Greg. It would be late morning. John wanted Ruthie to be there for it. "I will swing by the house and pick you up about quarter after ten. Okay?"

"Okay, I talked to Greg yesterday. He told me they were going to try to let Ian wake up today. What do you want to talk to him about?"

"If you object, we won't. However, we need to get Greg up to speed on the situation with Collins and tell him about the baby. Ian doesn't even know that Taylor is dead. You haven't told Ian anything yet, I take it."

"Not yet."

"He will need to make a decision and even though Jamie thinks he will just sign the release on the boy right away; I don't think that Ian will think it's that easy. I know him. Egan said the doc is concerned that this business is upsetting his recovery, but it can't be helped. If you don't talk to Ian soon, the state will have to. I think it would be better if it came from you."

"Gee, I win all the fun prizes, huh? I know you're right. We kinda came to the same conclusion about talking to him, stress or not. I never thought Jamie might talk to him. That would really throw him off the rails."

"I think it might. It would be best for you to tell him," John Kelly said. "Besides, it is your decision too."

"Well, not really."

"Oh Ruthie, don't even try to tell me that. You and I both know his decision will make a huge difference in your life. I'm afraid if you don't say how you feel now, it will be too late to say anything later. In a few days, all that will be left is the living of it."

"That sounds grim. Greg said they let Ian wake up this morning and he is now having some testing. They may have him sleep again this afternoon if the tests are too much."

"Seems like there is never a good time for him to talk," Ruthie shook her head. "Okay, I'll be ready."

Jamie, John Kelly and Ruthie met Greg in a small conference room. Greg started the meeting by telling them that the testing was difficult for Ian in the morning, but the doctor wanted him to keep awake all afternoon. He was in physical therapy now and would be back in his room in about an hour. The police explained the situation to Greg. Then Ruthie said, "I think that Ian can read that I'm not comfortable talking to him and that's why he's so upset. I don't know how to talk to him without spilling it about when those men broke into the house or anything about Tater."

"Tater?" Greg looked at her in surprise.

"That is what the little boy, Taylor, calls himself. He can't pronounce L's very well."

"You know him?"

Ruthie explained that Van, Egan and she had been seeing him.

"And Ian doesn't know anything about him, at all?"

"No, he doesn't," Jamie said. "Ian was pulled to a desk job after the Collins-Norris ring began to hunt down the other informants. There was no communication between Ian and any of them. So, he didn't even know that she was pregnant."

Greg put his hands on his forehead, "Yah, looks to me like he is going to be stressed. Oh well, there is the ideal situation and then there's the Meat Cleavers!"

Ruthie laughed and the cops looked at them both as if they were goofy. Greg didn't bother to explain, "I'll pass this along to Turner. May I make a suggestion? Can we go at this slowly? I'd like to have you policemen fill him in on all the cop stuff. I will check how he is doing with that information. If he is doing okay, then Ruthie can talk to him about this Tater. Otherwise, it had better wait until tomorrow."

Ruthie called Van and told her what was going on. "I'll call you when

I know if I can talk to Ian or not. It doesn't look like I'm going to get to watch Widey today."

"Egan and I figured as much. With your permission, we'll go over."

"That would be really nice. Tater will like to see you. He doesn't seem to be that excited about seeing me, anyway."

"Oh he does." Van stated. "You don't see it, but he watches your every move."

"Really?"

"Yes, really. We'll tell him that you couldn't make it."

"Thanks."

It was about one when the men emerged after having talked to Ian. They invited Ruthie to join them for a hamburger at the diner across the street. Over their burgers, John Kelly did most of the talking. "He knew that he had been stabbed. Greg had explained it to him. Greg said he took that in stride. But he didn't know anything about the break-in. He really went nuts over that. He is worried to death! He almost stroked out on us when we told him that you were in the hospital overnight. You're going to have to reassure him the baby is okay. Greg came in and gave him something to calm him a bit, but he was extremely agitated. He is now convinced that you will leave him and he is blaming himself, big time. You are going to have your work cut out for you."

"Should I tell him about Tater today?"

"Greg asked that you check with him before you go in to see Ian today. He needs to be reassured that you don't blame him for the break-in and that the baby is okay. Greg didn't know how much more we should lay on him today." Jamie looked directly at her, "I wish you and Egan wouldn't keep seeing the kid. If Ian has a brain in his head, he will simply sign the papers and put this mess into the history books. If I know Egan at all, we will have to get a restraining order to keep him away from the kid."

"Jamie, his name is Taylor, or Tater. Please don't call him 'the kid'. Aunt Van is well aware of how Egan is. It couldn't hurt for the little guy to have a friend. Everyone needs someone."

"Here we go!" Jamie growled, "I was afraid of this. If Ian says no, the next thing we will have to sedate Egan. You shouldn't have gone to see him."

"Well, I did. Van and Egan did, too. I don't think that any of us are sorry."

"Not yet," Jamie shrugged. "Be patient. It will come to no good."

John Kelly glanced at his brother-in-law, "Let's not borrow trouble. We seem to have an abundance of that already."

##

Van and Egan went to the Center. The woman greeted them warmly and asked, "The younger Mrs. Harrington couldn't make it today?"

"No, she had to be up at the hospital with her husband today. We thought that if you didn't mind, we could watch cartoons with Tater," Van said.

"I think he'll like that."

They went in and Tater looked up from his coloring. He smiled briefly and then his eyes darted back to the door. "Where is her?"

"Ruthie?" Van asked.

He nodded and Egan answered, "She was a bit under the weather and couldn't make it today."

Tater watched the man talk and then was silent for a long minute, "Her have code?"

Egan smiled, "Yes, that's it. Just a little cold."

The little boy sat a minute in deep thought and got up from the table. He ran over to a shelf and got a tissue from a box. He ran back and gave it to Van. "To her from Tater."

Without a thought, Van hugged him, "That is so nice, Tater. I'm sure she will love it."

He shrugged and went back to his coloring. The three colored for a few minutes until Wile E.Coyote came on television. The older couple sat on the sofa and this time, Tater sat between them.

After the program, they had to say goodbye. Tater said, "Watch Widey again?"

Egan gave him a hug, "You can plan on it."

Then Tater smiled and went back to his coloring.

On the way to the car, Egan said, "I think he must like us coming to see him. Do you be agreeing on that?"

"Yes, I do." Van smiled, "Let's not forget to give Ruthie that Kleenex. That was so sweet of him."

"I had a bit of a notion that he thought maybe she didn't want to come back. That's why I said she had a cold. I know I shouldn't have lied, but I felt the need."

"I know. I thought he was quite taken back that she wasn't there."

After their hamburgers, the cops had to go back to work. "Call and I will give you a ride home," John Kelly offered.

"Egan and Van were coming up. So, I can ride home with them. I know you have so much to do."

When Ruthie arrived back at the hospital, she checked at the nurses' station to speak to Greg. They told her that he had just gone to lunch and would be back in about half an hour. Ian was sleeping. Then she asked if there was a chapel and the nurse told her where it was. Ruthie spent some time in prayer. She asked for guidance about what to say to Ian and the courage to do it. She returned upstairs just as Greg walked up to the nurses' station. "Hi, I was wondering if you were around."

"I went to the chapel for a bit."

"I think we all need that. I spent most of my lunch mulling this over. He was so bent about the fact that you and the baby fell; I can't see how he is going to handle this. My guess is that he believes in families."

"Yes, he does. His whole family is close; however, some of them say he should just sign the little boy away right off, without seeing him or anything. They feel it will just cause trouble if he does anything else. What is your opinion?"

"It doesn't matter what I think," Greg pointed out. "I know what I would do, but that's me. Right now, he is so worried you're going to leave him, I have no idea what he would think about a child." Then he took her arm gently, "There isn't a right or wrong answer here."

"I know. Greg," Ruthie agreed. "What would you do if you were Ian?"

"At the very least, I would want to meet the child. If my Marcy was willing, I would want my son to be with us. It isn't just about me. He would have siblings and they would want to know that they had a brother. You know? Anyway, Ian is waking up now, so you go on in. If it seems that he is having trouble coping with all this; ring the buzzer. I'll be right down the hall. Okay?" He looked at her, "Good luck."

Ruthie entered the room and Ian was sitting up in his bed, but he had his eyes closed. She put her purse on the chair and went over to the bed. She watched him sleep a bit and then kissed his cheek.

He opened his eyes and took a minute to realize she was there. He put his good arm around her and held her close to him. The tears flooded his face as he kissed her. "My Ruthie. I was so afraid you hated me. I caused all this."

Ruthie kissed him back. "You didn't cause this. Don't be silly."

"I have to talk to you, but they keep putting me to sleep."

"I know. I need to talk to you. Greg says that we can talk today. Okay?"

He just held her as tight as he could, "I wanted you to have a good life. I've messed it all up. You were right. I should have told you right away about that girl. I knew it, but I just panicked."

"I get it, but we do need to talk. I know the guys dumped a pile on you earlier, but there is more."

A frown flashed across his face, "You didn't lose the baby, did you? John said it was okay."

"It is fine. The fall only mattered to my head."

"How is that? Are you okay? I can't believe I let this happen to you."

"You didn't *let* it happen. It just did. Besides, Aunt Van and I made short work of them," she giggled.

"John Kelly said that, but you were lucky." Ian's face was somber, "They wanted to kill you."

"I know, we know. The neighbor boys helped," Ruthie added. "You should see the staircase now. It is a total mess. Egan said that his insurance will pay for it, but I want to do something to repay them. I thought I might get them a week at this Country Inn place, so they can stay there while they steps are being refinished."

"That's sounds like a good idea. I'll pay for it."

"No, you know I have all the money from my father."

"That is yours. This is my mess."

"Ian, don't start dividing things. This is our mess and it's our money. We don't make divisions."

He looked at her and then took her back into his arm. He kissed her forehead, "I will make this up to you, I promise."

"No need. I didn't make it up to you when my nut-job sister shot you."

Ian answered, smiling for the first time, "No, and why was that, anyway?"

Ruthie giggled, "I slithered out of it!"

They sat just holding hands for a few minutes and then Ian asked,

"What did you want to talk to me about? Because I didn't trust you? Ruthie, I never told you about Taylor because she didn't matter. It was in the past and we weren't a real thing, so I just never thought to mention it. You knew I had been with women before you so I didn't think about it."

"I never had a problem with that. I was upset that you didn't trust me enough to tell me after the encounter at the Street Fair. I went crazy trying to understand why you wouldn't just tell me."

"I should have, but I was humiliated to have you think that I'd use someone like I used her. I didn't know what you'd think of me."

"You were a major jerk. I think she was in love with you and by using her, you hurt her worse than any old prison sentence."

"That was right to the old jugular." He hesitated, "She was just a hooker."

Ruthie glared at him, "You better think that over. Hookers are human beings and she was more to you than 'just a hooker.' You had an affair. Don't try to tell me that you had an affair with someone for a couple months and didn't care at all about her!"

"Okay, I liked her. Mostly, I felt sorry for her, not only because I knew what I was doing was wrong, but because I knew that she wanted more than anything to have a real home. That's all she ever talked about. Honestly, I used that. I never promised her I would marry her or even that we would have a home together, but I did let her believe it." Ian dropped his hand from Ruthie's and he sat still. "I felt guilty about it at the time and I have thought about it since. I confessed it and was told I was forgiven, but I still can't get past it. Sometimes when things are going really well for me, I think of what I did to her. I shouldn't have done it, but I can't fix it. There was really nothing between us." Ian raised his eyes to Ruth's, "Now she overdosed and is gone. All that's left is the guilt."

"Not quite," Ruthie said.

Ian got a puzzled expression on his face, "You mean you won't forgive me? You think I was too awful?"

"I think you were an ass, but that isn't it. Can I ask why you didn't take any precautions?"

Ian frowned, "Precautions? What are you talking about?"

Ruth took his good hand in both of hers, "Ian, Taylor was pregnant when she went to prison."

His expression froze in disbelief. A short time passed without a word and then he slowly began to shake his head no. "She couldn't have been.

She couldn't have kids. She told me that. She couldn't. That's an ugly mistake."

"How do you know?"

"She told me that she'd had a couple abortions when she was fourteen. When she had her third abortion at sixteen, the doctor told her she had so much scarring that she could never get pregnant. Why are you saying that?"

"She had a baby in prison. He was born June 20, 1968. She named him Taylor Collins. She didn't name the father."

Ian was like stone, not blinking, not moving. The monitor, however, reflected an elevated heartbeat and a spike in his blood pressure. After an agonizing endlessness, Ruthie said softly, "He was taken away when he was born."

Ian's eyes moved toward hers, "She was a hooker."

"I know, but she was about a month or so pregnant when she was arrested. She likely didn't even know it herself at that time."

"She was with a lot of men, if that's what you're saying." Then he pulled his hand out of hers and said without emotion, "I'm sure it was adopted by a fine family."

"No, he was placed with foster families. She never signed him over to the state. She wanted to get him back when she got out of prison."

"Did she?"

"No, Ian. She went back on drugs and never got clean enough to get him."

Indifferently, Ian said, "So, now he can be adopted."

"It's not that easy."

Ian snapped in anger, "She's dead. Now, he can be adopted! God only knows which john fathered it."

"Ian Sean Harrington! How can you be so callus?"

"Callus? What are you driving at? You come in here and tell me a load of crap I can't believe and expect what? She was a hooker. If she got pregnant, so? Give it away. Be done with it!"

"Taylor told her parole officer that O'Hara was his father. You were O'Hara. She never put your name on the birth certificate, but she said it was you."

"How could she possibly know?"

"The state needs to know before they can put the boy up for adoption. The boys asked me to sign the papers for the blood and DNA tests. I did."

"What? You signed to have me put in the running for paternity? Are you out of your mind? She wasn't pregnant and she couldn't have been! I would've known! Nobody ever told me she had a kid! This is insane!"

"The blood tests came back yesterday," Ruthie continued. "You are very likely the father. It won't be confirmed until the DNA is back in about eight more days."

"Me? Me?" he looked at her in disbelief and then the tears began to fall. "My god! What is going on? Why did you come in here and say all this stuff? Get away from me! I don't need this. I have to be hallucinating. Get away from me!"

He was beginning to overreact and Ruthie pushed the buzzer. Greg was there in a heartbeat and tried to calm him down. It wasn't working, so he dashed out to get a shot for him. Meanwhile, Ian was furious. With himself, Ruthie, Taylor and anyone else who came into this head.

"Please calm down, Ian. We can talk about this."

"I'm all done talking! This is all bull. Leave me alone. I don't want to talk to anyone. Just get out of here. Keep away from me!"

Greg overheard when he came in to give him his shot. Then he took Ruthie's hand and moved her back from the bed. "I'll meet you in the hall as soon as the shot starts to work."

A couple minutes later, he came out. He put his arm through hers, "I'll buy you a soda pop and we can chat a bit. Okay?"

Ruthie nodded yes through her tears and followed him down the hall.

A few minutes later, she was sitting in the gray vinyl chair in a tiny waiting room. Greg said softly, "I take it that it didn't go well."

Ruthie explained it all, completely, even though she hardly knew this person. She was telling him intimate details of their married life and all the while wondered why. Finally, she just cried. He put his arms around her, "I was afraid it'd be a lot for him. It needed to be done, and it is only sad that you had to do it."

"Shouldn't I have told him? Did I tell him the wrong way?"

"I don't know a right way. I think you did as well as anyone could."

"Now he hates me."

"No, don't think so. He is pushing back on unwelcome information. He has had to absorb a lot in a very short time. How long did it take you to absorb it?"

"A while and it was a little at a time. I never even told him that I have met the little boy." Ruthie cried, "He just told me to get out and leave him alone."

"I know he wasn't very nice about it, but I think that is exactly what you should do. Give him some space and time. Let him think it over."

"Greg, he was really furious. He acts like he has no responsibility to the child."

"He knows he has responsibility. That's what all the anger is about! Do you have a ride home? Someone I can call for you?" Greg said, "I think you should go home and give him at least a day to think this over. I will keep you informed. You have my word?"

"What about other folks? Jamie acted like he wants this settled ASAP."

"Don't we all? Jamie will have to wait. He will have a decision well before the eight days are up." Greg said. "Are you going to be okay?"

"I just give up. I hate this whole damned thing."

Greg agreed, "You and me both!"

Then they heard Egan talking in the hall. Greg ran out to invite Van and him into the tiny room before they went in to see Ian. There, they explained what happened.

Then Greg said, "I think it'd be wise to let Ian smolder a while. No company. I told Ruth that I'll keep you informed."

"You are on the right track of it, young man. He has to sit in the corner for a bit to consider his behavior. I only hope you can direct his head the right way, if he might ask."

"I don't know what is right for him." Greg assured them, "Somehow, I feel that he will have a different take upon reflection."

25

The ride home from the hospital was very quiet. There seemed to be no subject that mattered. They had all looked forward to talking to Ian and wondered what he would say. Now that it had happened, it seemed nothing was as they thought it would be.

Once home, they all changed clothes. Egan went out to give his car a wash and Van made coffee. "I don't know why I made it, I don't know if I want anyway. I can't imagine what how you must be feeling."

"I'm numb. I don't even know what to think. Matt told me to promise him I would not take Ian's first reaction as what he really wanted to do. I didn't think that he would be happy about it, but I never expected he would just say to sign *it* away, so coldly." Ruthie looked at the older lady, "Aunt Van, he didn't even hesitate. In fact, he acted like I made it all up just to rile him!"

"I think it is like when someone hears someone died, they often say that. 'No, it's not true!' It is a defense mechanism. He just needs some time now. It will be better tomorrow."

Ruthie cried and reached for a tissue. The box was empty and Van looked at her and smiled, as she got a new box down from the cabinet. "That reminds me of something that we forgot to tell you in all this hubbub."

Van explained to her about when Tater asked where she was. Van took the Kleenex from Tater out of her handbag. "This is from Tater for your code."

Ruthie cried even harder, "He is such a sweet little boy. I can't believe that Ian is just going to sign him away. What kind of person is he, Aunt Van?"

Van put her arms around her, "Don't jump to conclusions. Look how Egan had a fit at first. He is in a whole different place now."

Ruthie nodded, "I just hate all this. And the worst, nothing is resolved. Those characters are still up to Lord knows what, Taylor isn't buried, cops are watching our every move and Ian isn't home. As far as Tater, he still has no one."

Van laughed softly, "Oh yes. He has at least three people, right now."

"Oh good grief, I was supposed to call Matt. What am I going to tell him?"

"The truth. There is no need to hide it from him. Matt is a good soul and understands his brother." Van looked at the clock, "You might want to call before they milk."

"They are already milking. I'll call in about an hour." Ruthie looked at the clock, "I think I'll call Zach. He would be home now."

That night, after she had talked to Zach and Matt, she felt better. They both seemed to understand Ian's outburst, even though they didn't like it. They both felt he would get over it. They were going to talk to each other and then go talk to Mo and Carl. Ruthie took her bath and went to bed early. She worried she wouldn't be able to sleep, but she did.

In the morning, Greg called by six. "Ruthie, our boy had a terrible night. I talked to Turner. He agrees that Ian needs to handle this as best he can. Right now, he flops between being an angry victim and feeling like a monster. He is terrified that he really messed things up with you yesterday and asked me to tell you that he didn't mean it. I told him I won't do that. So, don't tell him that I did. Do you think you could come up this afternoon?"

"I'm not very certain I want another round of yesterday. I'm up to my eyebrows with all this."

"I can imagine. If you can't, we would like Egan to come up. He needs to talk to someone."

"I know. Someone will be there. I just don't know if it will be me."

"I understand. I won't say anything to him. His arm didn't give him a lot of problem last night. Maybe it figured he had enough going on."

"Thanks for calling Greg. Someone will be there. About what time?"

"He will be finished with therapy about three or four this afternoon."

"Okay."

Over breakfast, they decided to call and see if they could see Tater in the morning and then they would all go up to the hospital in the afternoon. Whoever felt up to it, would talk to Ian.

They were just finishing their breakfast when Mo called. She talked first to Egan, who answered the phone. He filled her in on all the details and answered her questions. Then he handed the phone to Ruthie. "Here, Mo wants to talk to you."

"Hello Mo," Ruthie started, "I'm sorry..."

And she cried. Egan took the phone back to apologize to Mo, only to find out that she was crying just as hard on the other end of the line. He and Carl had a long talk before he hung up. Then he said, "Carl and I are almost certain, if you can be patient, and we aren't telling you to be, but if you can..."

"What, Egan?" Van said.

The tall man shook his head, "We think Ian will calm down and be sensible about it. We think there is no need to throw the crystal in the trash just yet."

Ruthie looked at him and then at Van, who didn't understand him either. Then Egan went out to talk to Otis. Van turned to Ruthie, "I think he means it will be okay. Is that what you got?"

"Yes, I think so."

They called the Center and Mrs. Feldman told them that the children would be out playing in the morning. They usually didn't allow visitors then, but in this case, they would make an exception. The three arrived at the Center about nine-thirty.

Right after the red Cadillac stopped in the parking lot, a green, older model Buick drove past the parking lot and parked on the street. A man got out and the driver of the car drove off. The man walked across the street and sat on the bench at the bus stop. He was apparently waiting for his bus to stop.

Harringtons checked at the office and Mrs. Feldman took them out the side door to the playground. Surrounded by a ten-foot tall, chain-linked fence, there was playground equipment of all types, slides, swings and teeter-totters. There were kids jumping rope or playing catch. Mrs. Feldman waved for Tater, who was waiting his turn to go down the slide. He looked over at her and when when he noticed Egan, Van and Ruthie, he darted right over to them. Egan held out his arms to the little guy and picked him up with a big hug. The boy giggled and then looked at Ruthie.

"You okay?"

"Yes, I'm a lot better. I think your Kleenex helped me. That was so nice of you to send it for me."

"Good," he smiled. "Play ball?"

"I would love to," Egan grinned. "Is there one here we can use?"

Tater took him off to the box of balls. Mrs. Feldman turned to the ladies, "Tater rarely shows any affection to anyone, but he seems very comfortable with you folks. I'm glad that he has found someone to depend on."

They played catch for a short time and then the children had to go in. They told him goodbye and went to their car. No one noticed that the man at the bus stop didn't board either of the two buses that stopped. He just watched the playground. It wasn't until they left, that he took the next bus to leave.

At the hospital, they met with Greg before they went in to see Ian. Greg thought it would be a good idea for Ruthie to see him alone. "He is very sorry for his tirade yesterday. You two need to have a serious talk. Okay?"

Ruthie went into the room where Ian was standing by the window, looking out over the city. He didn't hear her come in and she came up beside him. She took his hand and he put his good arm around her. "I'm so glad you came back. I was terrible yesterday! Can you ever forgive me?"

"Already did." She hugged him back and they shared a kiss. He became a bit woozy and had to sit down. She helped him into bed, "I understand that it was a lot for you to take in all at once. I wish I had a better way of telling you, but I didn't know how."

"It wasn't you. It was me. It was just too much. I never in my life imagined that Taylor had a baby. I couldn't believe it. I can't imagine what you must be thinking of me. This wasn't fair to you at all. I should have been the one to make all these decisions."

"What would you have done?"

"I don't know. I want you to know that there is nothing that I will allow to destroy our marriage. Ever."

"We are the only ones that can do that."

"I should have been the one to deal with all this." Ian said thoughtfully. "I made so many mistakes the last couple days. I should have trusted you

143

right away. I was just shocked and honestly, I was afraid you wouldn't think I was nothing more than a creep for leading Taylor on."

"I did think so, but I also understand the situation. I think it is a bad, bad way to do business. But the past is the past."

"If the DNA says it is my kid, I will give him up, so it doesn't destroy our marriage."

Ruthie pulled back, "Don't you want to meet your son?"

"No. I don't want to mess up our life. How could you love me if I brought my kid into our lives?" He took her hand, "I don't want you to hate me."

"Ian, how would I feel about you if you could walk away from your own child without even seeing him? You wouldn't be the man I married if you could do that! What would stop you from walking away from our baby?"

"This is different."

"Is it? I don't think so. I looked at that little guy and I thought of Miriam. You always said you would take her into our home."

"Ruthie, that is not the same. She needs a family."

"So does Tater."

"Tater?"

"He can't say Taylor. He calls himself Tater."

"You've seen him?"

"Yes, and please don't be angry with me, but I had to see him. I caught hell from everyone but Van and your Mom for going to see him."

"Mom knows?" Then he shook his head, "Of course, she does. I suppose they all think I am a cad."

"No, they don't. Your Mom is planning on giving you hell, though."

"I can about imagine." Ian nodded. "I'm sure folks are lining up to give me a piece of their minds. God, did I ever make a colossal mess of things."

"I hope you aren't furious with me for seeing him."

"How could I be angry? I should have been the one to take care of it." Ian said and then became quiet for a minute and then asked, barely above a whisper, "What's he like?"

Ruthie explained their meetings and what he was like. A few times, Ian had to wipe tears away, but he listened quietly. He only interrupted to ask what Egan and Van thought. "I bet they think I'm an ogre."

"No. They don't. I think that Egan would take him home with him in a second. He thinks he is a fine lad." Ruthie added. "I think I can get it arranged so you can meet him soon."

"I don't know about that. Maybe I shouldn't see him. If I'm just going to put him up for adoption, why would I see him? I don't think that would be good for either him or me."

"Why would you put him up for adoption? He has a father." Ruthie hesitated, "Mrs. Feldman said that when Taylor came to see him, she told him that his Daddy didn't want him, but she would come get him soon. Then they had to tell him that she was dead. He has no one."

Ian cried. Ruthie held him and let him cry. After a couple minutes, he stopped and wiped his face, "I just want our lives to go back to where they were."

"That cannot be. You didn't know about him before. Now you do, and I do. He is a real person and he has no one to depend on. After he had that one bad placement they had to remove him from…"

"What happened?"

"I don't know the details, but they had to remove him and two other foster kids because it was an abusive situation. All they would tell me was that it had a profound effect on him. That is why they hadn't placed him again. They wanted to get him sorted around after that. Then Taylor got out of prison, so they thought it wise to just keep him there until they could see how that went."

Ian nodded. He looked out the window and then his face flooded with tears again, "Is there any reason that he might not be adopted?"

"No. Ian, could you live with yourself, knowing he is out there somewhere with the only thought of his family being his mom was dead and his dad didn't want him? You told me that you felt guilty when you were happy thinking about Taylor. How would you feel with our children, if you knew that you had a son somewhere facing Lord knows what?"

"I don't want to mess up our family! Don't you understand?"

"Don't you understand, he is our family? He is your son."

Ian grabbed onto her, "Could you stand to have him around? He is a little kid now, but he will grow up. Will you hate him?"

"I can't tell you about what I will feel years from now. I only can answer for what I think now. I'd never want to be responsible for standing between you and your son. Ian, he can be ours. It is up to you." Ruthie looked at him, "He has the right to know he has a family, and a brother or sister. And our baby has the right to know he has a brother."

Ian stared at the bed and then nodded, "He does. But Ruthie, this is a permanent decision. We can't go back on it later."

"I know that."

"God, I am so blessed to have you for a wife. I love you so much." Ian hugged her again, "Okay, I will meet him. But promise me that you won't tell him I'm his dad. I think that I should be the one to tell him."

"Oh yes. Believe me, I don't like making these decisions. In fact, I may not ever make another decision." Then she got a funny look on her face, "Although I did make another one I didn't tell you about."

"What was that?"

"Aaron said that the Collins had not claimed Taylor's body. They said in a few days she would be buried in the indigent cemetery, Potter's Field. You know how I feel about that."

He took her hand, "I know."

"I told John Kelly to not let that happen. If no one claims her, I want to get her a casket and a headstone in a regular cemetery. Everyone deserves that much." Ruthie went on, "John Kelly said he would let me know."

"Do you really want to do that?"

"Yes, I do. If she has a decent burial, then Tater will have a place to go see her grave. He will know that someone cared for her."

Ian shook his head, "Ruthie, I did like her. I felt sorry for her because all she ever wanted was a real home and somewhere to belong. I let her down."

"Not yet. I think that if you really had any feelings at all for her, you would want her to have a decent burial and raise her son. At the very least, he could have a home."

They embraced and both cried, "Okay," he said. "You set up a time when I can meet him, but I'm not making any promises. I do think I want to meet him."

"Good," She smiled. "I'm so relieved about that. I want a promise from you."

"What kind of promise?"

"That we won't do this anymore. I've been miserable knowing you were keeping something from me and trying to keep something from you. We just aren't good at it."

"I know we're not. Not even a little bit." He kissed her, "I promise, but you have to promise, too."

"I do." Then she giggled, "We better call Egan and Van in. I'm sure she has had to suffocate him twice already."

146

He looked at her, "You're right. I don't want to face him."
"Get over it."

The visit went well, even though Egan did give him some guff. "Lookie here, Laddie. Don't be pulling this again, hear me? It's too damned hard on me! I won't be giving you hell. Your Mom is plotting that out already. I will let her do it."

Ian got a slight grin, "And it will be a doozy."

26

The next morning was the first time Ruthie had a positive feeling when she woke up in days. She had slept well and felt confident that Ian would not sign Tater away once he met him. She knew that with all her heart. If he did, that would mean that everything in her life was based on falsehoods. She didn't, or couldn't, believe that.

John Kelly came over for breakfast. He was more relaxed than he had been in days. "I am so thankful that things are getting straightened out. I shouldn't talk out of school, but I have to tell you. Even Jamie told me last night, that he was relieved that Ian wanted to see his son."

"Jamie?" Egan's eyes flew open, "After all the ranting he did? The Chorus of Angels must have passed out cold! I guess there is hope."

Van smiled, "Yah, who'd ever think that a grown man could have a fit one day and then the next, befriend the little guy. Who, I ask you?"

"Okay, so I was a little hot-headed at first. I just hate stuff messing everything up." Egan defended himself. "John Kelly, do you know what we need to do next to set up this meeting?"

"I would imagine talk to Mrs. Feldman at the Center. They are loosening the restrictions after the blood tests came out as they did. Aaron talked to her yesterday and she was very pleased that your visits have gone well. She should be able to help us out."

"I will call her this morning," Ruthie said. "We will have to figure out where they can meet. Maybe I should talk to Greg first. Ian isn't going to be out of the hospital for a week or more yet, so they will have to meet there."

"Not ideal, but the DNA will be back in seven days now. They need to meet before then," Van added. "At least, these things seem more positive.

Even though we know there will be bumps in the road, the worst has to be over now."

"Which reminds me," Egan motioned toward the front door, "How long are we going to have cops sitting on our doorstep day and night?"

"For a while yet," John Kelly said. "We haven't heard any rumblings, but a few days aren't enough to think the Collins-Norris ring has slithered back under their rock."

They visited about the rest of the family and Ian's recovery. Just as John Kelly was ready to leave the house about nine, the phone rang. It was Aaron for John. He took the phone and listened intently, "Damn, damn, damn! I will. You sending more units?"

John Kelly hung up and his radio went off. He went out to talk to the officers our front and came back in. "Stay put. I will talk to you in a minute."

John went back outside. The folks in the house were dumbfounded. More police cars with sirens screeched up in front of the house. John stationed some of the officers in the backyard and then came back into the house.

"What's going on?" Egan asked.

"Something no one expected. This morning, the kids were playing outside at the Center. You know that place is pretty secure, because they have their share of trouble there."

Ruthie put her hands up to her face and started to cry. Van put her arm around her, "Is Tater okay?"

John Kelly shook his head, "We don't know. This morning, two men rammed the fence and knocked it in with a white four-wheel drive pickup. They jumped out and grabbed two little boys. Then they threw one of the kids back on the ground, but took Tater with them. Then they sped off."

"Was anyone hurt?" Van asked.

"The security guard was hit by the truck, but he is alive and on his way to the hospital. The children are all shook up and the little boy that was thrown out of the pickup has scrapes and such. There is little information."

"Did the cops get them?" Egan asked.

"The cops were called right away. They found the pickup abandoned about five blocks away. It was stolen yesterday afternoon. No sign of anyone. Apparently, they had another car waiting for them."

Ruthie was shaking so hard she had to sit down, "No sign of Tater at all?"

"Not yet." John Kelly said. "It is early yet. This was a blatant, reckless thing to do. I think they must have some addled plan. They had to know this would bring hell down on them! They are either desperate or crazy!"

"Do they just want Taylor's child? Because he is family?" Ruthie asked.

"Doubtful. From all we've learned, they just want money. They had no love for Taylor and resented her kid. I think we will hear something very soon."

"Has someone told Ian?" Ruthie trembled, "He should be told. I need to go to him."

"No," John Kelly said. "Aaron is on his way up there now. He will talk to Greg and tell Ian. We need you to stay put."

"Will the Center be okay?" Van asked.

"Yes, there is commotion now, but they will have things back to normal soon. They have plenty of security there now."

"That fence wasn't much help," Egan pointed out.

"A heavy chain-linked fence is usually enough. There is little one can do if someone is determined enough to drive through it. Especially if they have no fear of getting caught." John shook his head, "I'm afraid we have really botched this whole thing. We didn't figure this at all."

"How would you have known someone would take him?" Egan looked at the young man, "Do you think there is a possibility this was a random thing?"

John Kelly bit his lip, "No. Of course, anything is possible, but the odds are against it. He was the target. The only thing we can think of is this was Ian's kid and they wanted him."

The doorbell rang and it was an FBI agent, and some of his compatriots. Haversham was all business and took over immediately. "Any demands yet?"

John Kelly answered, "No, but we don't know if they might call the hospital to speak to Ian."

"Got Driscoll working that end. We should hear something soon. They want something. I doubt they just wanted to take him for ice cream."

"Will they hurt him?" Van asked.

"Who the hell knows," Haversham grumbled. "Can you show me where your phone lines are?"

The next hour passed with folks moving in and out of the dining room. It now served as Haversham's headquarters. The family heard through John Kelly's police radio that Ian had been informed and was struggling with the information. Turner wanted to put him to sleep, but the FBI wanted him awake if these men called. Besides, Ian refused to go to sleep.

The surveillance cameras from the playground were taken to the police station. The man driving the pickup was identified as Ted Collins. The other man, Bill Moss, was known by the street name of Mouse because he looked like one. Mouse was puny and jumpy, with a high-pitched voice. He made it all worse, by growing what passed for a scrawny mustache under his pointy nose.

When they reviewed the tapes, they saw that the day before, Mouse had been sitting at the bus stop across the street from the playground. Ted was spotted on the tape the day before, sitting across the street in a pale green Buick. They noticed the Buick drove by the Center several times in the last couple of days. The police put out an APB on that vehicle.

The four-wheel drive pickup was being towed to the police impound where the forensics team would inspect it. More cops were sent to the area where Collins had been hanging out before the Warehouse robbery. After that went bust, the remainder of the crew fell out of sight.

Ruthie began to berate herself, "Is it because we went to see him? Did we lead them to Tater?"

"Doubtful. They knew the kid was at the Center. His mom visited him there. They might not have known what he looked like, because they had never seen him that we know of. It is possible that Taylor had pointed him out to them anytime in the last six weeks or so. But it wouldn't have mattered. Once they got the idea to break in there, they would have been able to single him out."

"How?"

Haversham shook his head, "He has a name. They know it."

Ruthie went into the kitchen and plunked at the table with her head in her arms. John Kelly came out and put his arm over her shoulder, "I know Haversham should be nicer, but he's right. If they want to use him for something, they would've been able to get him. Most of the time, fences keep folks out. This time it didn't."

"What do you think they want?"

"My guess is money. That was the reason they broke into the warehouse, remember?"

"Why do they think we have money or anything?"

"Because you don't live in a cardboard box. This kind don't really care how you get it, just so you give it to them."

"If they don't call, then what? Maybe they just wanted to kill him or steal him."

"I'm rather certain they don't want to steal him. They don't want to raise him or anything like that. That I would bet my life on. Kill him? The only reason would be to hurt Ian. I don't know if they know he cares. My guess is money."

An hour or so later, the phone rang. Egan answered at the direction of Haversham. A gruff voice on the other end of the line said, "Let me talk to O'Hara's old lady."

Haversham had told them to try to keep whoever called on the line long enough so they could find out where the call originated. Egan answered, "I'm sorry. You have the wrong number. There is no one named O'Hara here."

The man cussed into the phone, "Don't be cute with me, idiot! I don't care what the hell name he's going by! Put his old lady on the phone!"

Haversham nodded to Egan, "Just a second."

He handed the phone to Ruthie, who was shaking like a leaf. The gruff man said, "You want to see that little bastard alive again, you need to listen good. I'm telling you once. Put $50,000 in a shopping bag. Nothing larger than a fifty. Take it to the park outside Villameade Mall. Set it between the bench and the yellow rose bush at four o'clock. Then get lost. If it's all there, we'll call to tell you where to get the kid."

Haversham shook his head no, and wrote on a piece of paper, "Ask him to repeat it."

Ruthie stammered, "Could you tell me again. I don't live here."

"$50,000 between the bench and yellow rose bush at Villameade Mall. Four o'clock."

"I don't have that kind of money."

"Then the kid is dead."

"How do I know he isn't already?"

The man barked, "You don't. Want to take the chance?"

Ruthie started to say that she didn't know how to get the money and he slammed the receiver down. She almost collapsed when he hung up. Egan helped her sit down and then asked the FBI agent, "Did you have time?"

"No, but we know which section it came from," then he talked to John Kelly. Ruthie had to go throw up and Van helped her.

John Kelly and Egan met the women in the kitchen. "They were able to get it traced to the Leather District. That is a help."

"I should have kept him on the line longer."

"He probably knew that he was being traced. Notice he didn't say to not call the authorities, because he knows we're in this already." John pointed out.

"I have to go to a bank."

"Ruthie, we can help you round up the money. It is quite likely that if you pay him, the little boy will be killed anyway... or already is dead."

"I have to try, John Kelly. I can't let him be killed because I didn't try."

Haversham came into the kitchen, "You say you could raise the money? Then I think you should. Kelly, you go with her and get it. We can rig up the shopping bag or something. We have to draw them out. We don't want them in the wind."

John Kelly took Ruthie to the bank. Since it was going to be a large withdrawal, she had to have approval from her brother, Zach. John Kelly arranged the phone call and explained to Zach what had happened. "Are you okay with it? We will try to get the money back, as well as the little boy."

"Not a problem, that was all blood money in the first place."

It took a few phone calls and some faxed signatures back and forth before John Kelly and Ruthie left the bank with a bag of money. As they got in the car, Ruthie shrugged, "What's wrong with people? How can they do this to a little boy who has no responsibility for any of it?"

"I don't know Ruthie. I wonder about that all the time. I think God should've flooded the whole damned works and started over fresh."

Ruthie laughed, "Then we wouldn't be here."

"True, but maybe His next batch would have turned out better!"

"Do you think they will hurt Tater?"

"I couldn't even guess."

It was almost one o'clock when John Kelly and Ruthie returned to the house. Jamie and Aaron had both just come over to fill them in and then Aaron was heading back up to the hospital. They had discouraged any phone calls between each the hospital and Egan's home because they wanted to keep the lines open in case Ted would call back.

"We found out that Mouse has an ex-wife who lives in the Leather District. We have sent someone over to check out the place. We want to see if there are signs of the little boy." Jamie said, and then he gave Ruthie a big hug. "We will get him back, if it's at all possible."

"I know."

"I'm sorry I was a butt head about things the other day."

"Forget it."

Aaron said, "Ian is a basket case, but he's doing okay. He had a good physical therapy session this morning before the phone call. Greg said he is beginning to make visible progress. His lung is healing and his doctor is very pleased with the recovery. Ian said to tell you he really wishes he could do something besides worry and that he loves you all. I have to tell you, he's having a terrible time. Blaming himself. I called my parish and Father Colter is going over to talk to him."

"Thanks, Aaron. That is a good thing. I appreciate that."

The conversation ceased when the phone rang. Everyone went back to the dining room. Egan took the phone and the man barked, "Put the woman on."

"She's coming."

They waited as long as they could put him off and then she answered, "Hello? Can I talk to Taylor?"

"No way in hell. Got the money? Give me the money and you can wipe his snotty nose the rest of your life for all I give a damn! Got it?"

"I do."

"Good, changed the spot. Two-thirty at the Cooper underpass. Drop the bag by the dumpster. There will be an address there where to get the brat."

The phone went dead and Haversham nodded, "Son of a –, he likely figured we would have the Mall staked out. That underpass has no one around and several access roads. It will be a bitch."

"So, what do we need to do now?" Egan asked.

"Get in the car and go to the Cooper underpass. Know the way?"

John Kelly interrupted, "Let me drive her. I'll wear one of Egan's shirts over my uniform. I don't want her to walk into this without any protection."

"Good idea."

Half an hour later, John Kelly and Ruthie were driving down the freeway in Van's car. Ruthie looked over to him, "What a crazy time this has been? I owe you a big one, John."

"You don't owe me anything. I'm a cop and this is my job. I feel terrible that we haven't been able to keep ahead of these dudes. We say they're dumb, but so far, they've been ahead of us."

"You shouldn't apologize for not thinking like a psychopath!"

"You are handling this well. I've been proud of you."

"Thanks," she smiled. "That means a lot. Considering the upchucking, bawling and ranting I've done, I think you probably have cringed a lot, too."

"Well, it makes it more interesting." Then he winked at her, "We will make it through this."

"What are the honest chances of getting Tater back alive? That poor kid. I wonder what is going through his mind?"

"Couldn't begin to answer that. We just have to pray for the best."

A few minutes later, John Kelly pulled over on the side of the highway and put the flashers on. He took the shopping bag and went under the bridge, where there was a dumpster. He set the bag in the pile of garbage next to the empty dumpster and looked for the note. It took him a minute because of piles of garbage strewn about. He opened the note and it contained an address. Then he ran back to the car and they left.

Ruthie looked at him, "See anything or anyone?"

"No, just garbage."

"Was the dumpster full?"

"Nope, not a damned thing in it! Why the hell carry something all the way down there and then set it next to the garbage can? People are nuts!"

Ruthie bit her lip, "Now what? Got the note? What does it say?"

"Just an address. As soon as I can pull over, we will radio in the address."

As soon as they got to a turn off the highway, they pulled into a gas station. John called the department and gave them the address. Jamie told him they were keeping the best watch they could on the location and so far, no one had picked up the bag. But it was early. He said he was sending someone to their location. A black and white would meet them on Whitehall and Franklin. John should go with them and one of the uniforms would bring Ruthie back to the house.

Ruthie was having a difficult time keeping it together, "I know you don't know either, but how long will it be? When will we get Tater back? I'm going crazy." She was crying now, "How can people handle it when it happens to a child they have raised from scratch?"

John Kelly looked at her and started to laugh, "From scratch?"

He broke into a belly laugh and so did she. They were just pulling themselves together when they met the black and white. "Gee, we better quit laughing or these guys will commit us!"

Ruthie nodded, "Look how somber they are?"

John Kelly looked at her and they both giggled again. "Damn girl. We have to be serious!"

Once they got out of the car, it was easy enough to become serious. One of the officers had bad news. They had found the house of Mouse's ex-wife. She told them that he, Ted Collins and this other guy had brought a kid over there and wanted her to keep him. She told them to get him out of there because she didn't want to be involved in anything like kidnapping. They took the kid and left. But at the time, the little boy was very upset but not hurt physically. They were transporting her to the station for more questioning. She did give him the name of the other man, Mark Mackee.

Ruthie cried harder and John Kelly have her a big hug. "Be brave. Go with this officer and maybe we will have this resolved very soon."

She nodded and kissed his cheek, "Be careful, John."

"I'll do that."

By the time Ruthie returned to the house, the FBI had more news. They had sent folks to scout out the address, but it turned out to be an empty lot. Nothing on it but weeds. They were having better luck with Mackee's name. They found that he had several family members living in the Leather District. They were looking into them. So far, no one had picked up the shopping bag.

Ruthie frowned, "How can they trust that someone else wouldn't stop by and pick up their money?"

Egan shook his head, "How many times do you randomly stop by a dumpster at an underpass?"

"About as often as I kidnap someone," she replied.

The phone rang, and the room's anxiety level rose. Haversham frowned, "Don't know why they'd risk calling again. Answer it."

Ruthie picked it up and said abruptly, "Yes. We did as we were told."

"It's me, Ian," Ian said, "I can only talk a minute, but I had to know how you're doing?"

"I'm okay, we are all okay," Ruthie smiled. "How are you?"

"I want to get out there and help. I feel worthless." Then she heard Aaron in the background, "I have to leave the line clear. I love you."

"I love you, too."

Ruthie hung up and ran upstairs to have a good cry. She tried to rest, but her mind was going wild. She took a shower and changed her clothes. Then she went back downstairs.

It was almost four-thirty when the police called. A man on a motorcycle had driven up the back way and through the ditch to get the shopping bag. The Boston Police were able to pick him up from above by helicopter, which followed at a distance to the home of Mackee's aunt. She was an elderly invalid who lived alone on the third floor in a small one-bedroom walk up. The police and FBI gathered to go in. John Kelly, Aaron and Jamie were there, too.

Ruthie begged Haversham to let her go to the hospital so she could be with Ian. He said no. "We need you here, just in case they call for any obscure reason. One of these others can go."

Egan said he would and Van could stay with Ruthie. Haversham had one of his agents take him to the hospital. Ruthie felt better, but not as good as she would have had she been able to go.

She and Van tried to keep busy. They played ball with Otis and then went back in the house. They took out some meat for dinner and then put it back, having decided they didn't feel like cooking. Finally, they just went in the living room to listen to the large grandfather clock measure out eternity with its baritone beat of the pendulum.

It was almost six when Haversham's radio went crazy. There was a lot of excited talking back and forth. Ruthie and Van heard men shouting, noise and gun shots. Then it was still. Haversham yelled into his radio, "Driscoll? Status!"

Worried looks passed between everyone assembled at the dining room table. Then a calmer voice responded, "Entry made. Two arrests and one man down. No sign of the boy, yet, but we just made entry."

Then Haversham grabbed another garbled call on the radio. After that, Haversham picked up the phone and called a number from his head. He did a lot of mumbling. Then he hung up and looked at the folks gathered in the room, "Two arrested and the other was shot dead. He fired on the police and was killed in the return fire. It was this Collins dude."

Frantically, Ruthie asked, "Anything about the little boy?"

"Not yet, Ma'am. He wasn't in the apartment, but they are searching the building. The aunt is pretty feeble. She said that one of the guys wanted her key to the basement. She didn't know anything about a little boy, but she can hardly see or hear."

"God, I can't stand this!" Ruthie held her head. "I feel like my head is going to blow off! Why don't we hear something?"

"It's a big building." Haversham stated, "And we want to do a thorough job."

"I know, but I just can't..."

The dank, dirty basement was filled with junk, mildew, cobwebs and debris. The FBI agents and local police divided into groups. The 20,000 square feet of concrete walls and floors, pipes and bare light bulbs also housed tangles of wires and an ancient furnace. There were a few rooms, some with doors and some not. The contents of these rooms were anyone's guess. There were old, rusting appliances in disrepair, boxes, broken furniture and old cabinets and closets. There were piles of bulging plastic bags, covered in the accumulation of at least a year's worth of dirt and dust. Hiding the body of a small child would be a simple task for almost anyone.

John Kelly was assigned the back part of quadrant four. He entered a pitch-black room and fumbled until he found a switch for a bare bulb, which flickered erratically. The room smelled of dirt, mold and mildew, making it difficult to breathe. There was a back room similar to a large walk-in closet that had no light. John Kelly flashed the beam from his flashlight around inside it. It was completely empty, save debris and what looked like a rodent nest in a corner. The cobwebs hung unsullied across the door and the corners. It seemed unlikely that anyone had been in there. Nothing had been disturbed for some time.

His eyes searched the area he where he was standing. He could hear the drip from some old, rusting pipe echoing in the room and the sounds of a few of the rescue team moving around. John Kelly swept the area with his flashlight and noticed the area in front of some decrepit kitchen cabinets had been disturbed. He did not know how recently, but before there was a chance for debris and dust to reclaim it. He pulled away some dilapidated boxes that were jammed up across the front of the cabinet. They were stacked about three piles out from the hideously painted kitchen cabinet. The paint was peeling and some of the wood was rotting.

John began moving the boxes out of the way, checking to see if they had been recently disturbed before moving them. Most had not and could not have been without falling apart. Some disintegrated as he moved them, leaving piles of old clothing and brittle papers strewn all over. After moving about seven boxes, he stopped to wipe some dust out of his eyes.

As he did, he thought he heard a whimper. The strong, athletic man froze, with his sense on high alert. He waited but didn't hear anything again. After a couple minutes, he asked, "Tater? Can you make some noise if you hear me?"

His heart was pounding so thunderously in his ears; he could hardly make out another whimper. When he did, he flew into motion. It was coming from that decaying cabinet. He shoved the boxes aside as fast as he could and studied the cabinet. The top of the cabinet was missing, so nothing could be in the top drawers or cupboards. Some of them had doors, in varying stages of disrepair. In the corner was one cabinet about eighteen inches wide and two feet tall. That door seemed intact, but was jammed. John Kelly tried to open it with his hands, but could not pull it lose. He questioned if it had been opened in some time. He was so anxious, he could barely manipulate his fingers around the door. He asked as confidently as possible, "Tater? Can you make a noise for me?"

This time he heard a whimper and he knew it was from the cabinet. He tried the door again and could not budge it. He studied it carefully with his flashlight. That is when he noticed, the two back hinges. The paint had peeled away from one hinge recently. Neither had a hinge pin. One was held by an old nail and the other had a narrow, wooden dowel-type thing jammed into it. John removed the nail and then pounded the wood dowel until it smashed apart. Then he pulled the door off backwards.

He ripped off the door to find two shelves. The top was full of boxes of old sink hardware, but the bottom held the treasure. There was a little boy, stuffed into an area about eighteen inches wide by sixteen inches tall. He had been jammed in headfirst. Only by his back with one arm laying on his spine and one leg jammed under him. The other was distorted into a contortion against the side.

John yelled to his coworkers, "Got him."

Then he spoke calmly, "I will get you out of there, Tater. It will okay now. You will be fine. I will get you out, quickly as I can."

He kept repeating words of encouragement while he tried to pull the boy out. The child was so jammed in, that he was unable to. He quickly threw out all the boxes of sink hardware and lifted the shelf off from above. Then he was finally able to remove the child.

The little boy was covered with sweat, dirt and tears. The lower part of his face was wrapped about three times all the way around his head with duct tape. John Kelly gave him a gentle hug and then took his scissors and cut the tape. That was the first time that the little boy looked at him.

John knew the child was laboring to breathe so he grabbed the end of the tape and ripped it back from his mouth. The boy screamed in pain, but then took a deep breath. Then he put his arms around John Kelly's neck and held him for dear life. John rubbed his back gently and soothed him, "It will be okay now, Tater. Everything will be fine. I'm sorry I had to hurt you, but I wanted to get the tape off. Can you breathe better?"

"Okay," Tater mumbled through his tears.

The little boy held on to the policeman with a death clench the entire time the other people arrived. John Kelly carried him to the ambulance.

The boy never said much but held onto John all the while. John Kelly held him in his arms all the way to the hospital in the ambulance.

Before they got out of the back of the ambulance, Tater looked at the policeman. "I sorry I wet my pants. Are you mad at me?"

John gave him a hug, "You are my hero. I wouldn't have been as brave as you."

"Does that mean you're mad?"

"No way, little man. I'm not one bit mad at you."

"Okay," the little boy buried his face in John's shoulder. "I don't want you to be mad. I'm sorry I got wet."

##

The phone rang and Haversham grabbed it. He listened for only a second before his face broke into a huge grin. "I'll tell them! You coming in?"

Ruthie and Van smiled expectantly while waiting for Haversham to hang up. "This John Kelly cop found the boy. The kid was stuffed in an old cabinet down in the back of the basement. He is shook up and scared, but seems okay. The paramedics are bringing him to the hospital. John Kelly insisted they take him to the hospital where your husband is. If you want, we can give you a ride there?"

"Yes, please!" Ruthie said.

Haversham said they would clean up the mess in the dining room and leave when they were finished. They decided to keep men posted out front, even though they were certain they had all of the Norris-Collins ring. They wanted to take no more chances by underestimating them again.

Ruthie and Van arrived at the hospital and went directly to the Emergency Room. The first person they saw was Aaron. He gave them a big joyous hug, "What a day! We got him. The doc is looking him over now, but thinks he will be okay. Egan is in the room with him. That little guy seemed really glad to see him." Then he hesitated and grinned, "There's no doubt about it. That little guy is a Harrington."

Jamie came up and shared the embraces, "Greg is coming down. He wants to talk to you. I would love to just hang out here, but Aaron and I have work to do back at the 'ranch'. We're leaving John here for you."

"Thanks you guys. Thanks so much."

Van and Ruthie went to the desk in Emergency and John Kelly met them. "He's okay, bruised and scared. The doc said they want to keep him in overnight, just to be sure. I already asked. You can go in with him."

Greg came up beside them, "I just talked to Turner. We wondered if maybe you would like it if we put Ian and him in the same room? We can move Ian to a double room and Tater can share it, especially since they both need police protection. This is a special request and I had to put my vacation on the line, so you better say yes."

Ruthie threw her arms around him, "I love you!"

Greg chuckled, "Well, that really changes things! Don't know what the wife will say!" Then he laughed, "Should I tell them you want them together?"

"Please. That will be wonderful."

"They haven't met yet, have they?" Greg asked.

"Not yet."

"I wouldn't introduce them tonight. Just first names, okay?"

"Okay."

Ruthie and Van were ushered into the exam room where Egan was talking with Tater. "Look who's here, Tater." Egan said.

He looked up with a surprised smiled, "Aunt Van and her!"

They both hugged him and then Van said, "I just wanted to say hi, but I need to talk to Egan for a minute. Would it be okay if Ruthie visited with you for a little bit?"

He nodded, "I'll talk to her."

28

After the nurse got him set up with an IV because of dehydration, Ruthie sat with him. "I was so worried about you today. Are you okay?"

He nodded, "This big huge truck came right into our yard and wrecked up everything! Mr. Hoddis got squashed! This ugly guy grabbed me and Jerry. He throwed us in that truck. The other guy there said a bad word and threw Jerry out! I think he got hurt. I was crying and the ugly guy put tape on my mouth. I cried cause I was so scared and mad."

"I bet you were. I can see the marks from the tape on your face. Does it hurt?"

"It scratches. I didn't like that. I hope Jerry didn't get dead."

"He is okay, Tater. I talked to the Center and Jerry is fine. He was worried about you, but he is okay."

"Good, cause he just got a new mommy and daddy. He is going to go live with them. He couldn't have done that if he was dead and stuff."

Ruthie hugged him, "Well, he isn't dead, so I'm sure it will be just fine. The policeman told me that Mr. Hollis, the security man, is doing okay. He will get a vacation from work for a couple days, but then he will be back."

"Good. Can I go back today? I want to see Jerry before he goes to his new house."

"I think you can leave tomorrow, but I'll tell you what. I will talk to Mrs. Feldman and make certain that you get to tell Jerry goodbye."

He nodded, "Good. Ruthie, I didn't get to see Widey for a long time."

"I know. None of us watched him today. We can see him tomorrow." Ruthie said, "You are going to sleep here tonight. Guess what? You will share your room with a friend of ours. His name is Ian Harrington and he wants to meet you. So, this will work out well. Won't that be nice?"

"Is he a little kid like me?"

"No, he is a grownup."

He shrugged, "Do Egan and Aunt Van know him?"

"They do. In fact, we are all good friends."

"I guess it's okay. Ruthie, I'm thirsty."

Ruthie helped him get some water and the nurse came in. "Are you ready to go for a ride with us, young man?"

He looked to Ruthie and she nodded. "He is ready. Will he be in with Mr. Harrington?"

"I don't know, but I know he is sharing a room with someone who is not in Pediatrics. Neurology, I believe."

"That's right. Can I come along?"

The nurse smiled, "That's up to Mr. Taylor."

"Tater," the little boy corrected her. "Her can come."

When they arrived at the room, Ian wasn't there yet. The nurses put Tater in the bed nearest the door and the other bed, by the window, was still empty. Ruthie asked, "How soon will Ian be here?"

"About half an hour. Dr. Turner is making rounds and then they will move him. Okay?"

"Great." Ruthie smiled, "Did you hear that, Tater?"

He shrugged and looked at the bed, "This bed is way big. I never knew about wheels for a bed."

"Yes, they use them in the hospital all the time. Pretty clever, huh?" He looked at her without answering, "Why did those bad guys wreck up our play yard?"

"I don't know," Ruthie answered. "Sometimes people aren't very nice. It is very hard to understand them."

"Is your friend nice?"

"He is very nice and I think you will like him quite a lot."

Tater started to cry and Ruthie put her arms around him, "What's wrong, Tater? Can you tell me?"

"Jerry is going to get a mommy and daddy. I want to see his new mommy and daddy. He and I both wanted them. I wanted to have a daddy but my Mommy said my daddy didn't want me. Was I a bad boy?"

"No. You are not a bad boy at all! I think your mommy was mistaken.

I happen to know that your daddy just didn't know where you were. Your mommy forgot to tell him."

"Why did she forget?"

"I don't know. I guess she was real busy."

"She got dead now. Jerry's first mommy and daddy got dead, too. They were in a car smash up and got dead. He was sad about it. But he is getting a new mommy and daddy now. He won't be in my room anymore. He is going to a new house."

Egan and Van came in the room and over to the little boy. "We picked up a couple things for you at the gift shop. That is, if you are interested."

The little boy just looked at them but never said anything. Then Ruthie said, "Tater, what do you think Uncle Egan and Aunt Van brought for you?"

He shrugged and said, "I don't know."

"Would you like to see what it is?"

"I guess."

Van gave him a coloring book. He looked at it and smiled. "Pages. For me?"

"It is all yours. Do you like it?"

He turned the pages and beamed. He nodded, "It is good. No coddors."

"Oh, gracious," Egan teased, "I think I put them someplace! Where would they be, Aunt Van?"

Van shook her head no and so he asked Ruthie. She answered, "I don't know where you put them, Uncle Egan."

Egan turned away from the boy and patted himself as if he was looking for something. While he was turned away, he slid a small box of crayons into his front pocket. When he turned back, he asked, "Tater, do you know where I put them?"

The little boy saw them sticking out of his pocket and smiled at the game. He pointed to Egan's pocket, but the man pretended he didn't understand. Then Tater giggled and pointed again, "In that pocket."

"Oh," he said. "Well I'll be jiggered! What are they doing here? Do you think you know what to do with them?"

He shrugged. Van moved the table over to the boy and Ruthie helped him get situated. Then Egan gave him the box and the little boy opened the lid. He looked at them and then picked out the green crayon. Then he giggled. "Egan coddor, too?"

"Don't mind if I do." The man said as he took a purple crayon.

Ruthie touched Van's arm, and they went into the hallway. "I want to try to catch Dr. Turner before he leaves. Okay?"

"Sure. You should do that. You might want to talk to Ian a bit before he comes over."

Ruthie was waiting in the hallway when Greg came out. "Oh, I didn't know you were here. Come in and you can talk to Dr. Turner. You should've just knocked."

"I didn't want to disturb something," Ruthie answered as they entered the room.

Dr. Turner turned and smiled, "Hello, Mrs. Harrington. I've been hearing about your adventures. You really know how to pass a quiet week in Beantown."

She laughed, "I'm ready for some quiet. I tell you, adventure is very overrated."

She went over to the bed where Ian was sitting. She kissed him and he gave her a big hug, "How is the little boy?"

"He is okay. He has a terrible rash from the duct tape they put around his mouth. It seems to be getting redder. He says it scratches him."

"I will check his chart, if you'd like. I heard he was okay, but sometimes the reaction to adhesives can be bad," Dr. Turner said.

"I know I react to it," Ian said, nonchalantly. Then he got a funny look on his face.

Turner didn't flinch, "That makes sense, now doesn't it? I'll check it. As for this guy, I think those loose ends in his wiring are finally beginning to mesh together. He hasn't had a spasm in about eight hours. His control is a lot better and his should be able to wash your windows when you get home."

"That will be nice!" Ruthie smiled. "They need it. Have you any idea how soon that will be?"

"Not yet. Another week in here and then we can send him to his Uncle's place. Maybe a week after that. Do you know how soon things will be settled with the little boy?"

"DNA should be back in about a week. Then I guess I just have to sign some papers."

Turner sat down, "I know this is not my business, but I would like to say something. With your permission."

"Sure." Ian said. "Any advice is helpful."

"I don't know how you feel about families. I can't tell you that adoptions or foster care are bad, because often it is wonderful. It is still a crapshoot, no matter how you cut it. Aside from this child, you have to realize that your decision will matter to any other children you will have. They have a stake in this. Don't fool yourselves. It isn't easy to walk away. It is not like dropping a letter in the mailbox. You will have many a day when you think about it. Be very cautious in this decision." Then he stood up, "But I'm rather certain that you will make the best decision possible. Now, I will go out and check his chart. I have to see another patient and then I'll stop in. I think they will be moving you soon."

He left and Ian gave Ruthie a warm embrace, "I was about nuts with worry today. I was useless. It helped when Egan was here."

"I know. I wanted to come up, but they said I had to stay near the phone."

"Is Tater okay?"

"He was very scared and suffered from dehydration and stuff. He's got bruises all over. They think those jackasses planned on just leaving him in that dirty old cupboard."

"That's what Aaron said. He was really jammed into it. I never thought Ted had brain cell one. He was a rotten excuse for a human being."

"Well, we told Tater that you are our friend and we wanted you guys to have a sleep over. He asked if you were nice. We said you were."

Ian frowned, "But certainly not reliable or dependable."

"Ian. Don't do this to yourself. You didn't know he even existed." Then she went on to tell him about her conversation with Tater about Jerry's new parents and his own mommy and daddy. "I don't know what he thinks about any of it. I'm leaving that all to you. I want you to know, though, I really want to take Tater home with us. After today, I can't trust fate. We may not be the best folks in the world, but we don't stuff kids into cabinets."

"I know Ruthie. I thought the same thing, but maybe he'll have a different take on it. Maybe he won't want to live with us."

"I've said too much already. It should be your decision. I did want you to know how I feel though."

Ian pulled her over to his chest, "I love you."

Greg gave a quick knock, "Quit your necking and let's get you moved.

Ruthie, can you grab his bag from the closet? We can have you moved over there in one trip if we play this right."

A few minutes later, they entered the room. Ian was in the wheelchair with his bag on his lap. Ruthie had the flowers the clan had sent and Greg carried a washbasin with his toiletries in it. The curtain was closed around the other bed. After Greg got Ian organized, he said, "Egan and Van, I would love to meet your little friend."

He went behind the curtain and Ruthie could hear Greg talking to the little boy. Ian took Ruthie's hand, and said softly, "I hope I don't mess this up."

She kissed his cheek, "You won't. You're good with kids. Do you want to be alone when you meet him? Or what?"

"Maybe just you here? Okay?"

"Okay."

Greg had asked Egan and Van to buy him a cup of coffee and then poked his head out of the curtain. "We are going to get some coffee for a bit."

He opened the curtain and they went out. Ruthie went over to Tater's bed. Ruthie said, "Hey Tater, our friend is here. Want to say hello?"

"I don't see him, Ruthie."

"Of course not, I'm standing in the way. Dumb me!" She stepped back and let the father and son see each other for the first time.

Ian's face was a study and he was motionless. Tater looked at him and then asked Ruthie, "Doesn't he know how to talk?"

Ruthie giggled, "Yes, he does. Don't you, Ian?"

Ian smiled, "Yes. I do. You are a fine looking fella."

Tater looked and shrugged, "You are good. Do you coddor?"

"I've been known to color in my day. Do you like to color?"

He shook his head yes, "Egan and Aunt Van gave me pages. You can help if you wanna."

"That would be nice. I think I might." Ian said, "I have to have help reaching the pages though. Do you think Ruthie would bring me one?"

"Her will," the little boy answered as he tore a page out of the coloring book. He picked out a blue crayon and handed it to Ruthie.

Ruthie handed Ian the page and Ian smiled, "Thank you, Tater. I will try to do a good job."

"Good." Tater said.

When Dr. Turner came in. He looked from one bed to the other, and chuckled, "Well, I don't need DNA."

Ruthie grinned, "Tater, this is Ian's doctor and he is going to look at your face. Okay?"

The boy shrugged, "It scratches."

"It looks very sore and tender. The chart said they were concerned about a reaction to the tape and they were right. I will order some cream to put on it, so it will quit bothering you. How does that sound?"

He shrugged, "Good. Do you coddor?"

"I used to when I was a boy. You're doing a very good job."

"Wanna coddor?"

"I would love to, but I don't have time. I want to get that cream for you. Okay?"

"Okay, bye."

Turner winked at Ruthie, "I'll be right back."

The guys colored and Ruthie watched them until Turner returned. He applied the salve on the little boy's face and the kid sighed. "Does it feel better?"

"Yes."

"I will leave it here in his bedside table. You can reapply it, as needed. The irritation should start to subside in a few hours." Then Turner looked at Tater, "I have to go see some other patients. Will you keep an eye on Mr. Harrington for me tonight?"

Tater glanced at Ian and then frowned to the doctor, "How?"

"Well, if he falls out of bed, push the button so someone can come and help him back in."

Tater looked at the button and shrugged, "Okay."

Dr. Turner said good night and left. After he went out of the room, Tater pulled Ruthie closer to him, "Does him fall out of bed?"

"Not very often. The doctor was just teasing."

Tater looked at Ian and then at the buzzer. Then he said, "Hey. Don't fall out of bed, okay?"

"Okay, Tater. I will be careful."

Tater nodded, "Good."

Greg and the older Harringtons came in and visited a bit. Then Greg went home for the day. "I know you want to spend time together, but everyone had a long day. You better shut it down when visiting hours are over, in about fifteen minutes. You can come back in the morning."

"Thanks, Greg."

Ian said good night. Tater looked at him and waved bye.

The visitors started to pick things up in the room. It was obvious that Tater was getting worried. "Is something wrong, Tater?" Ruthie asked.

"Is everybody going away?"

"No, Ian will be here."

The little boy looked at the other patient, "Will that ugly man come back?"

"He won't. The police put him in jail, so he can't bother you anymore. Guess what?" Egan said, "There are two police guys right by the door to keep watch. If anything scares you, you just yell and they will be right here. Okay?"

Tater looked worried, "I want to go to my bed at the Center. I don't want to be here."

Ian got out of bed and walked over to the little boy's bed. "What do you say, we ask Uncle Egan to put our beds a little closer together. I promise I will watch over you."

Tater thought, "I guess. Can we keep the lights on?"

"Unless the nurse says we have to turn them down." Ian took the little boy's hand in his, "You will be okay."

Ian looked down at his delicate little hand and then looked at Ruthie. He teared up. Without thinking, he gave the boy a hug. Then he said, "We will be okay. We are big guys, huh?"

"I'm just a kid."

"I know, but you are brave. I know that because you were so brave all day."

"You think so?"

"That's what everyone said. They aren't wrong, are they?"

"I cried though."

"I cry, too, sometimes. So does Uncle Egan. Everybody does, but that doesn't mean you aren't brave."

"Really?"

"That's a blasted fact."

As soon as the words left his lips, Ian turned pale. Tater watched him and mimicked, "That's a basket fact." Then he giggled.

The next morning, Ruthie was awake before the alarm went off. She was dressed and downstairs making coffee before Egan and Van came down. "Boy, you are really perky today," Van teased. "In a happy mood, are you?"

Ruthie hugged Van, "Yes, I really am. I forgot I could feel this good. I'm almost afraid to feel good, because that seems to be a signal for the other shoe to drop! I got Tater's clothes washed so he has something to wear home from the hospital."

Egan laughed as he opened the can of dog food, "Don't know why you didn't feed Otis already, seeing as how you were up before the sunshine!"

"What can I say? I'm a slacker!"

John Kelly called and said he would be over about nine to pick up Ruthie. He would take her to the hospital so she could see Tater before returning him to the Center. She said she would be ready. Van and Egan would be up to the hospital about noon and she could go home with them. They had plans to watch Wile E.Coyote with Tater in the afternoon and then see Ian that night. John Kelly thought it sounded downright boring since there were no shoot-outs or car chases! "You guys should be able to fit in an arson or bank job with all your spare time!"

John Kelly had coffee with them before he and Ruthie left for the hospital. "Our little wannabe kidnappers are talking so fast the spit is flying! They can't tell us enough," John chuckled. "Those life sentences are scaring the pants off them. The good news is that it seems we have dismantled the whole Norris-Collins ring. At least until they start getting out of prison. Hopefully, we will all be retired by then!"

171

"Being retired didn't help me!" Egan blustered. "I've never been in a crime wave in my life, until now!"

"Poor Egan! At any rate, we only have a few more things to check. If that is clear, the department will likely pull the security." John grinned and then reported, "Before we go to the hospital, I would like you to go with me to the cemetery. The morgue will only keep Taylor through tomorrow. There is a nice non-denominational one over on Parcell. Maybe you would like to get Taylor's plot there?"

Van nodded, "That has pleasant grounds and it is well-kept. One of my friends has their family plot there. I believe it is quite reasonably priced, also."

"We can pick out her casket there, if you still want to do it." John continued. "Should there be a service or what?"

"I don't know. Can I talk to Ian about it before I have to decide? I don't think any of her family could attend. They are all either dead or in jail."

"Her immediate family could attend, but would have to be accompanied by an officer. Hell, half the congregation would be law enforcement. What an outfit. Besides, they never seemed to worry about claiming her body." John said.

"I'll talk to Ian."

"Oh. Mouse said that Ted told him to kill the kid. He didn't want any loose ends and was afraid the boy could identify them. Mouse took him to the basement, but couldn't bring himself to do it. He scrunched him in the closet. He knew he would die there, but he figured that way, it wouldn't be his fault." John rubbed his head, "I never cease to be amazed how people justify things. The interrogator said 'Of course it would be your fault! You knew he would die.' Mouse said, 'Yah, but he was alive when I put him in there!'"

"I bet the little guy is sore today after being squished into the little space. I quake to think what was going through his little mind!" Van said. "It makes me shudder."

"Well, you ready, Ruthie?" John Kelly asked, "We have a lot to do today."

The cemetery was very nice. It was on a rolling hill and had many trees. Ruthie and John Kelly were able to decide on a plot quickly, because they didn't need a family plot. The casket took a little more time. The cheapest two were pathetic. As John said, "I have shoeboxes that are better built. If you don't want to spend more, I'll chip in. That's awful."

"I know, huh? I have the money. I like that one."

Ruthie pointed to a polished light blue metal one. John looked it over, "It's nice, Ruthie, but it is twice the cost of the cheap ones."

She looked at him, "Too extravagant?"

The business agent came up to them, "May I help you?"

The two explained the situation briefly and he listened carefully. "So, you mostly want something that looks decent, not costing an arm and a leg. You know, you will have to pay for the headstone or footstone, too." The man looked around and thought a minute, "Hey, we have a rental that is one step up from this that I can get you a low price on."

"A rental?" John raised his eyebrows. "I thought rental caskets were only in jokes."

"Not at all. Caskets are often rented for transport and for viewings. This one was used for a woman's viewing and service. She was cremated after the service and her ashes were interred in Oklahoma. This is a brushed charcoal metallic finish and has a soft pink interior, so it is feminine. Want to see it?"

The couple looked at each other and nodded. They left the cemetery forty-five minutes later, having purchased the gravesite, the rental and a modest but nice headstone. John gave the funeral home the necessary paperwork to pick up the body at the morgue. Ruthie said she would call with the rest of the information.

In the car, John Kelly shook his head, "This whole thing makes my mind bubble!"

Ruthie giggled, "Bubble?"

"Yah, well, you make babies from scratch!"

The two both laughed until they were crying. Then John looked at her, "You know, we do have a good time together!"

"I think chapters in Psychiatric books could be written about it, but we do. You will always be dear to my heart. I'm so glad that Ian turned to you. You have been my rock."

They went up to the room and knocked. There was no sound and they frowned at each other before they pushed the door open. The patients were both sound asleep. John Kelly looked at them both and said softly to Ruthie, "I sure hope Ian takes his son. Hell, I told Nancy that if he doesn't, I will."

"That's sweet," Ruthie nodded, "I bet Nancy had a different take on it."

"Not really. She said if I was serious, she would definitely consider it. You know, after Turk, we think we could raise almost any kid!"

"Turk is a live wire, no doubt."

Then Ian stirred and opened his eyes. He grinned and said, "Keep it down. There are sick people here, trying to sleep!"

They went over to his bed and Ruthie gave Ian a hug and kiss, while John grabbed his hand. They sat down next to his bed and visited quietly, "Did he sleep well last night?"

Ian shook his head, "No. He didn't really fall asleep until about four this morning. I'm not sure if they gave him something or not. He was scared being away from the Center and of the dark. He would start to fall asleep and then jerk himself awake with a cry. He talked a lot about being in the box, as he called it."

"I can imagine so," John Kelly agreed. "The area was so small, he was like a pretzel in there. I had a hell of a time getting him out. It must have hurt like the dickens."

"He told me that he couldn't get his air it was so tight. I don't imagine the duct tape helped."

"I doubt he would have lasted very much longer. As it was, he was in there at least a couple hours."

"How's he doing physically?" Ruthie asked.

"Turner checked him this morning. I put that cream on his face a few times last night, and it seems to be getting better. He is quite sore today and was running a slight temperature. Turner was going to leave it to the pediatrician, but thought he could still go home today."

"Did you get any sleep?" John Kelly asked.

"Oh yah, not steady, but I've slept away the last week or so! Last night, is the first time I've actually done anything in a long time. It felt good."

"How did you guys get along?" Ruthie asked.

"Very well. He's really worried that Jerry will be gone before he gets back to tell him goodbye."

"I talked to Mrs. Feldman. Jerry isn't leaving until tomorrow afternoon. They are having a party this afternoon for him. Cupcakes and stuff. Tater will get to be there for that."

"That's good. He was pretty worried about that." Ian said and then got lost in his thoughts. After a silent time, he said to John Kelly, "I want to thank you for rescuing him. I owe you a lot for doing all this for me. This disaster was all my fault."

"No, it wasn't. Don't start that or I'll slap you. Besides, I would've never got to know Ruthie this well, if all this hadn't happened." John grinned. "We've actually had some fun together."

Ian took her hand, "That's why I love her so much. I'm really a lucky devil. I don't deserve this."

"That's what John and I said! We don't deserve this!" Ruthie giggled.

They discussed the arrangements for Taylor and decided that there would be no service, but Ian was going to talk to Father Colter when he came up later in the morning. "Is that soon enough?"

"Yes," Ruthie agreed. "Ask him about Tater. Like if he should go to the service or if he thinks something should be done?"

"I will. He talked about her last night. He told me that she said she would come and get him. They would have a house together. She talked about having a home a lot. I guess because she never really had one. He also told me that she said his daddy didn't want him. I almost said something, but he went on to tell me that you said Taylor had made a mistake about that. He said that you said maybe his daddy just didn't know where he was. Thanks for that, Ruthie. How soon before the DNA comes back?"

"Six more days." John answered.

"Do I have to wait for the test results or can I just sign for him now?"

"The state will want that for proof. I take it that you have decided to keep him?"

"I'm leaning that way, but I really don't know."

John Kelly looked him straight in the eye, "What is the decision you are trying to make?"

"Huh?" Ian frowned, "It is a major decision. He will be ours forever."

"To my way of thinking, he already is. The only decision is if you are going to accept your position." Then he stopped himself, "I'm sorry, Ian. That was way out of school! I have no right to say anything. It is a big decision and it is yours. I guess I feel close to him because I found him in that hideous closet."

Ian studied him for a minute, "No, you have every right to say what you think. I appreciate that. It helps. Part of my concern is how everyone else will react. I don't want him to be treated like a leper."

"Good lord, Man!" John retorted. "That's just a cop out. Some folks will treat him like that if he is a foster kid. I've met the North Dakota clan. Those guys would never do that. As far as Colleen and Vivian approving, they never approve of anything! In fact, if they thought something was a good idea, I would have to rethink it!"

Ian laughed, "Amen."

Tater tried to turn over when they laughed, but it hurt his arm. He had a bit of a whimper and Ruthie went over to him, "Can I help you, Tater?"

"My arm is twisted over. It hurts. That man put it in my back when he put me in that box. I sure didn't like him."

"I don't think he was a very nice man. Should I ask the nurse if you can have something so it won't hurt so bad?"

He shrugged and then noticed John Kelly. He looked at him with recognition, but never said anything. John came over to him and smiled. "Hello, I don't suppose you remember me but I saw you yesterday. How's it going?"

"Good. You took me out of the box."

"That's right. I did." John took his hand, "You look a lot better today than yesterday. Did you have a good rest?"

"It was good. Do you know Ian?"

"I do. He, Ruthie and I are all friends."

"Aunt Van and Egan, too?"

"Yes sir."

"Do you live in the same house?"

"No, I live with my wife and our kids."

Tater nodded and thought, "Good."

Ruthie had gone out to the nurses' station and the nurse came back in with her. "Hello, little man. This lady told me your arm hurts?"

He said it did and she looked it over. "I will call your doctor and see what he wants to do. Will that be okay?"

"Okay."

Ruthie and John visited with Tater while Ian went to his physical therapy. They were there when Tater's doctor came in. He introduced himself as Dr. Walker. Ruthie was going to leave while he examined him, but Walker suggested she stay, if Tater didn't mind. He didn't.

He checked the rash from the duct tape and then his limbs. He was good with the little boy and when he was finished, he said, "I am glad that

Dr. Turner gave you that cream from you face. It seems to be doing the trick. Does it feeling less itchy?"

Tater nodded, "It is good. No more scratchy stuff. Ian put that smooth stuff on it."

"Good," Walker grinned, "I bet your bones all hurt today, huh?"

"Pretty a lot. I think it is because they were squished yesterday."

"I think you are right. I will have the nurse give you a pill to help them quit hurting so much. Can you swallow pills?"

"How big are they?"

"Just little."

"I can little ones."

"Okay," the doctor grinned, "Then you can go home. How does that sound?"

Tater answered matter-of-factly, "I don't have a home, but I go to the Center. I want to get there before Jerry leaves. He got a new home to go to, so I won't see him anymore."

The doctor gave him a little hug, "I'm sorry. I forgot you live at the Center. So Jerry got a new home, huh?"

"Yah, he says he thinks it will be good. They have a dog named Spider! Isn't that a funny name for a dog?"

"It is," the doctor agreed. "I will make certain that the folks at the Center know that you need to see me tomorrow. Okay?"

"Okay."

Ruthie dressed Tater in the clothes that she had washed. They were what he was wearing when he was kidnapped. "You made them clean again?"

"I washed them at Aunt Van's."

"I used to like this shirt, but not so much anymore," Tater frowned.

"I understand. Mrs. Feldman will probably let you change when you get to the Center."

They started to say goodbye. Tater gave Ruthie a hug and then told Ian goodbye. "I hope you get well so you can go to Aunt Van's house. Ruthie says she has a TV, so you can watch Widey there."

"I will do that. We will see each other again, soon. Would you like that?"

"It would be good."

"Well, young man, you ready for a ride in my police car?" John asked.

Tater got a worried look, "Am I in rest?"

"Not at all. We are just riding in the car to the Center."

"Okay. That would be good. I can tell Jerry about it."

After they left, the room became quite quiet. Ian took her hand and pulled her over to him. Then he gave her a tender embrace, "You are good with him."

"That's very easy to do."

"I can't believe John said what he did about Tater. He seems pretty definite about what he thinks I should do."

"He told me this morning that he and Nancy talked about it. If you don't want him, they are going to try to at least be named his foster parents."

Ian was dumbfounded, "Really? He said that? Why? Doesn't he think I will do the right thing?"

"He never said that. He just said that if you don't want him, that's what they want to do."

"It isn't that I don't *want* him. Of course, I do. I just don't think it is going to be a simple thing to do. I don't know how you're going to handle it. You will have a new baby in a few months. That will be a lot."

Ruthie laughed, "Good night, Ian! A lot of women have a toddler and a new baby. That's no big deal. Are you interested in what I think? Is that what is really bothering you? I can tell you, if you want to hear it."

He leaned back in his bed, "I'm not sure I do. I don't think I will like it."

Ruthie just smiled. He sat there for the longest time, playing with her hand, "Okay. Tell me."

"I wonder if the problem is that if we bring Tater home and you introduce him as your son, folks will know that you weren't a saint all your life. Most folks can get away with their fooling around and no one ever knows. Once there is a child, everyone knows beyond a doubt. Too many people think that gives them the right to pontificate about it."

Ian put his arm around his wife and cried, "Yah. I did think of that. I think it really bothers me."

Ruthie held him a minute and then said, "To hell with them. It is none of their business and besides, few people are so virtuous that they don't have a skeleton or two in their closet."

"You think I should just step up to the plate, don't you?"

"Yes, the responsibility is yours already. The only question is if you will take it."

"I know." Ian said quietly, "I almost told him last night. I know once I tell him that he is my son, there will be no way that I can say, 'but I don't want you.' Ruthie, I do want him."

"Then there is no dilemma, is there? It is only a matter of waiting until the DNA comes back."

"I don't know how much I should see him before I tell him. If I'm around him a lot, he is going to wonder how come I waited so long."

"I don't think you will get to see him much before the tests come back. He can't come up the hospital. Greg and Turner went out on a limb so you two could bunk together last night. The only reason they got away with it, is because you both needed guards at the door."

"Does he have security at the Center?"

"There is some there, but John said they are going to likely pull the security today. It seems that bunch is disbanded now and pose no threat."

Ian kissed his wife again, and it became passionate quickly, "I want you so much."

"Well, we have to wait. This place is like Grand Central Station."

"I don't think I care."

Father Colter stopped by a little later and the three had a good visit. Since Ian had never heard any mention of a Collins having a religious faith of any kind, Colter suggested that he contact a chaplain friend of his to do a short interment service for Taylor. "I feel there should be something. Then maybe Ruthie and your aunt and uncle could take Tater so he knows that someone did something."

"Okay," Ruthie said. "That's a lot like we did for my family. Is Tater too young?"

"Not really. It won't mean anything to him now, but someday he will remember that something was done. It may matter then or not, but at least he will know it was done."

"Thank you," Ruthie said. "Too bad we don't have more time. We will have to do it tomorrow or the next day."

"Remember, Tater has that cupcake thing for his little friend, Jerry, tomorrow."

"I will talk to Mrs. Feldman, so he can do that. I know it meant a lot to him."

"How did your visit go with Tater?" Father Colter asked Ian.

"It was okay," Ian explained. "He was rather shook up about being kidnapped and put in that closet, but I think we got along okay."

Father Colter raised his eyebrows, "I imagine I'd be a little shook up about that, too! What are your feelings about the child? Do you think he is yours?"

Ian shook his head, "Yes. I would be shocked if he wasn't. I don't know what to do though. I don't want to mess up our marriage over him, but I do think I'm his father."

"Do you have a lot of reservations, Ruthie?"

"The only reservation I have is how I would feel about Ian if he could walk away from that little guy. I realize that it isn't a piece of cake raising a child, but it might not be raising our baby either. I want to do the best I can to give that little fellow a home."

Colter looked at Ian, "So, the ball is in your court. You will get a lot of criticism from some folks about it, no matter what you decide. Just remember 'he who is without sin, throw the first stone.' Some sins happen to produce children. We have all sinned in some way for whatever reason. That is why we need forgiveness. It is a wise person who accepts that. I personally feel the world would be a lot better place, if everyone would get off their high horse and be realistic. A little humble pie isn't too bad, with Worcestershire."

"You think I should recognize him as my own?"

"If he is, he is. You can lie to the world, but you'll have a much more difficult time lying to yourself. And know what else? There are some in your family that already know about him and they will give you a piece of their minds, too. Some will be upset you didn't recognize him."

"My brother-in-law told Ruthie that he and my sister are thinking about taking him if I wouldn't."

"Now, just how would that work out? You would see him on family reunions. Ian, you know what you need to do. You need to do it."

"You think that I shouldn't let them take him, even if I don't."

"If you don't take him yourself, you have absolutely no right to say anything at all about where he goes! I'm just pointing out that you'd have a devil of a time living with it."

"They are good people."

"I don't doubt it. And I would be happy he had a home, but I don't think you would be able to cope with it very well."

"I know. I was just wondering. I mean then Ruthie and I could have our own lives."

"Is you new baby going to be inconvenient sometimes?"

Ian frowned, "What is that supposed to mean? I'm not like that."

"That's my point." Father Colter stood up, "I really have to go see another patient. Ruthie, here is my phone number. Let me know this afternoon about your decision on the interment." Then he put his hand on Ian's arm, "You are a decent man. Do what is in your heart and you will be fine. I'll see you tomorrow."

The priest left and Ian was silent for a long time. The orderlies came in and took Tater's bed out of the room. They moved Ian's bed back in the middle. After they left the room, Ian broke into tears. "Ruthie, I hate myself. Why can't I just say I will take him? What's wrong with me?"

Ruthie sat next to his bed, "Maybe it is because you feel badly about things with Taylor. That is a thing apart. Tater has nothing to do with that and shouldn't be the one to do the penance."

Ian hugged her and then pulled her close, "I know. I want to keep him, but I'm afraid."

"Afraid of what?"

"That he will remind me of her. His hands are just like hers."

"I noticed. He has very nice hands. He is both of yours. One thing that you can give him, that no one else is able to do, is a little knowledge of his mom. John and Nancy would be wonderful parents, but they didn't know her. You can tell him about her good qualities. He needs to hear that, too."

"Will it upset you?"

"If I was Taylor, I would want you to raise our child."

Ian held her a long time and then said, "Okay. To be honest, I don't think I could stand to leave him."

Ruthie kissed him, "I didn't think you could."

"How many days left?"

"Six."

"Are you going to tell Mom?" Ian asked.

"No. You are, but it would be best when things are more definite. I don't want to have to go tell everyone a change of plans. I will tell Egan, Van and John though. Egan would probably be hauled up on kidnap charges if you let him go!"

"He seems pretty attached to him, and vice versa. They aren't going to like it any better when he is in North Dakota."

"No, but they can visit." Ruthie pointed out. "I hope you aren't upset because I told you about John and Nancy."

"Not at all. I would have expected no less from them, actually. They didn't mean it as a slam against me."

Ruthie agreed, "I'm sure they didn't. They thought that way he would be in our family and Egan would still get see him. They would never want to hurt you."

"I know, but it did give me that last push. When Colter said, if I sign him away, then I have absolutely nothing to say about what happens to him… That's a hard piece of candy to chew. I do want to have something to say."

"So, I think that as soon as we find out the results, you can call your family back home. Then I will get Suzy to organize someone to help her set up the empty room as his. He will need a room."

"I thought the blank room was going to be the baby's room."

"No, the blank room is closer to the bathroom. I think the baby will be fine in the little room. When the baby gets bigger, we can reorganize. Okay?"

Ian grinned at her, "Does your mind ever stop? You have curtains up already, don't you?"

Ruthie giggled, "Actually, I was thinking green seems to be his favorite color."

He was kissing her again when Egan and Van came in. "Let's get out of here, Van. They are acting like hormone-crazed teenagers."

"We have news," Ruthie smiled.

"I decided, depending on the DNA results, we are going to keep him," Ian stated.

Egan beamed and Van gave him a hug. Then Egan asked, "What if the tests doesn't show paternity? You still gonna walk away?"

Ian looked at his uncle, "I am certain they will be conclusive, but if not, I'd still like to get custody of him. I don't know how we would do that. I guess we need an attorney."

"I'll call my mouthpiece. He's pricey, but a bulldog and works fast. Say, speaking of which, did you hear about the $50,000?"

"No. Not a word," Ruthie said. "Never even thought about it."

Egan chortled, "John Kelly, Jamie and Aaron are out buying a yacht this afternoon! Think that solves the mystery?"

Ian laughed, "Sounds like it."

Egan got serious, "Aaron called before we left the house. They found the money in the walk-up. It is impounded now at the station. That Mouse is talking to his attorney and wants to plead guilty. The other dude is leaning that way. If he does too, the money won't be needed for a trial and you should get it back right away. Otherwise, they will have to hang on to it until after the trial."

Ruthie shrugged, "I'm just so glad we got Tater back in one piece."

"I am anxious to see him this afternoon." Egan said, "Is his face better?"

"Yes," Ian said. "It was clearing up pretty well by morning, but his poor body hurts all over from being jammed in that small space. He sure didn't want the lights out last night. The nurse said we could keep the night lights pretty high last night and he was okay with that."

The nurse came with Ian's dinner tray, "Gourmet delights have arrived," she laughed.

"I can hardly wait," Ian smiled back.

"Eat up, because you have an afternoon jam-packed with exercises. You spent your morning leisurely hosting guests, so this afternoon you have to work it off."

"We're just leaving." Egan chuckled. "Don't like either work or exercise! Want me to call my attorney, or do you have someone you want?"

"No, yours is good. If he kept you out of jail all these years, he must be on the ball."

Over lunch, the three discussed Taylor's arrangements. Van felt that they should have someone say a few words graveside. They would talk to Mrs. Feldman and defer to her opinion on if Tater should attend.

After lunch, they went to the Center and discussed it with Mrs. Feldman. She thought about it and asked, "Are you folks going to be there, but none of her family?"

"Yes," Ruthie explained. "We won't go if there's no graveside service. Her family has shown no interest in her passing. If they are going to be there, I won't be. I don't think that Tater should be either."

"My feelings exactly. I would've said no to him going at all, except that he was very happy when she came and he thought he was going home with her. He was devastated when she didn't come back. It was almost good to be able to tell him that she died. Maybe he will think that she would have come back but she was ill. Between you and me, it was doubtful she would be able to get clean, but who knows."

Ruthie explained they would be taking him when the DNA came back, but even if the tests didn't prove that Ian was his father, they would want to try to adopt him or something. "That might be a little tricky, because you live out of state. But I would be very happy to go to bat for you. I need to visit with your husband, however."

"I understand." Ruthie asked, "How is Tater doing today?"

"Pretty sore. He has been only watching television since he got back. He was tickled to get to see Jerry and very happy that he will be at his cupcake party." Mrs. Feldman got out of her chair, "He is in the playroom now, resting on the sofa, waiting for Wile E.Coyote to come on. He'll be glad to see you."

After cartoons, Mrs. Feldman wanted Tater to take a nap and he didn't argue. "I can sleep, but not in the dark. Ian left the light on for me last night."

"We will turn on the side light for you, okay?"

"That will be good." Then the little boy hugged everyone goodbye.

By days end, they had done a lot. Arrangement were made for Taylor to be buried Saturday morning. The cemetery offered to bring her body out the night before, so they would meet the county's deadline. Ruthie had talked to the chaplain, Reverend Carson, and then gave the information to the folks about her headstone.

Ruthie had a long talk with Zach and Matt that night. Then she took a hot bath. She was asleep before her head hit the pillow.

The next morning, Egan called his attorney and he said that he would have time to see Ian and Ruth at the hospital around three. Ruthie was disappointed, but Egan said that he and Van would go watch Wiley with Tater. She decided seeing the attorney was more important.

Mrs. Feldman called about ten-thirty to report that she had brought Tater back from the doctor's appointment. He said he was doing well. He wanted to see him the following week, but it looked like things were on track.

She said that she could either bring Tater to the graveside service for his mother, or allow him to go with a policeman. Since John and Nancy had already said they were coming, as well as some of Ian's other family, Ruthie said she would have John come to pick him up.

Vivian and Colleen had refused to go, as if going to the burial of a hooker would somehow tarnish their exemplary souls. The rest said they were coming anyway. Egan laughed, "I don't think as many would have come had those two pillars of virtue had not thrown such a hissy fit about it."

Before Ruthie left for the hospital, Aaron called and said that both kidnappers had pled guilty. There would be no trial and she could retrieve her money on Monday. "Thank goodness, I was concerned we would have to be here for the trial."

"Yah, you would've had to. Ruthie, I wanted to tell you that I'm glad that you and Ian want the little fellow. I think he will have a good start in life. Terrie and I know that."

"Thanks, Aaron. It would have been almost impossible to turn our backs on him after all this."

"John was very taken with him. He told me how the little boy clung to him after he got out of that cupboard. John held him until the paramedics arrived. He told me the little boy was so brave and apologized because he had wet his pants. John couldn't get over that."

"He is a good little boy. He certainly has had a lot to face."

"Well, things can be better for him now."

Ruthie arrived in time to see Dr. Turner. When Ian asked if he could go to the burial, Turner said no. "You have not spent as much time healing as I had hoped. I thought keeping you in the hospital would help the process; but somehow, you managed to turn it into an adventure on a jungle gym. Unless you are very adamant, I think you need to not risk anymore chances of tearing those delicate loose nerve endings I tried to thread together."

Ian looked at Ruthie, "Do you think I need to be there?"

"No. The service will only be a few minutes, but you will have to be out of the hospital a lot longer than that. I think the doctor is right."

"I should be there, but I don't want to have another surgery." He looked at Turner, "Okay, I'll be good."

Turner laughed, "Yah, I can about imagine. When I come in tonight, you will likely be swinging from a trapeze! You give me bleeding ulcers."

After Turner left, Ian asked, "Did you see Tater this morning?"

"No. He had his doctor's appointment this morning. Then they are having that cupcake party to celebrate Jerry's new family. Van and Egan are going to watch Wiley with him while we meet with this attorney."

Ian's face fell, "I just wondered how he was doing."

"Mrs. Feldman said he is really sore, but the doctor said that is to be expected. He wants to see him next week. Other than that, he is okay."

"I was worried. That one arm really bothered him and his other leg."

"She said the doctor thought his leg was twisted badly, but not out of place. It will just take time."

He nodded, "Did you talk to any of the clan?"

"Yes, Matt and Zach. Carl had taken Mo out on a date for dinner in Bismarck. He thought she needed a break."

"I'm sure Mom needs a break." Ian said. "I bet she's been about bananas."

The couple visited with the attorney, Mr. Walsh. The abrupt, fireball of a man said he would get things in 'swinging order,' as he put it. "When we get the DNA, we will be able to run the bases. Do you want to adopt him, too, Mrs. Harrington?"

"Yes, I want to do that. Will that be a problem?"

"We need references, et cetera, but unless you've blown up a federal building or whipped up a batch of smack in your kitchen, we should be good. Will you want him to have a different name?"

They looked at each other, "No, I guess not," Ian said. "Unless Ruthie doesn't want him to be called Taylor."

"That's his name! My God, he should be able to keep that much! I think we can just add Harrington. He can be Taylor Collins Harrington. What do you think?"

Ian thought a minute, "It sounds good."

"Sounds to me like he could run for president with a moniker like that!" the lawyer laughed. "He'd have my vote!"

They spent the next hour giving Mr. Walsh reference names, addresses and other required information. Before he left, Mr. Walsh suggested they call all the folks they had put down for reference, so they would know what was going on. Then he gathered his papers and left. "Talk to you on Monday."

Ian looked at Ruthie, "Well, I guess I have some people to talk to. Can you close the door and help me make the phone calls?"

"Sure."

"I don't want to have to do this."

"Ah, piece of cake," Ruthie giggled.

The next hour, Ian talked to members of the clan, the loosely organized group of friends and family from North Dakota. Not one of them gave him anything but best wishes and support. Then he called his Mom.

She picked up the phone and he said, "Hello Mom. It's Ian."

"Ian? Is everything okay?"

"It is, Mom. Ruthie called you yesterday evening, but Matt said Carl had taken you to town for dinner and some relaxation."

"Don't make it sound like a romantic dinner! It was more like medication. Do you have any idea what havoc you have wreaked on your poor old mother? Joshua's Trumpets! You nearly had me draining the whiskey barrel! Laddie, did you forget my lecture on the birds and the bees? And condoms? Where was your head? In your pants? I can't believe it! That was just unbelievable!"

"Mom, I was undercover."

"It sounds like you spent too much time under the covers! Don't give me your excuses! Carl already sang me that sweet song about it being done for the good of mankind. Don't you be thinking that I bought it for a minute! You were thinking like an alley cat! Tell me now, do accountants have anything like this undercover work?"

"No, Mom, they don't."

"Good! Then, I won't be waiting for another surprise from you. Hear me? Next time, I won't pretend to be a bit nice about it. It had better never happen again or I will make your birth retroactive!"

"Geeze, Mom. I just wanted to tell you that the blood tests came back that I am his father, but the DNA tests aren't back yet. Ruthie and I talked about it today with Uncle Egan's attorney. We're going to keep the little boy. If the DNA proves he is mine, it won't be more than getting a few papers signed. It the test says he isn't mine, we'll have to apply for adoption or foster care."

"Ruthie says he looks just like you."

"He does, Mom. I knew he was mine, the minute I saw him."

"So you did see him. Tell me about it. Did you tell him you are his daddy?"

"Not yet. We thought it is only five more days and we can tell him the facts. But if he isn't mine, belongs to one of your other sons. He is definitely a Harrington."

"I hope he has more sense than this lot I already have! Boy, when I meet God in His Glory, He is going to have some serious explaining to do!"

They spent the better part of an hour talking and in the end, Mo said, "I have to state as a fact, Ian. If you would have not accepted that little tyke, I would have pulled you with a sunburn naked by the ears through a cactus patch! At least you have some sense, although my guess is that Ruthie had a bit to do with that."

"Yes, Mom, Ruthie is the best."

"That she is. She's only made one mistake in her life. Want to guess what I think that is?"

"No," Ian answered, somberly. "I know. She should have married someone more deserving than me."

"Put nicely. I might not have been so kind." Mo calmed down, "Ian, my dear son, I love you and I know you're doing the right thing. You and Ruthie will be fine parents for this little one. What is his name?"

"Taylor, but he calls himself Tater."

"Why not a Tater? We have a Gopher and a Kitten. Guess we were needing a Tater. Take care my son. We will talk soon. Carl and I will lie to the folks that call for references. We will say you are okay."

"Thanks Mom."

"Oh, my laddie, it is not so easy as a 'thanks Mom'. I'm thinking I will be deserving some fancy fussing over from you until the next of my flock flies against a wall! Knowing this organization, it won't be long. Oh, did I be telling you? I had a few phone calls from Vivian and Colleen. They both said they had been warned not to call, but that merely put them off for a minute or two. I hope they don't be a bother to Tater."

"No, I don't think they will. Their husbands wouldn't allow that."

"Good. Oh, I need a new rosary. I wore my beads right through to the nubs with this last little escapade."

"Okay, Mom. You got it."

32

The morning was dreary, overcast and threatening rain. The forecast suggested light showers but clearing in the afternoon. Breakfast was quiet at the Harrington household. Otis was having trouble with his arthritis, so Egan brought him into the laundry room to curl up in an old blanket.

Breakfast was almost over when Ian called. He spoke to Egan a bit about Otis and then asked to talk to Ruthie. She took the phone, "Good morning. How are you today?"

"I'm so lonesome for you I can hardly stand it. I wish I was there."

"I wish you were too, but it won't be long now. Dr. Turner said just another week. You seem to be getting a lot more motion back in your arm now."

"I do and I can do more every day. Mostly, I'm just relieved I don't get those horrible spasms anymore. I miss you. Today is going to be awful, and again, you're doing it all. I will be in here while you pull the load."

"Not really. You have to get well and take care of us. Your family is bigger now and will be bigger again soon. You have to get your strength back."

"You know that's not true. I can't believe how I brought so much down on you. I only wanted to make life good for you."

"Apparently you forget how your arm got bummed up in the first place! Yea gads, traipsing around the entire country after my family of lunatics. Turnabout is fair play. Now, unless we have some branch on a family tree we have overlooked, I think we are about settled down. What about you?"

Ian chuckled, "I guess that's one way of looking at it. But remember, we didn't know about this branch at all."

"You didn't do any other undercover cases, did you?"

"No. Just this one. There should be no more surprises. Goll, Mom would kill me."

"Carl said you owe him one for keeping your Mom in North Dakota. If she would have made it out here, it wouldn't have been pretty." Ruthie said. "Oh, I talked to the headstone people. They are going to put Taylor's name and dates on it and then on the bottom, write 'At home with God.' Think that will be okay?"

Ian fell silent. After a minute, Ruthie asked, "Ian, don't you want that?"

He could hardly talk, but said, "She would love that. Thank you, Ruthie."

"I hoped it would be okay. John Kelly and Nancy are going to pick us up and then we'll get Tater. The rest will meet us there."

"Who is the rest?"

"Aaron and Terrie, Patrick and Marge are bringing Lonnie, James and Frank are coming together."

Ian was surprised, "All of them?"

"Well, Egan thought it would make Tater feel good to know that some people cared. He thought we should, so we are going to do it. Some of us are going to have brunch then, before Tater has to go back. He is excited about the big cupcake party for Jerry later today."

"It's nice they do that, but it must be hard for the kids."

"Yah, there must be a lot of mixed emotions about it."

"What a rotten world we live in."

"If we don't like it, I guess it is up to each of us to try to make it better. Huh?"

"Ruthie, I hope today isn't too much for you."

"It won't be. We will tell you all about it this afternoon. Okay?"

Ruthie and John Kelly went into the Center. Even though Mrs. Feldman usually had Saturdays off, she was there. "I wanted to make sure that Tater had a ride today and then I couldn't miss the cupcake party."

"Will Tater get a new roommate?" John Kelly asked.

"We think that maybe he will just go to his new home," Mrs. Feldman winked. "Five more days? Right?"

"Right," Ruthie answered. "Do you have any idea how soon we could take him home?"

"If the DNA comes back on Wednesday, by Friday. You know,

everybody has to sign a paper they rarely read, to make it all official. I'm familiar with your attorney and he doesn't let grass grow under his feet! He plans his day with a stopwatch! He will have the papers all ready to go and the pen to sign them with!"

John grinned, "Is that good or bad?"

"I don't know, but I tell you. Some of these guys fool around so long that I wonder if the realize that a child is growing while they piddling around." Mrs. Feldman laughed, "But that won't be the case with this guy. I will go get Tater."

Tater came into the office and was dressed very neatly. He grinned when he saw John Kelly and then went over to Ruthie to take her hand. "She told me you were coming and we are going to bury mommy today. Are Egan and Aunt Van coming?"

"They are in the car. And so is my wife, Nancy. You will get to meet her," John picked him up.

"It she coming to say goodbye to my mommy too?"

"Yes. Is Ian?"

"The doctor said he can't leave the hospital today. You know his arm isn't well yet."

Tater nodded, "It is pretty messed up. It sorta hangs like a drip, huh?"

"It is much better than it was."

"How did he hurt it? Did he fall out of bed?"

"He got hurt at his job." Ruthie answered quickly, "Ready to go? Mrs. Feldman, we thought we would take him to brunch with us after the service. Is that okay?"

"That would be good because the children will have their lunch while he is gone."

Tater's eyes darted toward her, "The cupcake party?"

"That will be at two o'clock. You will be back way before then."

"Good," Tater nodded.

When the small group gathered at the burial site, the casket was already there. Reverend Carson met Ruthie and Tater and they visited a few minutes. He was a very warm and kind man. Ruthie was pleased that he took time to visit with Tater a bit on his own. Apparently, they talked what happened to people when they 'got dead.' The chaplain handled it very well.

Ruthie whispered to Van, "How do you ever get good at explaining that to a little kid?"

Van shook her head, "I don't know, but I'm sure glad someone knows how."

The folks gathered around the casket and the chaplain spoke briefly about Taylor. The entire service was geared to Tater, not the adults. Before they lowered her casket, Reverend Carson gave Tater a flower to put on his mom's casket. Then he helped him do it and stood holding his hand until she was lowered into the grave. Then he gave the little boy a hug and they all walked away. At the car, he told Ruthie that if they needed anything or if Tater needed to talk, they should feel free to call him. Anytime. Egan invited him to join them for brunch, but he said that he had another commitment. Then he waved goodbye and left.

Egan looked at Van, "Folks like that make me think there is good in this world."

Van shook her head, "Really? Is this a new revelation?"

"You know what I mean." Egan groused, "So, I think we are going to Adam's Breakfast House, right?"

Nancy smiled, "Yes, that is where I made reservations."

Everyone who had attended the service was impressed by how nice it was. Frank O'Hara went out of his way to tell Ruthie, "I was so wrong. I thought you were being all stupid sentimental, but I am glad I was a part of this." He looked over to Tater who was visiting with Egan and John Kelly, "And he seems like a good kid, and he is definitely a Harrington. I think you guys are doing the right thing. I plan on telling Colleen to keep her big trap shut. It would have been good for her to be here today."

Tater was mostly quiet, but while the adults had a last cup of coffee, Lonnie took him outside to watch the ducks in the park next to the restaurant. Otherwise, he stayed beside Egan or Ruthie as much as he could. When they got back to the Center, he gave John Kelly a big hug. "Bye. I have to go to a cupcake party now."

He smiled at Nancy and said, "You look like Ian and that Jamie guy. Do you know Ian?"

"Yes," she smiled. "He is my brother."

"Oh. Good." The little boy shrugged, "I don't have one of them."

It had drizzled and fiddled around all morning, but was in a full rain by the time they got back to Egan's place. John Kelly and Nancy had to hurry to pick up their kids from the neighbors, but made plans to get together later on in the week.

Egan, Van and Ruthie sat in the living room just mellowing out, planning to go up to see Ian. Before too long, they woke up to Otis barking to go outside. They had all fallen asleep and it was four o'clock.

"My goodness," Aunt Van said. "I bet Ian thinks were forgot him."

"We must have needed the rest." Ruthie surmised, "The rain and the cozy house were just too good to pass up."

"As soon as Otis comes back in, we should go. I imagine Ian is beside himself," Van suggested.

"Matt said they had a long talk on the phone and he felt that Ian was very settled in his decision. I'm glad that he talked to him. You could have knocked me over with a feather when Frank talked to me today!"

"I heard that, too. Good. Colleen and Vivian need to think before they go off the deep-end all the time." Van smiled, "Let's get moving. Otis is heading back to the house."

A bit later, they entered Ian's room. He was sitting quietly, no television on, just watching it rain. He smiled when they came in, "I thought you'd had enough of me today."

"Not yet." Egan smiled. "How did your therapy go today?"

"Pretty good, I guess. I squeezed that stupid ball to about 60%."

Egan crossed his eyes, "If you think that is good, I'll take your word for it."

Ian took Ruthie's hand when she kissed his cheek, "How did it go this morning?"

Sunday morning, Egan, Van and Ruthie went to Father Colter's parish for service. They attended with Aaron's family. After mass, when they shook hands at the door, Ruthie thanked him for telling them about the chaplain. "Reverend Carson was fantastic. He did a beautiful job."

Colter beamed, "I'm glad you liked him. Carson and I have been friends for years. We served in Korea together. I will likely see you tomorrow when I go see Ian."

Terrie, Aaron's wife, thought they should all try the new seafood restaurant after mass. It was a nice place and overlooked the busy harbor. While waiting for their dinners, Aaron looked out over the fishing boats docked to unload their catch, "I wonder if people would want to overlook a herd of cattle being unloaded at the slaughterhouse while eating a steak."

"Now why did you go say that?" Egan frowned, "What goes through that head of yours? You scare me."

"And you don't know the half of it." Terrie laughed, "Oh you guys! Vivian called me last night. She had a million questions about Taylor's service yesterday. Jamie wouldn't tell her a thing. He told her if she she wanted to know so much, she should have gone herself."

"What did you tell her?" Van asked.

"Only a little. I said the chaplain was nice and the service was short." Terrie giggled, "Then she asked about the little boy and I said, "He looks just like Jamie."

Egan's mouth fell open, "You didn't!"

"Yes, I did. I could hear her gasping for air and I enjoyed every minute of it. Then I said, 'Oh, sorry. Gotta run. I'll call you later!' I could just hear her hyperventilating!"

"You have a mean streak," Van laughed. "Good for you!"

196

That afternoon, Egan and Van dropped Ruthie at the hospital while they went to visit friends. They said they would be back in the early evening, but if she needed a ride sooner, to call. It was nice that she and Ian had time alone to visit. They needed an unhurried conversation.

They discussed the service, the adoption and decorating Tater's room at home. Ian talked a lot about his relationship with Taylor. It became obvious to Ruthie that he didn't love her, but did feel guilty about using her. He said she was a lost soul and never really had anyone that gave a darn about her. He knew he treated her the same way. He said that he and Father Colter talked a lot about that and he was helping him work through it. "I know there is no real excuse for what I did. I shouldn't have let her think I loved her. No amount of groaning about it is going to change that. Colter says I just need to show my respect for her as a person, by giving her son a home. I really want to do that."

"Ian, Tater isn't just her son."

"I know that, but I meant that if the DNA comes back saying he isn't my boy. Ruthie, I know he is. I really like the little character. We didn't have a lot of time to visit, because he was feeling so horrible. We did talk though. I can't imagine how it would feel to be in that cabinet. It gives me the creeps."

"He said his leg still hurts, but it is better. His face is just a little red from the tape, but it is almost healed up. I noticed he babies that one arm quite a bit."

"He said that man didn't have room for it, so he shoved it in his back. How long do they think he was in there?"

"About three hours or so."

"Does he talk about it yet?"

"Mostly he talked about the cupcake party."

"Were you going up to see him today?"

"No. Today is Jerry's last day, so Mrs. Feldman thought it might be best to let it go today. We are going up tomorrow morning. The kids are getting a new slide and teeter-totter after Ted smashed up the other one. So, they get to play on it in the morning. Egan bought some Tonka toys for their sandbox to give them. He was upset that they only had one truck. He went to the mall and came home with a tractor, bulldozer and something else. He can't wait to give it to them."

"He is a good person," Ian chuckled.

"He and Van have signed up with Mrs. Feldman to help out at the Center from time to time. She was glad they did."

"I bet he'll be there every day."

"Most likely."

Monday morning, Mr. Walsh, the attorney, came up to see Ian and Ruthie about eleven. "Got most everything in order. Those folks in North Dakota sure like you guys. I couldn't round up that many people to say good things about me in a month of Sundays."

"We think a lot of them, too."

"Well, I already talked to this one Family Court guy and he thinks that they can cut a few corners. We are hoping to have this all done by Friday, next Monday at the latest."

"Really? Even if the DNA results aren't as we expect?"

"Yah. The state isn't all that excited about housing another child if they don't have to. You know, the coins in the old pocketbook clink pretty damned loud. They will give tentative papers, but of course, Child Services will have to do a couple follow up visits before it is final. I hear you'll have to come back to get your arm okayed from the doc. We can try to set up the final hearing at that same time."

"Turner thought about two to three months after I go home."

"Good, we can work with that. I'm anxious to meet this little guy. Well, gotta go. I need to set some fires!"

"What?" Ian asked.

"Some folks love to dawdle. Bugs the hell right out of me. I found a hot poker gets them moving."

Ian laughed, "I bet it does!"

Tuesday morning, the three went up to the Center to watch the kids play on the new playground equipment and Egan presented them all with the Tonka toys. Tater was so proud it was 'his friend' that gave them to the kids. Even the little girls took turns playing with them.

In the afternoon, Ruthie and Van watched Wiley with Tater. Egan had some work he had to get done, so he couldn't make it. Tater tore out a colored page for him, Ian and John Kelly. "Give the pages to them so they don't forget me."

"They wouldn't forget you," Van said. "I know they will love them."

"Good."

Ruthie went up to visit Ian Tuesday evening, while Van and Egan went to a movie. Ruthie gave Ian the page and he was very moved by it. "He is a sweet kid, isn't he?"

"Yes. John Kelly really liked his, too."

"I was thinking, Ruthie, what would you think about asked John and Nancy to be his godparents?"

"Oh, Ian. That would be wonderful! That is really a good idea. Do you think that Father Colter would baptize him?"

"Probably. But you said he really liked that Carson."

"Yes, but Carson is Protestant. Maybe he could attend, though. Since he and Colter are friends," Ruthie said.

"If we can do this before we leave, I would also like to invite Greg and Turner with their families. They have been so good to us. Greg and I spent many hours talking about this mess."

"I agree. I will talk to Mrs. Feldman and see if they have rules and stuff."

"Oh I'm sure. There are rules about everything." Ian became very quiet and he took Ruthie's hand, "Maybe we shouldn't say anything until tomorrow when we should know."

"I am praying that it is conclusive that you are his father. Then they just need to wait with my adoption, but it sounds like there would be little problem with that."

"I need to know something, though." Ian looked at her with worry, "Has part of your love for me died with all this?"

"No. I think it is stronger. You are still my hero; only your white hat just has a little dust on it." Ruthie kissed him, "I know that even though things can rattle us; if we keep talking, we can work it out. Our relationship has been tested and stood strong."

"I love you."

Wednesday morning, John Kelly came by to give Ruthie a ride to the hospital so she could wait with Ian. They made a pact that whoever would hear first would contact the other. Ian was in physical therapy when she came into his room. Before he returned, Father Colter arrived. He and Ruthie had a long talk about step parenting. Colter said, "Even though I never had any children, I have noticed that folks that think taking a child into their home is a big deal, usually make it a big deal. Of course, the consideration is a big deal; but once you make the decision, it shouldn't be. You treat them like any other family member and they will be. If you always treat them like they are different, they will be."

"Our friends always say if you can tell someone is a stepchild, you're doing it wrong."

"That's good," Colter nodded. "Your clan sounds like a wonderful bunch of folks. I think they would be fun to know."

"Sometime, you should come out and visit. I think you and Carson would have a lot of fun. But mind you, you would end up milking cows and riding horses. If you time it right, you could come for the big cookout in July. That gets a bit blood-thirsty!"

"Really?" Colter grinned.

"Yah, last year two recipes were eaten before the judge's even got a taste! This year, we are having security!"

"You know, Carson and I do make a mean grilled lobster. I'm afraid you folks wouldn't have a chance," Colter taunted.

"Okay, I will send you an invitation and a set of the rules. I just need your address."

"Oh, we couldn't afford to come out there, stay and all."

"We have room for you to stay and we'll get your tickets. I just need your address."

By the time Ian returned to his room, those two were exchanging addresses. "What's going on here?" Ian chuckled. "I turn my back a minute and look!"

"Yes and worse—Carson and I may just come out to beat the pants off you in July when you have this cookout thing." Colter laughed.

"I kinda figured I wouldn't win this year, since Kid's brother-in-law is coming from San Diego. He owns a restaurant chain in California."

"You didn't mention that, Ruthie. You padding the ranks with a ringer?" Colter asked.

"No, he will likely take the Italian food, but he won't the rest."

Ian got back into this bed, "Heard anything?"

"Not a word, yet. I was hoping you would hear this morning, because I have an appointment at one. So, I will have to take off before long." Colter said. "Could we have a word of prayer?"

They had just said amen, when the phone rang. Ruthie and Ian grabbed each other's hand and Ruthie handed the phone to Ian. "Hello. Yes, this is he. Good. We've been waiting."

Colter and Ruthie watched his face to read a reaction, but he had a poker face. Then he thanked the person and put the phone back in its cradle. After he hung up, Ruthie said, "Ian, I can't stand it. What is it?"

He broke into a huge grin, "He is my boy. The test was 99.999% sure. He is my little boy."

There were hugs all around and then Colter said, "I'm so relieved. Now I don't have to wait all afternoon to find out. It is a blessing, you know. Well, I'm sure you folks have a million phone calls to make, so I will leave you to it."

"No," Ruthie said. "Wait, Ian has something to ask you."

A look of concern crossed the priest's face, "What is it?"

"Could you baptize Tater before we leave Boston? We would really like that."

"You had me scared a minute." Colter sighed with relief, "I would love to."

"We were wondering if Reverend Carson could be there, too?"

"I'm sure he would be pleased. You get the information to me and we will do it. Talk to you later."

The next hour was a flurry of phone calls. The phone calls to Walsh and Mrs. Feldman were the most exciting. Walsh said he would send his girl right over to get the lab analysis. Mrs. Feldman said she would come up to the hospital to see Ian in about half an hour. "We can talk over how to handle telling Tater and making the transfer."

Ruthie giggled, "And planning his cupcake party."

"Oh yes! Another cupcake party! The kids will be excited."

Mrs. Feldman arrived within the hour. Ruthie had helped get Ian ready for company. Ruthie greeted Mrs. Feldman and then introduced Ian. "Now I understand why you knew Tater was Ian's boy. My goodness, there is a striking resemblance!"

They visited for almost two hours and went over a lot of procedure and paperwork. Finally, they discussed telling Tater. "I would suggest, and mind you it is only a suggestion, that you tell him when it is just the two of you. Ruthie can come in later, but you really need to tell him one on one. It is important to keep two things in mind: little children have little idea how they can be born without their mother and father knowing about it. Another thing, if you butter a tale now, you will have to eat that piece later. By that I mean, tell him as much of the truth as he can understand, but leave it at the truth. Anything you say that isn't the truth, is something that you will have to explain later. He knows his mommy couldn't keep him because she had to be in this special place. When she got out of that special place, she came to see him. He never knew it was a prison or correctional facility. Just a special one. Then, of course, he was told she died. He still doesn't know that the bad guys had any relationship to him or her. I would leave it that way for a few years. It would serve no good purpose for him to know now and it could upset him. What you tell him, of course, is up to you. Do you know of a good children's counselor where you live?"

"Yes," Ruthie explained about her niece. "I'm sure that Dr. Samuels would see Tater."

"That would be good for him and also, help with the adoption process. I'm very pleased about this. And I am also pleased that I met Van and Egan!" Mrs. Feldman laughed, "It will be wonderful to have their assistance. Most of the kids already like them. Friday or Monday will be Tater's last day at the Center, but if you want to take him for outings before then, just let me know. We can work around it. Okay?"

"I was thinking would it be okay to tell him tonight? Or would it be better to wait until tomorrow?"

"It's up to you. He is your son, Mr. Harrington."

Ian beamed, "Thank you. I think that maybe we should tell him tonight. What do you think Ruthie?"

"I agree. I can pick him up and bring him up here this evening? When is his bedtime?"

"Eight or eight-thirty." Mrs. Feldman looked at her watch, "They will be eating their dinner in about ten minutes. So, give him a little time to finish."

After she went out of the room, Ian pulled Ruthie to him and embraced her, "I can't believe this. I hope I don't screw this up. I want him to be happy about it."

"Don't expect a miracle. He has learned to not let himself get excited about promises. He has been let down too often." Ruthie gave him a big kiss, "I think Egan and Van should be here any time now."

"We are here," Egan dashed over to Ian's bed. "We just talked to Mrs. Feldman! Let's go get our Tater."

34

Van, Egan, Ruthie and Tater met Greg in the hall, outside Ian's room. Greg waved to them and then squatted down to be at Tater's level. "How was the cupcake party?"

Tater grinned, "It was good. Jerry's new mommy and daddy brought two kinds of cupcakes and Kool-aid."

"Did you get some?"

"I had a chocolate one with white frosting and sprinkles on it. The Kood-aid was purple. Then we waved goodbye to Jerry."

"That sounds like a good time."

"It was, but now my room is sad. It looks sorta empty without Jerry."

"I bet, that's too bad."

"No, it's good. He got a new home, so it's good."

"Well, that is very nice. Guess what?"

The little boy shrugged, "I don't know."

"I know someone that is anxious to see you? Can you guess who?"

Tater looked at him and squinted, "My doctor?"

"No, you silly rabbit. Ian!"

Tater giggled, "I know that. I want to see him, too. When is he gonna get all better?"

"He might get to go home in another week."

"Good."

Then Greg said, "I need to talk to these guys, so can I take you into to see Ian? These guys will come in a bit."

Tater turned to Ruthie and asked, "Did you hear?"

"That would be great, Tater. You go in and we'll be along soon."

"Okay," He grinned and took Greg's hand.

Together they went into Ian's room where Ian was waiting, sitting in a big chair. Tater looked around the room and frowned, "Where did my bed go?"

"Oh," Greg answered. "We took it to a different room for someone else to use, since you could go home. Is that okay?"

"I guess. I just thought it would be here. I forgot it has wheels."

"Well, I'm going to talk to those grownups, so you can visit with Ian."

Tater said, "Okay."

Ian called him over to the chair, "Hi there. How are things going today?"

"Good."

"Would you like to climb up on my lap?"

Tater thought, "What if I hurt your arm?"

"We will be careful. Okay? I have something very grownup to talk to you about."

"Greg said the grownups are coming back. I'm a little kid."

"I know, but it is you that I want to talk to."

Tater froze and stood a few feet from Ian. "Was I naughty?"

"Not at all."

"Good," Tater nodded and shyly moved over to lean on the arm of the chair.

Ian put his good arm around him, "Did you know that I knew your Mommy?"

"Ruthie said so, but she said the doctor said you had to stay in bed and couldn't come when we told her goodbye."

"I know. I was unhappy about that. Well, this is very important. I knew your mommy before she had to go to that special place. We were friends. When she went away, we weren't allowed to talk to each other anymore. I didn't know that she had a baby boy. You. I didn't know about you."

"Yah, I was her baby but I had to go live someplace else because they don't let kids play where she was at. So I had to leave."

"I know. It wasn't until after your mommy got out of that place that we even knew where each other was."

"Oh."

"I didn't know about you being born or anything." The little boy shrugged as Ian continued, "Then Ruthie was shopping at this store and met your mommy. She left before I could talk to her. We asked John Kelly to help us find her again, but she died before we got to talk."

"I know. Me, too. She was going to come get me so we could have a home, but she got dead first. She said my daddy didn't want me, but she did."

"Well, she was wrong about that, Tater."

"How do you know? Do you know my daddy?"

"Yes," Ian looked into the little boy's eyes. "Tater, I am your daddy and I do want you."

Tater stiffened and stepped back, "Why didn't you tell me?"

"I just did. We had some tests done and look at this paper I got today." Ian reached the paper from the laboratory, "See, this one. It says right here, Taylor Collins. That's you and Ian Harrington, that's me. Father and son."

The little boy looked at the paper and studied it. "I don't know all these marks."

"I know, but that is what it says. You are my little boy. And Tater, I would love to have you come to my home and live with me."

Tater stiffened again, "For how long?"

"Forever, if you want."

"True?" He looked at him doubtfully, "When?"

"Well, we have to have a judge sign a paper and then we can pick you up. So, in two days."

Tater shrugged, "What if you forget?"

"I know you have no reason to trust me, but I hope you can. Ruthie and I want you to live with us and be our family."

"You mean like a mommy and a daddy? And I will be the boy?"

"Exactly like that, except that I am your real daddy."

"Why didn't mommy tell me that?"

"Because she thought that I got lost while she was in that place."

"You guys should have kept better track. Mrs. Feddman writes us kids down so she knows where we are."

"We should have, Tater. We really should have. But I promise you that you will always have a home with Ruthie and me. I am your daddy and Ruthie will be your new mommy, if you want?"

"Will Egan and Aunt Van be at your house too?"

"No, we live in North Dakota, but we visit a lot. So you will get to see them."

He shrugged, "Do you have coddors at your house?" Tater was so low-key, he could have been talking about picking out a breakfast cereal.

"We do, and coloring books."

"Good. Do you have a TV? Ruthie says Aunt Van does. I like to watch Widey."

"Yes, we have a TV and you can watch Wile E.Coyote. You will be in our family. Will you do that? Would you like that?"

"Does Mrs. Feddman know?"

"She does and she says that as soon as you have your cupcake party, you can come with us."

"Do I have to live at the hospital, too? I don't have a bed here anymore. Greg let another kid use it."

"No, you will stay with Ruthie, Egan and Van."

The boy nodded unemotionally, "That would be cool."

"And when I get out of the hospital, I will stay there for a while too, until the doctor says I can go home. Then you will come home with Ruthie and I." Ian said, "I would be very happy if you would say that you will do that."

Tater looked around, "It sounds okay, if Mrs. Feddman says."

Then Ian smiled, "Can you give me a hug? I would really like that."

The little boy gave him a brief hug and then asked, "What kind of cupcakes can I have at my party?"

Ian chuckled, "I don't know. Shall we talk to Ruthie and Van about that?"

"Okay."

Then Ian got up slowly out of the chair and moved toward the door. Tater stood beside him until he got up and then took his hand. They walked together to the door. Just before they got there, Tater looked at Ian, "It will be good to be in a family."

"It is our family, Tater. Yours, mine and Ruthie's."

The little guy looked up and smiled, "Good."

The patient and the little boy walked slowly to the waiting room where the grownups were visiting. Tater was holding Ian's hand when the others saw them. Ian smiled, "Tater said it would be okay to be part of our family."

Ruthie jumped up, gave Tater a big hug and then kissed her husband. The others all waited their turns and then Greg said, "You better get back to your room, Ian."

The group went back into Ian's room and Greg disappeared. They were engrossed in a deep conversation about Tater's party when there was a knock at the door. Greg came in with a tray. He had a little cake with a candle on it. "I thought we needed to celebrate."

Tater looked at him, "Is this your birthday?"

"No, young man. It is to celebrate you finding your home!"

Tater giggled, "Like my first cupcake party?"

"Just like that," Greg grinned as he set the tray down.

He set the paper plates and plastic spoons aside and lit the one candle. "Now, you and your daddy need to blow this out, together."

"And Ruthie, too?"

"Good idea."

They blew out the candle and then Greg cut the tiny cake into six little pieces. They all ate their cake and Greg said, "Okay, I hate to be a party pooper, but visiting hours will be over soon."

Egan nodded, "And we have to get Tater back to the Center before his bedtime."

Tater nodded, "Until I can be at your house."

They all said their goodbyes, and Tater finally gave Ian a hug. "This is way cool."

"I'm glad, Tater." Ian smiled, "I think it is, too."

When Ian hugged Ruthie goodnight, he said, "I don't think he is all that excited."

"Remember what I told you. He probably doesn't really believe it yet."

"No, I guess not."

That evening, Ruthie was almost asleep when she heard the phone ring. Van came and knocked on her door. "Ruthie, it's Ian. Can you talk to him?"

"Did something happen?"

"No, he just sounds like he needs to talk to someone."

"Sure, I'll go downstairs and take it there."

When she said hello, Van told them goodnight and hung up her line. Ruthie said, "What is it, Ian?"

"I don't know. I just feel terrible. I want to be home with you. I guess I... oh... I don't know."

"I think I do. I think you hoped that Tater would be more excited about the news. Honey, he doesn't do that. He has been disappointed too many times to let himself be excited."

"But he seemed more interested in the cupcakes than in the fact he found his dad."

"He has only a vague idea of what having a dad means. How can he feel one way or the other?"

"I know. I guess it was such a big deal for me, I expected it would be to him."

"It will be, but it will take time. He will need to know that he can count on what you say and that you will come through with it. It will be a gradual thing. Just hang in there. I don't think it will take him that long to realize that you are a man of your word."

"Am I?"

"What?"

"A man of my word? I sure left Taylor high and dry."

"Yes, Ian. That was not an ordinary situation. What did Father Colter tell you? Look, Tater is as happy as he will let himself be. If Mrs. Feldman told him tomorrow that he would never see you again, he would just shrug his shoulders and think, 'I figured as much'. You need to be patient."

"I wish you were here."

"Do you want me to come up?"

"No, that would be silly. I hate being away from you."

"You have the blues. Honey, try to get some rest and tomorrow will be brighter. Tater didn't say no and he was as happy about it as he gets."

"Do you think so?"

"Yes, I truly do."

"I love you."

"I love you, too. Will you be able to sleep? Maybe you should ask the nurse for something."

"No, I don't want to do that. I'm just being a sap. I ignore a kid his whole life and then when I finally get my head on straight, I expect him to be excited about it. It wasn't very realistic. I guess I should be glad he will even talk to me."

"Now you are being silly. Try to rest. The sooner you get home, the sooner you can start building a relationship with your little boy."

"I know. I will grow up," Ian said. "I guess a man should at least try to be a little more grownup than his son."

The next morning, the sun was shining brightly and Egan was the first one up. He had made breakfast for the ladies, "Waffles and scrambled eggs. Sit and eat. Then we can get moving."

"What is the hurry?" Van asked.

Egan shook his head, "I was thinking we have to get Tater's room ready."

"He can use the other room upstairs. The bed is already made up and everything. What else do we have to do?" Van yawned.

"Plan this cupcake party and does he need clothes? What time should we go over there today? Think it is too early?"

"Good grief, Uncle Egan. It isn't even six o'clock yet. It is way too early." Ruthie took a drink of her coffee, "Mrs. Feldman doesn't even get there until eight."

"We should be there first thing. We have to plan this all out. I think that next week I need to take Tater fishing. He's never been. I asked him and he told me."

PJ Hoge

Van took his hand, "Don't you think that maybe Ian would like to come along?"

"Sure. I meant when he gets home. I have to reserve spots on a fishing boat ahead of time, you know."

"I think a little fishing trip would be better. Ian can't be on a sea-going vessel this soon."

"Oh, you might be right. Okay, I will find us a place to fish off the docks."

"Much better." Ruthie smiled, "Ian and I want to ask John and Nancy to be his Godparents and have him baptized before we go back to North Dakota."

Egan got excited, "Good idea! We need to take Tater shopping to buy a suit. John Kelly and Nancy, good choice. We will have a dinner here afterwards. Okay, Van? Family and who else?"

"We can do it someplace else and Ian and I will pay for it. You guys have done so much already," Ruthie said.

"We will do it here! It will be a grand event! I'm thinking we should have a big dinner. Who do you want to come?"

"Mrs. Feldman, Reverend Carson and we asked Father Colter if he will baptize him. He said he would. And then we wanted to invite Greg and Dr. Turner." Ruthie said, "I think we should find a place to have a dinner afterward. That is too much for you guys to do."

Egan frowned, "I guess, what with the stairs and front entrance all messed up. What do you think Van?"

"If you want it here, we can do it. My concern would be that Ian will just be home from the hospital and too much commotion might not be good for him."

"Okay, but I want to help pay for it. I insist!" Egan said, "That little laddie would likely have never found our family, if it hadn't been for me!"

Ruthie and Van looked at each other and shook their heads but Egan never noticed. He was off deciding about if he should lend Tater a fishing pole or buy Tater his own.

About eight, Mr. Walsh called. He said that he would meet Ian and Ruthie at the hospital about ten to sign papers. Then he would tell them what to expect for the rest of the time. He was rather certain that they could pick up Tater on Friday. He was going to call Mrs. Feldman and sort it out with her.

Ruthie called Greg and asked how Ian was. He said that he and Ian had a long talk when he got in at seven. Ian was feeling much better about things now. Greg said that he would make sure that Ian was back from his therapy by ten.

Ruthie called Mo and Carl, to share the news. They were excited. She spoke with Mo for some time about Ian's disappointment. She listened and then said, "Oh that sounds like my Ian! His heart was racing ahead of his brain! He will do okay. He was just excited and forgot the little tyke doesn't know what a wonderful thing this will be. I'm thinking Tater will come around sooner than you think. He has had a plateful before him for some time and will have to scrape off the peas and broccoli before he can enjoy the dessert!"

Ruthie giggled, "Thanks, Mo. You are the best."

"Ain't I just? So, now I have to tell Carl. He is remodeling the whole Gopher room. Matt and Zach are ready to strangle him. He decided that his one wall of cubes for the kids needs to be expanded. Would the man be content to add another wall? Not my Coot! No, by George! We are shuffling those storage cubes for the kids around like so many building blocks! Please tell Egan that Carl already bought a shovel and fishing pole for Tater. So, if he gets him a fishing pole out there, he can keep it there for him to use."

"My goodness, who would have thought that a fishing pole is the most important thing you need when you get a new child in your family!"

Mo laughed, "Well, the baby twins, Ben and Beth, each have one already, and a shovel. They can't even sit up yet! You know, it isn't just Tater. I mean you and Ian are expecting, as are a few other clanners. Carl is thinking at least four new cubes!"

"Dr. Turner thinks that Ian can leave the hospital next week and then be able to return to North Dakota the following week."

"That will be grand. I'm so anxious to meet the little one and to have you and Ian home again. By the way, your garden, house plants and kitty are looking fine."

It was a few minutes to ten when Egan and Van dropped Ruthie at the hospital. Egan had a list of shopping he felt he needed to do and Van was going to hold on to the checkbook. Ruthie had just entered Ian's room when Mr. Walsh came in. From what he said, things were on the fast track. The papers were scheduled for Friday morning delivery. They should be able to bring Tater home with them right away. Then he walked through the adoption protocol for Ruthie. It all seemed straight forward. That could be finalized when Ian came back for his checkup. Then the man shook hands and dashed off to 'set more fires." When he left, Ian looked at Ruthie, "Can you imagine being married to him?"

"Not for long! I would have to suffocate him!" Then she gave her husband a long, loving kiss. "I missed you so much. Are you feeling better now?"

"When you kiss me like that, I can't wait to get home. I can hardly stand it."

"I meant do you feel better about Tater's reaction now?"

"Yes. Greg and I had a long talk this morning. He really is a good person. He has been such a brick through all this. He explained to me that the world looks different to Tater than to me. I needed to hear it. He didn't pull any punches."

"Good. I love him. I bet his wife is a sweetheart. What's her name, Marcy?"

"Yes. He talks about her all the time and his little girl." Ian took Ruthie's hand, "I would like him to be a Godfather for Tater, too. If you don't mind. If he hadn't slapped some sense into me, I don't know if I would have had the courage to do the right thing."

"You would have, but he was a great help. Do you know if he would want to be? What faith is he?"

"He is Episcopalian and his wife is Baptist. They go to the Methodist church that is a block from their house! He said both their families had a fit about it, but there is something really nice about being able to walk to church."

Ruthie thought and smiled, "I think it would be. Would you ask his wife, too?"

"No, just him. Tater would have three."

"Sounds great." Ruthie smiled, "Now we have to go meet with Mrs. Feldman this afternoon and then make arrangements for the cupcake party. I don't know what kind of cupcakes is he favorite."

Ian beamed, "Well, I do! He told me that night at the hospital that his very favorite is bubblegum. I told him that I had never tasted that, and he said he had one when this one boy went to his new home. The cupcake had blue frosting. He said it way cooler than chocolate."

Ruthie giggled, "Okay. I guess we need four dozen for the party."

"Do they have that many kids at the Center?"

"Mrs. Feldman says that is their maximum capacity. But they always want that many and what they don't use, they freeze. They usually have about thirty kids, moving in and out."

"I don't think I could do her job," Ian said.

"I know I couldn't." Ruthie shook her head, "Egan is manic about helping at the Center. Van said that is the most excited she has seen him in a long time. He is not someone who is apathetic about anything."

"I did notice a sparkle in his eyes when he talks about those kids," Ian said. "I think he loves it when they all say hi to him."

"You should see him, he sits on the floor and plays car with them. He had to give up on hopscotch, because he almost fell over. The kids thought it was really funny!" Ruthie explained. "They have to do a background check on them both and it should take a couple weeks. Then they can be permanent volunteers. Mrs. Feldman is very excited about it."

That afternoon, Ruthie, Van and Egan went to the Center and watched Wile E. with Tater. They visited for a while and Tater seemed much quieter than usual. After the cartoon was over, Van and Egan visited with Mrs. Feldman about the cupcake party. Ruthie sat down in the rocking chair and pulled Tater over by her. "Can you and I have a talk?"

Tater shrugged. She held her arms out, "Will you climb up on my lap so we can talk a little private?"

He gave her a piercing look, "No. You are just going to say I'm not going to your home."

"Tater, you are coming to our home. I want to talk to you about that."

"You don't want me now?"

"You can come live with us tomorrow and you are our little boy. Forever. There was no change and we want you in our family, very much."

The boy moved over toward her, "You sure?"

"Positive. In fact, this morning, Ian and I were talking about your cupcake party. He said you told him that bubblegum is your favorite. Was he right?"

The little boy's face lit up, "He knew about when I said that?"

"Yes, he did. Is that right?"

"Yes, with blue frosting."

"What kind of Kool-aid do you think we should have?"

He leaned on the arm of the chair, "I think red would be good."

"Okay, red it is."

"Tomorrow?"

"Yes, if Mrs. Feldman says we can have the party after lunch, you will be at our house tomorrow night."

"Are you just saying that?"

"No, it's real, Tater."

"I will have to bring my clothes. Are you going to bring them to your house?"

"Of course."

He looked at her, "Is Ian going to change his mind?"

"No. He and I talked to the attorney this morning and signed the papers."

"Is that so he won't forget where I am?"

"He won't forget you." Ruthie assured him, "These papers will tell everyone else that you are our boy."

"That's a good idea." The child nodded, "Ian let me see the paper that said I am his real boy. I like that paper. Is he going to show it to everybody?"

"No, we have to keep that in a very safe place so it doesn't get lost or wrecked. What we are going to do is put our last name on the end of yours, so everybody will know."

Tater frowned, "I don't know it."

"It is Harrington. Your name will be Taylor Collins Harrington. Then everyone will know you are our little boy."

He thought and then nodded, "That would be good. How do you say that name?"

"Hair-ing-ton."

The little boy repeated it. "Harrington. The same name that Egan has?"

"It is."

"Cool."

36

Egan went over to watch Widey with Tater, while Ruthie and Van were home baking the bubblegum cupcakes. Tater asked Egan if Ian was coming to the party, but he told him that his doctor said no. Tater frowned, "All the new daddys and mommys come to the cupcake parties. What am I going to do? Maybe he doesn't want me to be his boy."

"No, Tater, he really does. You know how his arm is. The doctor is afraid that it will hurt his arm more and then he won't be able to move it. Will it be okay if Van and I come to the party?"

"Yes, but my new daddy should be here. Every time, the new daddy is here."

"I will ask Dr. Turner. Okay? But do you promise to be a big boy about it if he says no? We don't want Ian's arm to be messed up forever, do we?"

"No, but all the new daddys come." Holding back tears, he shrugged, "I guess it is okay if he can't. The other kids will say I made him up."

"Let me find out, okay?"

When Egan got home, he told the women. "I don't think that Turner will let him go, do you? He wouldn't let him go to the burial and that was only a couple days ago," Van said.

Later, at the hospital, they told Ian. He said, "I hate to have Tater be disappointed the first thing. I will ask Greg."

Ruthie went out to catch Greg before he went home and told him the situation. Greg shook his head no. "I don't think Turner will go for it. I know how important it is to both Ian and Tater, but Ian still has a lot of mending to do."

A bit later, Turner stopped by. "So, I hear tomorrow is Tater's cupcake party. Greg told me that is when the kid's get to show off their new mom and dad." He looked at Ian and shook his head no. "You are going to be my undoing. I hope you realize that."

"I know. I wouldn't have asked, but I've not been there for him in his whole life. Now the first thing that matters to him, I let him down. I guess he'll have to get used to it. He is a tough little kid."

Turner sat on the stool by his bed, "This is completely against my better judgment, my religion, my training and everything sensible but I will relent. Mind you, it is not for you, but for that little guy and because Greg pleaded. He said he'll go with you. You have to be in the wheelchair."

"I can walk." Ian said. "There is nothing wrong with my legs."

"No, it is your lung, arm and especially your brain! I want you to stay in the wheelchair. You are weaker than you think. If you fall over, you could land on your arm. It is also to remind you and everyone else, that you are not well. No wheelchair, no go. At the rate you are going, I don't think you will ever let yourself heal up. You have to sign a form releasing me and the hospital from responsibility if you mess everything up. We will make your arm as immobile as we can. Greg will take you over there and bring you back. No lifting or moving that arm! If you tear those loose ends I mended, I will wring your neck. You can only be there about half an hour. Then you have to come back. Hear?"

"Thank you, thank you, thank you."

"And you have to promise that you won't ask me to bend anymore rules. My god man, the only thing you didn't ask for was to do your own surgery." Then he looked at Ruthie. "I have no idea how you can put up with him. But then, I think of his uncle! Egan explains a lot."

Egan furrowed his brows, "What do you mean by that? I'm a good influence."

"Okay," Turner laughed. "This will add one day on your sentence. I hope you are aware of that."

Ian held out his hand and Turner squinted at him. "I'm not kidding around about this. You've had two surgeries in two weeks. This is no joke."

"You have my word."

Turner shook his hand and rolled his eyes. Then he stood up to leave, "I can't imagine why I don't find that encouraging!"

That evening when they got home, Van said, "Turner was really pretty nervous about him going. I'm not so certain that he should."

"I know he shouldn't," Ruthie agreed. "But in this case, I think it is important, not only for Tater but for Ian. We will make him be careful."

"Should we tell Tater?" Egan asked.

"I don't know, what do you think?" Ruthie said, "What if something goes awry and he can't leave? Then it will just be another broken promise."

The three decorated while the children finished their lunch. The party would be in the playroom.

Mrs. Feldman brought out Tater's things that were all in one large box. Egan and Van took them to the car while she took Ruthie aside. "Tater's had a bad morning."

Ruthie sat down, "What's wrong? Doesn't he want to come home with us?"

"He really does, but he is upset that his new daddy won't be here. It is a thing with the kids that everybody gets to see the new families. He is afraid they will think that he just made it up that he has his own daddy."

"He told us that. Dr. Turner said last night that he can come. Greg is bringing him, but it is against the doctor and hospital protocol. We didn't tell Tater, because we didn't want something to come up at the last minute and have him be shattered again. If Ian's vitals and tests weren't adequate this morning, he would've had to stay."

"I understand. You said he is on his way?"

"Yes, Greg called a bit ago They are on their way."

"I will call Tater in before the kids get finished with their dinner. He should know before he cries. Would that be okay?"

"Of course, I don't want him to cry on his special day."

Mrs. Feldman went to get Tater. Ruthie was just setting the paper plates and napkins out when Egan and Van returned. With them, came Greg and Ian who was holding a big bouquet of helium balloons. Ruthie ran over to him and gave him a hug. She told them what Mrs. Feldman had said.

Just then, she came in with Tater. He looked around and his face lit up like the Fourth of July! "You came! Mrs. Feddman, my own daddy came!"

"I said I would if Dr. Turner said I could. He said I had to stay in this chair, but I could come for a little bit."

Tater ran to his daddy and dove for his lap. Greg had to catch him before he landed on Ian's arm, "We must be very careful of the arm. You can hug this side of him."

Tater crawled up on his lap, very carefully, and then gave him a kiss on his cheek and hugged his neck. Ian had the happiest tears a man could have. When Tater saw his tears, he worried, "Did I hurt your arm?"

"No, Tater. You just made me the happiest man in the world."

"Now the guys will know you are real and I didn't make you up." Tater hugged him again. "This is so way cool!"

The party went well. Everyone enjoyed the bubblegum cake, Kool-aid and balloons. Greg and Ian could not overstay the half an hour, so had to leave before the party was over. Tater seemed to be a happy kid. He hugged his Daddy and Greg good bye and even got to walk to the car with them. Ruthie and Tater waved goodbye before they went back to the party.

After an hour, they picked up the mess and put the room back in order. Tater told all his friends goodbye. They waved and thanked him for leaving the balloons for them, except the green one. He wanted to bring that home because if was from his daddy. All the way home, the little boy asked a million questions. He was anxious to see Egan's house and especially his TV, since Wiley would be on soon. Mostly, he repeated over and over how happy he was when Greg brought his Daddy in. "My eyes just didn't know they were seeing him! I told them, that is him!"

At the house, Ruthie took Tater's hand while Aunt Van unlocked the front door and Egan brought in the box of his things. They came in the entry and Tater looked everything over. He smiled and said, "It is cool, but the steps are icky."

"Yes, we had a bit of trouble recently and they are being repaired. The workmen will be here on Monday to do some more work on them," Egan replied.

"I can help you work," Tater said. "I am pretty strong for a boy."

"Good to know." Egan said, "You hang on and I will introduce you to Otis."

Egan ran upstairs with Tater's things and Tater looked at Ruthie, "Who is Otis?"

"Uncle Egan's dog. He is very old and can't move very fast, but he loves little boys. You just have to remember to be gentle with him."

"I will. Does he look like a Widey Coyote?"

"No, he is a Basset Hound. He is low to the ground with long, droopy ears and a sad looking face."

"What's he sad about?" the little boy asked.

"He isn't. He just looks like he is." Aunt Van answered. "Come, I will get you a doggie treat to give to him when you meet him. Okay?"

Egan came down the steps and gave Ruthie a big hug. "I'm so glad Ian insisted he come. It meant a lot to Tater."

"I think it meant a lot to Ian, too."

"I know it did." Egan shook his head, "I don't know of one of my kids or Mo's kids that could have got everything they owned into one cardboard box when they were almost four-years-old. Where is he?"

"He and Van are getting a treat for Otis," Ruthie smiled.

A little later, the group, including Otis, were watching Wile E. Coyote on Egan's television. Tater petted Otis while he watched his favorite show. Every so often, he would look at the grownups and giggle.

Egan took Tater for walk around the house and yard, showing him all sorts of things. Then they ate a quiet dinner and talked to Ian on the phone for a little while. Tater was really tickled when Ian asked to talk to him. Tater told him about Otis and Egan's red shiny car. Then he said, "Is your doctor mad at you? Did your arm get bad again?"

"No. He checked it and said it was okay. But I have to go to bed early tonight."

"I have to go to bed at eight. Mrs. Feddman says kids get out of sorts if they don't go to bed at eight. Do you think she's right?"

"Yes, she probably is."

"Daddy Ian, how is you when you're out of sorts?"

"Crabby." Ian chuckled. "Some of us grownups get that way, too. We both should go to bed, don't you think? You have a good sleep. I love you, Tater."

Tater giggled and handed the phone to Egan. Then he cuddled into Ruthie's arms and gave her a hug, "My daddy said we both had to go to bed now."

"How about a bath first?"

"Do you think I'm dirty?"

"I think you were playing on the playground and with Otis. What do you think?"

Tater looked at his shirt, "And I got bubblegum cupcake on my shirt!"

After Tater's bath, Ruthie brought him downstairs to tell Egan and Van goodnight. They were sitting on the patio watching Otis. Tater gave them both a hug and said, "Thank you for coming to my party."

Van gave him a big hug, "It was our pleasure."

"I wouldn't have missed it for the world." Egan said, "How 'bout I carry you up to your room and then Ruthie can tuck you in?"

"I can walk."

"Nope, I will give you an airplane ride!" The man laughed as he held the boy so he was like Superman going up the stairs.

There was a lot of whirring, swishing and airplane noise accompanied by tons of giggles before the plane landed in Tater's bed. The Egan hugged him goodnight, "Sleep tight. Remember, in the morning you have to help me polish the Cadillac!"

"Okay, Egan."

Ruthie sat down on the edge of his bed, "Do you have everything you need?"

Tater looked around, "Are you going to keep the door open?"

"Yes sir, and my room is right across the hall. Uncle Egan and Aunt Van are right next to your room. If you need anything, just shout. We will be right here."

"Can you keep the light on?"

"Of course, and guess what? I almost forgot that I have a special present for you. Wait right here!"

She ran out of the room and came back with a Wile E. Coyote plush toy. "You can sleep with it and then keep it, if you want. I don't know if you will like it. Think you would like this?"

The little boy hugged it and then hugged Ruthie. "I will like it a lot."

"It is from me and your daddy. It is yours."

Tater hugged her very hard, "I'm a pretty lucky kid, huh?"

"So are your daddy and I. You settle down and I will read you a story. How does that sound?"

"Okay. What are we going to read about?"

"I have two books. One is about horses and the other is about boats. Which one?"

"Boats would be good."

"Boats it is."

A few minutes later, Ruthie tiptoed out of the room, leaving the lamp on and the door open. The little boy was sound asleep with his Wile E. Coyote stuffed under his arm. He was so tired, that he barely stayed awake more than a couple pages of the book, but he did hold her hand while she read.

She went downstairs and called Ian. They talked for only a short time because Ian was wiped out, too. He was so glad he had gone to the cupcake party. "I finally feel like he was really glad to be our family. I was so worried."

"I know you were. I love you, Ian."

"I love you, too, Ruthie. And don't think I don't know that if it hadn't been for you, today would have never happened."

Ruthie told Egan and Van goodnight and said that she was going to take a bath and hit the sack. They both agreed they were all tired out from all the excitement themselves.

Sometime during the night, a little boy came into Ruthie's room and crawled into bed with her. When Ruthie heard the alarm in the morning, she looked over and saw Tater, curled up around his stuffed Wile E. Coyote. She smiled.

Saturday went by quickly. Ian was not allowed visitors, because Dr. Turner wanted him to really rest. He did talk on the phone to Tater that evening.

Tater had a lot to tell him. He explained about his car polishing lessons. Uncle Egan said he was one of the best polishers he had ever met. Tater was proud of that. He met the big neighbor boys, Jeremy and Jason, who helped him play basketball. He really liked that.

"Aunt Van let me help her make a pie for supper. I never did that before."

"What kind of pie did you make?"

"I don't know," the little boy said, "But it has cherry things in it."

"Sounds very good. I will be anxious to taste it."

"I don't know. We might have to cook another one. Egan gave a piece to Jeremy and Jason, so it is pretty much gone now."

"It must have been very good then."

"Are you sad now?"

"No. I think Aunt Van can make me another one."

"And me, too."

"Of course, that will be what makes it special." Ian chuckled, "What are you going to do tomorrow?"

"We are going to this place in the morning. I can't remember what they call it."

"Mass?"

"Yah, that's it. Have you been there?"

"Yes, I go every Sunday."

"Are you coming, too?" the little boy was excited.

"No, Dr. Turner said I have to stay here and get well."

"I know. He doesn't want you to wreck your arm."

"Ruthie told me that you are going to John Kelly's to have dinner after Mass. Is that right?"

"Isn't that good? Aunt Van said we are having chicken. I love those sticks a lot."

"What sticks are those?"

"Like, I forget. Those things that you bang for noise."

"Hm, I don't know. Do you like the wings or the legs? Oh," Ian guessed, "Drumsticks?"

"That's it! They are so cool!"

The four got dressed and into the shiny red Cadillac. Tater was very proud when Egan said it had the best shine of any car in Boston! Then they went to Mass. He sat between Aunt Van and Ruthie and watched everything with wide-eyed interest. When they left after the service, Father Colter shook his hand. "How are you today, young man?"

"Good," Tater said.

"I know your daddy."

Tater nodded, "So do I. He's in that place for sick people, but he is getting better."

"I know. We will see you again, soon I hope."

"That would be good."

When they got to John Kelly's house, Tater's eyes were as huge as saucers. "Does he have this big house?"

"Yes," Ruthie smiled. "He and his family."

"He must have a big family," Tater said.

Egan answered, "His dad lives with them. He can't see very well, so they take care of him."

"Why don't his eyes work?"

"He got a sickness in them."

"He should go see my Daddy's doctor. I bet he could fix him."

They went up to the door, but John Kelly opened it before they got there. Tater grinned broadly, especially when John picked him up and gave him a hug. Then Nancy came out to invite them in. Inside, they met the rest of the family. There was Big John, John's father, and the children, Tony, Tammy and Turk. Tony and Tammy were twins that were nine-years-old and Turk was seven. The older kids just said hello and went off to do whatever they were doing before. Turk, however, took Tater's hand. "I'm your cousin."

Tater looked at Ruthie and shrugged, "What's that?"

"It means that one of your parents is a brother or sister to one of his parents."

Tater frowned and then asked, "Is it a good thing?"

"It's a great thing," Egan said. "You and Turk are cousins."

"Okay." Tater shrugged.

"I can show you stuff, if you want?" Turk asked.

Tater looked at Ruthie and she said, "Sure, if you want to." Then she smiled at Turk, "Maybe not far because this is all new to him."

"I know. I can just show you our dog."

"Egan has a dog. His name is Otis."

"I know Otis," Turk said. "Our dog is named Rascal. He's in the backyard. Want to see him?"

Egan said, "I can come with to tell Rascal hello."

After the three went out back, Nancy asked, "How is it going?"

"Good. There is a lot of new stuff for him, but he is doing quite well. Still terrified of the dark." Ruthie explained. "Mrs. Feldman says he was never like that before the kidnapping. He talks about 'that box' a lot. He is very hesitant about anything to do with closets and stuff like that."

John Kelly shook his head, "Don't blame him. I tell you, I've even had dreams about it. How in the hell anyone could do that to another human being amazes me."

Nancy raised her eyebrows, "Well, I'm glad he did. He was supposed to kill him, you remember. I know it was horrible, but it is better than the little guy being dead."

They turned and looked at her in shock, "Why didn't we think of that?"

John Kelly kissed her cheek, "That's why I love you. You always find something good in everything."

Dinner was fun and Tater was happy that he was allowed to eat his drumstick with his fingers. He and Turk each had one. He had a lot of fun with Turk, who told him all about Ian and Ruthie's house. Turk was extremely knowledgeable about it. He told him that it didn't have any big trees to climb, but maybe some would grow. Tater was glad about that, he guessed.

Turk told him about Charlie and CJ, his best buddies out there in North Dakota. He said they would be his friend, too. He would have his Mom call so he could tell them to be. Tater thought that was a good idea.

Turk explained that Grandpa's place had a lot of fun stuff for kids. "You are a lucky duck to get to live by there. I wish I could, but we live here. We are going to come visit before school starts, or after it does. So I will get to see you in a few days. See, we go on a big plane and then Grandpa picks us up in his car. We drive a hundred hours to get to his house."

"Will you be so old when you get there?"

"No, just a little."

"Does he have a red Cadiddac, too?"

"No. Dad, what kind of car does Grandpa Carl have?" Turk yelled.

"A Mercury."

Turk turned to his little cousin with authority, "He has a Mercury."

Tater raised his eyebrows, "Is that good?"

Turk asked his dad, "Is that good?"

"Yes," John Kelly laughed. "It is a fine car."

Turk turned to the little boy, "It is a fine car."

Tater nodded with his newly acquired wisdom, "Good."

That evening, Tater talked to his Daddy on the phone, "That Turk kid was pretty good. He told me about your house and Grandpa's. He said that you don't have a doggie, but that Grandpa is getting one."

"Yes, Grandpa will probably have his dog before we get home, so you will get to meet him."

"Turk said I should call and tell him if it is a good dog. Can you help me? I don't know what kind that is?"

"I'd be glad to." Ian said, "Mostly a good dog is the kind that you love and loves you."

"Like a coyote?"

"Coyotes don't like living with people. It makes them nervous. They are much happier to live with other coyotes. Maybe when we get home, we can see if we can find a dog that you might like. Would you like that?"

"Don't you have one?"

"No, we have a kitten. Her name is Sprite."

"I never had a kitten. Is she fun?"

"She likes to play with a feather on a string."

"That sounds sorta dumb."

"It is fun. I'll show you when we get home. Okay?"

"Okay. Turk says he is going to tell these other guys to be my friend. I think they are Chardie and CJ."

"Yes, they will be glad to be your friend."

Later when he was telling Ruthie goodnight, Ian said, "Yea gads, Turk told Tater that Charlie and CJ would be his friends. I don't know how scary that will be. Those two lunkheads invented the word mischief."

Ruthie giggled, "What's the fun of being a little boy, if you can't be mischievous?"

"Do you remember when Charlie put that container of chicken poop in the refrigerator?"

"Oh, I forgot about that."

The next afternoon, Van and Ruthie took Tater to see his doctor. Dr. Walker examined him. After the exam, he suggested that Van and Tater could go out to find a book in the waiting room while he talked to Ruthie.

As she sat in the chair across from his desk, she felt panic setting in. "What is it? Is he okay?'

"His leg is a lot better, but his arm is still very sore from being twisted so severely. However, if he does his exercises, he should be back to normal in a few days. How is he doing otherwise?"

Ruthie explained about his fear of the dark and aversion to closet-type places. "Actually, I think he is doing very well, considering."

"So do I," Dr. Walker agreed. "That experience would take some time to get over for anyone. Is there someone that you will have back home for him to talk to?"

"My niece, as I told you before, had a horrific early childhood, and she sees Dr. Samuels. He's a psychiatrist and a friend of my brother's. Zach is a pediatric surgeon there."

"You think that Dr. Samuels would be your choice to look after Tater?"

"Yes."

"I would like to send Tater's medical records... Well, all his records, to someone back there to assure continuing care. Who would you suggest? Your brother or Dr. Samuels?"

"My brother. I can give you his clinic address and phone number. He will oversee his medical care and he would be the one that would set up an appointment with Dr. Samuels in the first place." Ruthie shot the doctor a worried glance, "Are you expecting a problem?"

"No. However, we know there is already one. Adults can have a difficult time dealing with trauma from an abduction. He has that and a whole new set of people and situations to deal with. It isn't going to be a walk in the park." Dr. Walker noticed her expression, "I'm not saying that you and your husband will not handle it well. It is just that some of these things will require more than what the average person is equipped to deal with."

Ruthie nodded, "I do know that. I guess I was just hoping that a chocolate chip cookie would solve the problem."

"Oh, if that was the case!" Walker smiled, understandingly. "I will call your brother and we can have a talk. Then I will send off Tater's file to him. I would like to see him next week, if you can. It would be helpful if he would exercise his arm a little more, but he is doing okay. When he comes in to your room at night, visit with him and then take him back to his room. Don't make a big issue about it though. Okay?"

"Most of the time, I don't even wake up. He just crawls in bed. When I realize he's there, he is already asleep. Should I wake him?"

"Only if it is early in the night. Remember, Ian will be home next week. I assume you share a bed. How many people can sleep in one bed, especially if one person has an injured arm?"

"I know, huh?" Ruthie nodded, "I did think about that. I just don't want to scare Tater or be too strict with him."

"You have to keep certain rules. No matter what. If you give in to his every whim, you will create a monster that will take an army of swordsmen to control. You don't want that. However, don't make him sleep in a dark room or go into a closet. Give that some time. It would be good if Tater could get some confidence with the other things in his life before he has to face that."

"You know," Ruthie said quietly, "Someday he is going to want to know about his real mom and what happened. That will be a nightmare."

"Depends. There may never be one big revelation day. It may just come out in bits and pieces over time. Don't try to keep it buried. That gives it more power."

"Ian and I are expecting a baby in October. We haven't told him yet and don't know what to say?"

"A lot like you told me. You can tell him that he will have a new brother or sister. Behave like it is something that he can be happy about. He might really like that." Dr. Walker leaned back, "I will call your brother. I feel good about Tater's situation and I think that he will do well. Could you make an appointment out front for next week?"

Ruthie stood and shook his hand, "Thank you, Dr. Walker. I appreciate you taking time with us."

38

Tater and his daddy talked on the phone each day and compared how they were doing with their 'exercises'. After Ruthie explained to Tater that the exercises for his arm were like Ian's therapy, he became more interested in doing them. They would compare notes and decide how much harder they had to work to heal up.

The week was rather quiet and pleasant, compared to the previous time. The family did their chores, Tater and Egan polished the car and the ladies did the housework. Otis loved having a kid around and the little boy loved him. The neighbor boys came down almost every day to play ball and talk about cars.

Ruthie and Ian asked John Kelly and Nancy to be Tater's Godparents, and they were delighted. Greg was very moved when he was asked and could barely talk. "I have never been asked before. I don't know if I will be good at it, but I would consider it an honor. Of course, I will!"

Ruthie talked to Father Colter and Reverend Carson about the time and place. Then she and Van made the arrangements. The baptism would be at Father Colter's church and afterwards they would go to the restaurant that Nancy had chosen for brunch after the burial. They could have a private room there and there was a beautiful park right next door.

Invitations were given to Dr. Turner and Dr. Walker. They were also extended to Ian's family. The expected repercussions from Vivian and Colleen were less than anticipated. Apparently, Jamie had really given Vivian a lecture about it, while Colleen had received a stinging lecture from her mother. They let their disapproval be known, but were much more restrained. The baptism would be on the last Friday Ian's family would be in Boston. They were scheduled to head back to their home in North Dakota on Saturday.

Because he had no other distractions and few visitors, Ian was able to make a lot of progress that week. Dr. Turner said he was living proof that turmoil in one's life had a lot to do with their physical health. His release was scheduled for Saturday, if he signed in blood that he would behave. He did.

Ruthie had spent a lot of time the next nights after the doctor visit, taking Tater back to his room when he wandered into her bed. They would visit and she would take him back to his room. It was showing a little success. He didn't crawl into her bed, but would stand on beside her and tap on her shoulder until she woke up. Then they would talk and find a book to read, so he could so back to sleep. He rarely slept more than two or three hours without getting up and checking to see if she was there.

Thursday, Egan had an idea. At breakfast, he announced that Otis was getting lonesome at night. He asked, very officially, if Tater could help him take care of Otis. The little boy was more than willing to help. That night, they made a bed for Otis on the floor by Tater's bed, so he could sleep there. It worked well and Tater didn't come into Ruthie's room at all. However, in the morning, Tater's bed was empty. He and Widey were sleeping on the floor with Otis.

Egan asked Ruthie if she would allow that and she smiled, "Who can say no when you see that little guy with his arm around that old dog. They both love it. I only have one concern."

"What's that?"

"What's going to happen when we go home?"

"Hm. I would say you could take Otis, but he is really too old to be in quarantine, travel and all that. Doggone it! I thought it was a good idea."

"It is a great idea. I think I need to make a phone call."

Ruthie talked to Ian and then she called back to North Dakota. She talked to Kid, a friend of theirs who trained dogs. She told him the situation and he said he would see what he could do. "Does he or you have a preference what kind of dog he would like?"

"He loves Wile E. Coyote, but I know coyotes don't domesticate. So, I can't tell you. Otis is an ancient, overweight Basset Hound. I really don't think that he would care."

"I'll see what I can do," Kid promised. "How soon will you be home?"

"About a week or two."

"I will try to find one right away then. Tell Ian hi for me and you guys take care! Sounds like your last week has been downright boring!" Kid laughed.

"Boredom is very underrated. I love it."

"I can imagine. I will get something lined up for you. Not to worry."

Later that evening, Kid called and was very excited. "Ruthie! Guess what I can get? It is called an Alaskan Klee Kai. It is like a miniature husky or wolf dog."

"Would that be safe for Tater?"

"I talked to the vet in Minot who knows a guy that knows this lady in Alaska that started breeding them. She said that they are very intelligent and curious. They are very active and don't particularly like strangers. They are great family dogs if the children are careful with animals. Is Tater? Because these dogs don't put up with having their tails pulled and things like that. They have a tendency to hunt, so they have to be introduced cautiously to other pets. I can handle that for you. They are very smart and train well. I can get one. The woman is leaving today to visit family in Flin Flon. She has some she isn't going to breed, because she wants only ones whose markings are symmetrical of something. She said if I drive up to Flin Flon, she will bring one for us."

"I don't know. I've never heard of them before."

"This lady says that they are like a miniature husky. They have very expressive faces and she has a grey-white, a brown-red and a mostly white. I think the brown-red would look the most like a coyote, but it will not get bigger than about sixteen inches tall and about fourteen pounds. I would love to work with Tater on training him and that would also teach Tater about caring for animals."

"You sound like you want one!"

Kid chuckled, "I do. Honestly, I saw the photo this guy had of one. He was visiting the vet in Minot and I fell in love. I think I will get myself a grey-white one. I don't know what I think I need it for, but I just love it. Here, I wanted to raise cattle dogs! This lady says she just started breeding these dogs, so they aren't registered or anything fancy. They tolerate the cold very well. The pups she has for sale are weaned and mostly housebroken. They are three and a half months old. She doesn't want to keep these for breeding, so will sell them. We have to promise to spay them. What do you think?"

"I have no idea. I will call Ian and have him call your right back. Okay?"

"Great. I will wait right here by the phone. I need to let that lady know tonight."

Ruthie called Ian and he called Kid within minutes. "Hi. Ruthie told me you have just the ticket for us."

"I don't know, Man. You know it is a newer breed. It has predatory instincts and needs to be trained well. The lady said the breed is protective and good with kids, especially the females, but won't tolerate bad treatment. What do you think?"

"I think that Tater is very careful with Otis. But we don't know anything about training a dog; or a kid for that matter!" Ian laughed.

"I will be happy to do it. I told Ruthie, I'm thinking about getting one myself. I saw the picture of a gray-white one and fell in love. These guys all have very expressive faces and are surprisingly vocal. I think one that is red-brown, she called it Cinnamon, would look like Wile E. Coyote. If you think you'd be interested, I will go up to Flin Flon and get Cinnamon for you and Campfire for me."

"Campfire?" Ian chuckled, "What a name for a dog!"

"I kinda like it," Kid laughed. "And after all, why would a dog want to be called Puddles? Remember, I have a horse named Rapunzel! Well, I am supposed to call this gal back. She needs to know how many pups to bring and they are leaving in the morning for Flin Flon."

"You will train it?"

"Yes, sir, and work with Tater."

"Okay. If the dog turns out to be flighty or something, can you find him a different home?"

"I will do that."

"Okay, talk to Mom and she will give you a check for the lady. How much is this dog?"

"I guess about $100, and we have to promise not to breed them. So we will have to get them fixed."

"That's fine by me. Pups would be about all we need. Okay, I'll call Mom. And have her put a commission and travel in for you."

Kid laughed, "We will split the travel because I think I am going to get me a Campfire."

"You are really a nut. I hope you know that."

"I'm not the only one. Kevin is at home pleading with his wife right now so he can get one, too!"

The next morning, Kid called Ruthie. "Guess what? Kevin can get one. I called the lady and she will meet us in Portal. Then she will handle the border crossing and all that and we won't have to drive all the way to Flin Flon. So, I don't want any travel o expenses or commission."

"You should, you know."

"No, I shouldn't. That's final."

"Thanks. Ian said the one you want is named Campfire?"

"Yah, isn't that cool?"

"I guess. What is the name of the one that Kevin wants?"

"Qannik, (KUN-nik). It means snowflake in Inuit and she is white and the markings are a light gray." Kid grinned, "Sounds pretty. I hope we aren't all falling off a cliff with these guys."

"Oh Kid, it wouldn't be the first cliff we ever fell off!" Ruthie laughed.

Ian and Ruthie discussed the puppy on her next visit. "We are out of our minds. This is a new breed and not many steps down from a wolf. Tater loves Otis and he doesn't look any more like a coyote than an alligator! I don't think he would care a lick if he had a big old black lab."

"I know," Ian smiled. "But I think it is cool. I mean, I want it."

"Men!" Ruthie shook her head, "Kid says they tend to hunt. What if he tries to kill Sprite?"

Ian took her hand, "Kid says he will introduce them."

Ruthie stared at him, unconvinced, "Now I have to worry about a little boy with claustrophobia, a dog that thinks it's a wolf, a cat that may end up dinner and a husband that is worse than all the rest!"

Ian laughed, "I know! Don't you just love it?"

"I hope you realize that Tater probably can't even say Cinnamon."

"You and I both know that he will call his dog Widey."

"Maybe so, but will the dog know?" Ruthie got a funny look, "Is it a male?"

"Female. Don't worry, we had to promise that we would get them all fixed. The lady doesn't want people all over breeding them. Besides, we are going to have a new baby. I think we will have enough going on in our world, that we don't need puppies."

"Thank goodness." Ruthie kissed her husband. "Well, tomorrow is the big day. After your tests tomorrow morning, we will hear when to pick you up. Ready to come home?"

"You have no idea how ready."

It was about eleven when Dr. Turner called. "I'm doing myself a favor and returning your guy to you. Pick him up as soon as you can. He scares me to death!" Turner laughed. "I have to say, caring for him has been the most unbelievable experience that I've ever encountered! I will admit though, this last week when he decided to be a patient instead of Boston Blackie; he has made a lot of progress. He will need to go to therapy every morning for about three hours, but other than that, just try to keep him from jumping out of helicopters!"

Ruthie giggled, "I promise. We will be there in about half an hour, depending on traffic."

Ruthie and Van went in to get him while Egan and Tater waited in the red Cadillac. Ian stepped out of the wheelchair at the hospital door and took a deep breath! "It feels so good!"

Tater and Egan got out of the car, to help them put his things in, and Tater gave him a big hug. "Now, we are a really family. Right?"

"Right, Tater. We are a 'really' family."

After a light lunch, Ian took a nap. That afternoon, he was able to sit on the patio and watch Otis and Tater play together. Egan visited with him. "He's doing well, you know. His nights are challenging, but otherwise, he is a good little guy to have around."

"I have to say, Mrs. Feldman runs a good organization. After all the horror stories I've heard, I was worried."

"I think that is mostly some of the homes where the kids are placed. One has to remember though, that a lot of homes where kids live with their real parents aren't any picnic either."

"Amen to that."

That night Ian read his little boy a story and tucked him in. It was a pleasure for both father and son. Otis took his spot next to the bed. In the morning, Tater and Widey were on the floor again, but his time, Tater thought ahead. He brought his pillow with him.

The last week in Boston was fun. They mostly relaxed and enjoyed the company of each other. Tater was getting used to the routine and he and Ian spent a lot of time looking over the books about coyotes and wolves that Uncle Egan brought them from the library.

Kid called and said he and Kevin had met the puppy lady in Portal. They were delighted with their puppies, and started calling Tater's puppy 'Widey' to get her used to her new name. Kevin took his puppy, Qannik, home right away. But Kid had his hands full. Since he was still living at Schroeder's, who had a housecat, he had to keep the puppies in a pen in the barn. It was warm and safe, but the puppies didn't like it. Schroeder's family dog had eight pups and the Klee Kais were joined there by Carl's little Beagle, named Peanuts. Peanuts was about ready to go home, but Carl didn't want him until he was housebroken. Carl and Mo were the neighborhood babysitters, and as Carl put it, had way too many unhousebroken creatures around as it was!

Kid worried, because it would set back the housebreaking program with the pups in the barn. But they all had the idea to go outside to the bathroom. The worst thing was that all of those dogs loved to howl. Not simply bark, but howl. Nighttime usually led to a symphony, which everyone had horrid suggestions how to cure.

Finally, Kid gave up. He grabbed an old blanket and pillow and spent his nights in the barn. Kid figured he could last until Ian and Ruthie got home. The next day, they would take delivery of their dog and he was dropping Peanuts off at Carl's place. Kid was given permission to bring Campfire in the house, if he wouldn't hurt the cat. Rag's pups would be outdoor dogs, so it didn't matter.

Friday morning, Ian and Ruthie took Tater to the cemetery to put flowers on his mom's grave and so he could tell her he was going to North Dakota. He worried that she might be mad about it. They told him that she would be glad that he had a new home and would not feel bad, but he thought he should tell her goodbye.

Then they got ready for his baptism. They had spent some time talking to him about God and Jesus. Father Colter helped them and explained that he didn't have to know very much since many religions baptized infants. It was more so Tater would be comfortable with the baptism.

That evening, the Harringtons, Reverend Carson, Greg's family, Mrs. Feldman, Drs. Turner and Walker met at the church. Little Taylor Collins Harrington was baptized. He was well-behaved and didn't get frightened at all. Then they had dinner at the restaurant by the park. He got to play outside with Lonnie and his new best friend, Turk. He didn't get weepy until he had to start telling everyone goodbye. There were a lot of hugs and kisses and several tears. But there were also promises that they would see each other again. Since Ian's follow-up appointment was in early September, as was the finalization of Ruthie's adoption, they would all come back. They would get together again for a visit.

That night, Tater couldn't sleep. He came into Ruthie and Ian's room and patted her on the shoulder. When she woke up, he was crying silently. She sat up and scooped him into her arms, "What's wrong, Tater?"

"I think I should stay here with Egan and Van. You can go."

"Don't you want to be with us?" Ian asked as he came around the bed.

"Yes, but what's going to happen to Otis? He will be lonely and then what?"

Ian hugged his son, "I talked to Uncle Egan and he said that Otis can sleep in their room."

Tater thought about it and frowned, "Are they going to sleep in his bed? He can't sleep on top of beds, so I sleep with him. Will they? Cause he gets sorta scared if he's by himself."

"I don't know. I think we can talk to Uncle Egan about that in the morning."

Tater nodded, "Okay." Then he stood for a bit and said, "Can I sleep with you when we get to the other place?"

Ian picked him up, "We will work something out. You have my word."

Tater studied his face, "Does that mean no?"

"No, it doesn't. It means that there might be a surprise or two for you when we get to our home. I promise we will work something out that you won't mind."

"I guess."

Ian walked with Tater back to his room and they looked at some picture books for a while until he got tired again.

When Ian crawled back in bed, he cuddled with Ruthie, "I feel for the little guy. I know I don't like sleeping alone."

The next morning, there was a long, tearful goodbye between Tater and Otis. The little guy walked all around the yard with a face as droopy as the old Basset Hound. Egan looked out the window, "The poor tyke. I would feel bad, but I doubt the lad could take anymore despair."

Van rubbed her husband's back, "Your face is just as long. I'm surprised he wasn't more sad about leaving the Center than he was. He was there almost a year."

Ruthie agreed, "I thought about that too, but you know there was a big turnover there. Jerry was the only one who was there as long as he was. Besides, he likes you guys. I'm going to miss you, too."

Egan called Ian and Tater into the house, "Come on guys. It's time to go to the airport. Just think Tater, it will be your first real airplane trip. Won't that be exciting?"

Tater shrugged, "Will you tell Jeremy and Jason goodbye for me? I think I forgot to tell them."

Egan picked him up, "I will remind them, but you did tell them. You will see them again in no time. When you get back, we will have our stairs all fixed up again. You know, Otis, Van and I are going to stay in the country next week while the house is getting fixed. So, we won't be here anyway. Okay? No long face, little feller."

"Okay," Tater gave him a big hug. "I like it here."

"I liked having you here. When you come back, we will all be here waiting. Okay?"

The bustle of the airport and all the new sights served to distract Tater from his discontent. He sat by Aunt Van all the way to the airport. He had an emotional farewell to the red Cadillac, that was only appreciated by Egan. The older couple went with them as they checked their bags and got settled in the departing gates. Ian and Egan took Tater to the big windows and they watched planes land and take off. Then they were called to begin boarding. By the time they got on the plane, all of them were in tears, but there was little doubt that Egan took it the hardest.

Inside the plane, the young couple and their son found their seats and settled into their places. They had Tater sit between them. They decided if he wanted to see out the window, he could do it when they changed planes in Minneapolis. This time, they felt more comfortable having him between them. Ian sat by the window, so his bad arm had protection from bumps by the side of the plane. Ruthie didn't mind sitting in the aisle.

Ruthie watched Tater who was fascinated by all the seatbelts, overhead baggage and stewardesses. He had three short of a million questions, but about every tenth question was, 'do you think they miss us already?' Every time, his parents assured him that Van, Egan and Otis were thinking about him the same as he was thinking about them. They promised when they got to North Dakota, they would call so he could tell them about the trip.

Ruthie wasn't certain that he liked the take-off until it was over. He gripped Ian's hand with both of his during the whole thing and didn't let go until they were level in the air. Then, and only then, did he giggle. She remembered the first time she flew with Ian. She did almost the same thing.

The little boy's excitement turned to boredom within a short time. However, the stewardesses served breakfast right away and he thought their carts were cool. After he ate, Ruthie gave him his Widey comic book to look at. He was asleep in no time. Ian had lifted the seat arm up, so the little guy could cuddle by him. Ruthie smiled as she watched her husband with his son. When he noticed, he reached over and took her hand. "Remember our first trip?"

"I was just thinking about that."

"Tater gripped my hand about as hard as you did."

By the time they arrived in Bismarck, it was about seven-thirty in the evening, with an hour time change. They were all glad to get off the airplane and move around again. Matt and Carl were there to pick them up.

They greeted the weary travelers and met their new family member. After hugging his sister-in-law and brother, Matt knelt down to the little boy, "Hello Tater. I'm your Uncle Matt. I am your daddy's brother. I am very glad to meet you."

Tater shrugged, "Hi."

Then Carl introduced himself, "I'm Grandpa Carl."

"I'm Tater Coddins Harrington. This is my real daddy and my new mommy."

"I'm very glad to meet you." Carl said, as he shook his hand. "Did you have a good trip?"

"I guess so. Did we, Daddy?"

"Yes, we did." Ian answered, "And we are very glad to be home."

"Well, we are almost there. Let's go get our bags and get on our way. Mo and Diane have big kettle of soup waiting for when you get there, so you can eat before you go to your house."

"Great." Ian said. "Even though we were fed, airplane food doesn't quite cut it."

When Carl brought the car up, Tater looked at it. "Is this the Mercury car, like Turk said?"

"It is. Very good, young man."

"I helped Egan wash the red Caddidac. He says I am a good worker so I can work for you. We can make it shine."

"That's good to know. I will take you up on that."

Tater took Ruthie's hand, "Does that mean yes?"

"It does," she smiled.

Because of the long evening light on the northern prairies, Tater was able to see a lot of the countryside on the way to Grandpa Carl's house. However, it was cloudy and became dark before they turned into the yard almost an hour later. Tater did not like that. He was familiar with city nights, where there were streetlights. Rural nights had darkness. Black darkness scared him.

Once he was in the house, he was scooped up by his Grandma Mo. She gave him a huge hug and kisses, "Well, if you aren't the most beautiful Leprechaun I've been blessed to lay my eyes on! Joshua's Trumpet! It is a certainty that he belongs to you!"

While Carl Kincaid was a big man with an imposing build, Mo was short and cuddly with auburn hair, large blue eyes, big friendly dimples and a welcoming demeanor.

As Mo hugged her son, Tater took Ruthie's hand. "Do you know what she said?"

"Yes, I do. She talks like Uncle Egan," Ruthie said. "You'll get used to it."

Tater raised his eyebrows in disbelief.

Then Matt's wife, Diane came over to him, "Hello. I am Aunt Diane."

Diane was about five-seven, slender and had a gracious, gentle manner. Matt, was taller than Ian, with the same coloring, dark auburn hair and bright blue eyes but a slimmer build. He and Diane were both very friendly and liked children, and Tater liked them.

After all the greetings, Ruthie looked around, "Where is everyone?"

"We thought it might be nice to have a quieter get-acquainted meeting," Diane explained.

Ian agreed, "It has been a long day."

Before they ate, Ian asked to use their phone. "We promised Egan we would call when we arrived."

Tater listened and added, "And me, too."

"Of course," Carl said. "Wouldn't have it any other way."

The conversation was short, but Tater did get a chance to check if Egan remembered to have Otis in their room. Egan replied, "I just moved his bed in our room before you called. He's already to go to sleep."

"Will you talk to me again?"

"We will be talking tomorrow. Okay?"

"Okay. Bye," the tearful little boy handed the phone back to his dad and ran quickly to Ruthie for a hug. "Egan said we can talk tomorrow."

"That's great, Tater."

Grandma Mo asked Tater, "Do you want to eat first or look around?"
Tater shrugged and took his Daddy's hand. Ian suggested, "Since we are getting tired, maybe we should have some soup first. What do you think?'

Tater nodded, studying his Daddy the whole time. Then he wiggled his Daddy's hand and Ian bent down to him, "What is it, Tater?"

"She looks like you."

Ian smiled at his Mom, "That's because she is my mommy."

Tater raised his eyebrows with a giggle, "You have a mommy?"

"Yes. That is why she is your Grandma. She is also Matt's mommy and Jamie's."

"Is she John Keddy's mommy?"

"No, but she is Nancy's mommy."

"Does she know about Turk?"

Maureen smiled, "Well, I do for certain! He is one of my Leprechauns too!"

Tater looked at her, "What is that thing?"

Maureen picked him up, "See Laddie, in the country where all the Harringtons come from, there a little people. They are called Leprechauns. They are smaller than you. They live in the forests and make shoes! They are like fairies or sprites."

Tater turned to Ruthie, "Is your kitty a sprite?"

"That is her name, but she is a kitty."

"There is a lot of stuff to know about here." Tater said as he sat on the stool Grandpa put out for him.

"It just takes a bit of time and you will have it all figured out."

"Okay."

After they said grace, they ate their potato-leek soup. "Wow!" Ruthie said, "I really like this. Is it a new recipe?"

"No, I just haven't made it for a while." Mo looked at her grandson, "Do you be liking it?"

Tater nodded, "It is good. What are those things?"

She looked where he was pointing, "I heard that you like bubblegum cupcakes. Is that a fact?"

Tater nodded, "Yes."

"Well, I made some. After your soup is gone, maybe you would like one."

Tater looked at his Daddy, "Can I?"

"If you finish your soup, you sure can."

Over their soup, Ruthie and Ian caught up on all the neighborhood news. There was little conversation about their own adventures, although everyone knew about it. Because of all the phone calls while in Boston, their friends understood the situation with Tater.

After his soup was gone, Tater got his cupcake and was very happy about that. Grandpa Carl asked him what he wanted to see first, "Would you like to see your fishing pole and shovel? I heard that you wanted to see the slide in the house, or your cube?"

Tater shrugged, "Daddy, Egan and I went fishing with John Keddy and Turk one day. We went to the park and there was a fishing place. I got a baby one, but we had to put him back in the water so he could play."

"Sounds to me like you are quite the fisherman. Well, I got you a fishing pole and shovel of your very own. It is outside in the shovel shed." Carl smiled, "We can go out right after we have our coffee."

"You mean out there?" Tater pointed to the large patio windows that opened on the pitch-black prairie.

"Yes. It isn't far from the house."

Tater looked out the windows and then said, "It is dark out there."

"We can turn on the light."

"A big light? Will it be light all over out there?" Tater patted his Daddy's arm, "Can I go see it in the sunshine?"

Ian put his arm around him, "You sure can. Carl, I think Tater would rather see it in the daytime."

Carl nodded, "Fine idea! Then we can see the ducks, too!"

"You have ducks? I fed some at this one park."

"I do. When you come back, I can show you the whole yard. We can see the shovel shed at the same time."

"Okay," Tater said, as Ruthie wiped the frosting off his cheek.

"So, want to see the slide?"

"I guess so."

Carl, Matt and Ian went with him to the bedroom hall where Carl had built in a playground slide to the basement. It was inside a closet and was actually there to be used in case of a tornado. Carl worried if he could get all the children downstairs in a hurry, so he devised this. In the basement, the slide's landing was a large mattress inside the reinforced room where they would be safe from a tornado.

All the safety measures escaped Tater. He didn't like the small closet-type space the top of the slide was in. Nor did he appreciate the fact that the slide disappeared into the darkness below. He looked at it from the center of the hall while clinging to his Daddy's hand with all his might. All he could do is shake his head no. Matt and Carl both realized he wasn't comfortable and decided to find something more fun.

When they came back into kitchen eating area, Mo asked, "Did you be thinking you would like to slide down there?"

Tater shook his head, "No."

Then Mo realized by the expressions on the men's faces what was probably wrong. "Oh, well then you don't have to. There is plenty to do here."

Carl said, "We thought we might go into the Gopher Room and show him the toys and his cube."

Diane asked Matt to help her put Mo's crockpot on the high shelf and the rest of the group went into the Gopher Room. It was a large, open room directly off the kitchen eating area. Most the kids Mo and Carl babysat for loved to dig, either in sandbox, garden or any place there was dirt. It was their major activity. So, they were called Gophers and the Gopher Room was their playroom.

On one long wall of the Gopher Room, Carl had carefully built 'cubes' for each of the children. They were about three feet tall and eighteen inches wide. Inside each was a coat hanger and the rest of the space was for their toys, mittens or whatever they brought along when they came to the Petunia Patch for the day. It was their very own cube. They were painted the child's favorite color, inside and out, and the outside of the door had their name and a picture of their favorite thing, since the littlest kids could not read. The kids all loved their cubes and usually made a bee-line for them as soon as they came in the house.

The family went into the Gopher Room, which had children-sized tables and chairs and shelves on another wall with children's books, toys and games. Except for the huge, uncurtained sliding doors that looked out into the darkness, the room was comfortable for Tater. It was a lot like the playroom at the Center.

Then Carl motioned to the cubes, "You have to see these, Tater."

It looked like a wall of cabinets, brightly colored with pictures on the front of each door. "Can you pick out which is yours?"

Tater moved by Ian and put his arm around his Daddy's leg.

Carl said, "Lookie here Laddie, this one is green! Is that a color you like?"

Tater nodded with hesitation, but tightened his grip on Ian's leg.

"And who is on the door?"

Tater barely whispered, "Widey."

"Yes, this is your very own cube. I have a fine surprise for you! I built this just to your size! Come, see what's in your cube," Carl beamed as his opened the door to the cube.

Tater screamed and ran out the door toward the kitchen. Matt was just coming into the room and caught him. The little boy was shaking in terror. When he realized he was caught, he started to hyperventilate and cry. Carl and Mo looked at each other in shock, and Ruthie and Ian both suddenly realized what had happened.

Ian went to take his son, "Tater, it's okay. It is not a bad cabinet. You don't have to go in it."

"I want John Keddy." Tater pleaded, "John Keddy! He will help me!"

Ruthie was rubbing his back, "Tater, John Kelly is sleeping now. We are so sorry. This isn't a bad thing. Turk has a cube here, too. John Kelly would think it was okay."

The little boy tried to take a breath, but could hardly inhale. Ian and Matt took Tater into the living room and Ruthie explained to the rest of them. "I think this is too much for him. Ever since he was kidnapped, he is terrified of the dark and closet things. That man scrunched him into a small cabinet smaller than the cube. The man almost dislocated his arm because he didn't fit. When we said 'this is just your size' that is probably what he thought."

Carl turned pale, "Oh my God. I never in my life wanted to

frighten him. How could I have been so dumb as to do that? He probably hates me."

"Carl, don't blame yourself. Ian and I never thought of it either and we should have. We both knew that is why he didn't like the slide. He has told us both that it very dark here. We just never imagined this."

Carl looked at Mo, "Do you think I should talk to him?"

Diane patted his arm, "Let me go see how he is doing before you do. Okay?"

In the living room, Matt and Ian were comforting Tater. He had calmed down a lot but was still trembling. Diane knelt down by him, "You better now, Tater?"

He looked at her in anguish, "I think I'm going to throw it!"

Ian took him and dashed to the bathroom, where the little guy threw up his soup. Ruthie went in and helped them get cleaned up. Then they talked a bit. While he was sitting on the bathroom counter, Ruthie hugged him, "Tater. We are very sorry you became frightened. This is nothing to be scared of, really. Grandpa would never hurt you, ever."

"I don't like that box."

"We know," Ian said. "We feel just terrible that you got scared. Can you come out with us now?'

"No. I want to go back to the Center. It's good there."

Just then, Carl came to the door, "Tater."

The little boy looked at him in panic, but Carl continued to talk calmly, "There is someone on the phone that would like to talk to you. I called John Kelly and told him the big mistake I made. Will you talk to him?"

Tater put his arms around his daddy's neck in a death grip, "I guess."

Ian took him out to the phone and sat down, while Matt held the phone for Tater. When Tater heard his voice, it was the first time he relaxed. Tater said, "I want to come back to the Center. Can you come get me?"

John Kelly talked calmly to him, "Tater, my buddy, I promise you that if there is anything that you should be frightened of, I will come get you."

"Okay."

"You know what? I don't think this is one of those things. I know Grandpa Carl and Grandma Mo very, very well. They would never, ever hurt a little kid. Ever. I am positive about that. Okay?"

"He said he made the box my size!"

"He meant that it is big enough for your stuff and you can reach it. He never puts any kids in the cubes. Can you ask Matt to show you? There are no kids in any of the boxes."

Matt said, "I will move to the Gopher Room phone and we can open all the cube doors. Okay?"

Tater was not very happy about it, but since he was in his Daddy's arm, he figured he could look. He wouldn't let his Daddy go all the way into the room, however. They stood in the doorway. Ruthie held the phone while John Kelly talked calmly to him. The rest opened all the doors of all the cubes. There were only toys, shoes and sweaters in them. Then Tater said to John Kelly. "There is just stuff in them."

"See, I told you. Turk has one, too, and he loves his cube."

"Matt showed me his rocks he has in there."

"Yah, he collected them when we were out there. Do you feel better now?"

Tater didn't answer and then John repeated the question. Tater answered shyly, "I feel like a stupid kid."

John Kelly chuckled softly, "You have no reason to feel like that. You didn't know. I might have made the same mistake myself. You know, Carl used to work for the FBI. Do you remember? Those were the folks who helped us find you? That is what Carl used to do for his job, so I know he would never hurt you. In fact, I know he feels really bad that he scared you."

"I'm sorry I got scared."

"You never have to be sorry for that. Tater, will you be okay now?"

"I guess. I love you, John Keddy."

"I love you, too. And I know something else, Grandpa loves you, too." John Kelly said, "Are you okay now?"

"It is okay."

"I have to go back to sleep now, okay?"

"Bye bye." Tater said and handed the phone back to Matt.

Tater put his arms around his daddy. Matt thanked John for taking the time with Tater. "I'm very glad you called. That little guy damn near died in that box, so I can understand his terror. I think when I get to work tomorrow, I might make a trip over to lock up and kick the crap out of that degenerate that put him in the cabinet!" John Kelly said. "Call anytime. Hope I helped."

"You really did. Thanks again" Matt said as Ian said into the phone, "You're the best!"

Mo came over to Tater and said softly, "Should we just let these guys close all these doors and turn off the lights. Maybe you would like another cupcake, since you didn't keep yours in your tummy very long."

Tater looked at her and shrugged, "Maybe just the frosting."

"We can do that," Mo smiled. "Come, Daddy can help you climb up on your stool."

They all had another cup of coffee and then got ready to leave. Matt and Diane were going to drop them off at their house on their way home. At the door, Carl couldn't stop apologizing. When he gave Ian a quick hug, Tater looked at him. "I'm sorry I was a scaredy cat."

"I'm sorry I frightened you. I don't know where my head was," the older man said.

Tater grinned and pointed to his forehead, "Right there!"

Carl chuckled, "Well, I guess you are right! Do you think we can be friends?"

"Okay, but I don't want the box. You can give it to somebody else."

"How about we just keep it? In case, you ever want to use it. Then you will have it."

Tater looked at him, "I won't."

41

Matt and Diane helped them carry their bags into the house and upstairs. They said that if they needed any help with anything, to give them a call. Ruthie and Ian were certain that they were fine, but thanked them. "I really appreciate your help." Ian said, as he gave his brother an embrace.

"We are just glad you are home."

Ruthie smiled, "Yes, thank you."

Diane gave Tater a hug, "You take care of these guys for us. Can you do that?"

Tater nodded, "I guess."

"I know you will. Maybe I will see you tomorrow?"

"If Mommy and Daddy say we can."

Ian nodded, "I don't know how much we are going to do tomorrow. It looks like we might need to slow the new experiences down a bit."

Matt nodded, "I understand. Just turn off your alarms and get some rest."

Ruthie went into the kitchen where all their mail was stacked neatly on the counter. Ian went to the refrigerator and opened it, "Look! I think Mom was here! Fresh milk, bread and leftovers!"

"Are you hungry?" Ruthie asked.

Tater had joined his Daddy in front of the refrigerator. "No," Ian replied, "Just checking what we have in here. Right, Tater?"

Tater nodded. Then they heard a soft meow. Tater's face lit up and he looked at Ruthie, "Did you hear that?"

"It sounds like Sprite. I know a secret way to call her." Ruthie giggled, "Let me open a can of her cat food first."

Ruthie put a can of fresh food in her dish and then turned on the can opener. Sprite came running like a flash. Tater giggled, "She comes quick!"

Ian chuckled, "She thinks whenever she hears the can opener, she is getting fed!"

He and his son petted Sprite while she ate. Tater asked if he could pick her up, but Ian suggested that they wait until Sprite was finished with her dinner.

After Sprite ate, Ian put her on Tater's lap for a couple minutes. He petted her a couple times and she left. Tater shot a worried look to Ian, "Is she mad at me?"

"No, she does that. She'll be back later. She goes wherever she wants."

"Oh." Tater looked at her. "Now what?"

"What do you say we go check out your room?"

The little boy took his Dad's hand and they went upstairs. Ruthie turned out the lights and followed them.

Upstairs, Ruthie turned on all the lights. First, they went into Ruthie and Ian's room. Tater looked all around and then they went to the room next to it. The walls were a light green, the ceilings white and the carpet, bedspread and curtains were a medium green. Mo and Carl had fixed it all up for Tater. The sheets were Looney Tune characters, and Tater was especially delighted when he found a Wile E. Coyote on them. They showed him his bathroom and helped him into his pajamas. Then Ian turned on the two nightlights, one in his bathroom and the other in the bedroom. He and Tater picked out a book and they sprawled across the bed to read. Ruthie went to take her bath.

When she was dressed in her bathrobe, she came back in with Tater and Ian went to take his shower. She and Tater read until the little boy couldn't keep his eyes open. Then she kissed him good night and went out of this room. He had his Widey stuffed toy under his arm and seemed to be sound asleep.

She and Ian crawled into their bed and he put his arms around her, "I'm surprised he went to sleep that fast. I thought that must have really scared him tonight. Gee, Dad felt awful."

"The night isn't over," Ruthie said. "I felt badly for Carl. I don't know why we didn't think of it."

They were kissing passionately, when they heard a scream. They both tore down the hall to find Tater shaking and crying. It took a bit to get him settled down and then they started back to their bed. They no more than crawled in, when Tater was tapping on Ian's shoulder. "Daddy, that bad man is in my head! He keeps pushing me in the box. I don't like this house."

"I think it is just because it is all new. What do you say? Think that you might want to sleep with us tonight? Would that help?"

"I don't know. I might have to go back to the Center, huh? It was only a little bit scary there."

"I think you will quit thinking about that bad man very soon. Ruthie and I are here and we won't let anything bad happen to you. Okay? We locked the doors and checked the house. We are safe. The bad man is in jail and besides, he doesn't know where we live. Okay?'

"I guess." Tater said as he crawled in bed between them, "I don't think people should make dark boxes. I don't like them."

"I know, Tater." Ian kissed his son, "Now, if you are going to sleep here tonight, I need two promises."

"What are they?"

"That you don't wiggle all over and that you don't talk all night."

Tater giggled, "I won't."

The night was not quiet and peaceful. Tater woke up crying several times and it was obvious that the scare earlier had brought all his fears back to the surface. By the time morning came, they were all glad to get up. Tater was very happy that it was daylight.

He stood looking out the window for a long time and enjoyed it when Ian helped him see the trees by Matt's house and by Grandpa's place. He was happy to see Sprite and even happier when Sprite came into his room.

His room was 'prettier' in the daylight and he had a lot of fun trying to find all the Widey's on his pillowcase. When they were all dressed for the day, they went downstairs to the kitchen. He ran over to the refrigerator and reached as high as he could to open the door. Then he stood there like Ian had done the night before, "Come look, Daddy! We have milk and stuff in here!"

Ian chuckled and they stood there checking out the fridge for a while. Ruthie made cereal for breakfast and they had a quiet breakfast. Ian decided that maybe they didn't need to do anything except relax that day. They could miss Mass and dinner with the clan. They were all tired and wanted Tater to feel more settled before he had anything new to deal with.

The phone rang. It was Kid. He had talked to Carl and was going to bring Peanuts over to his place this afteroon. "I was wondering if you would like me to bring Widey up for you in about an hour? I heard you had a little problem last night, so I can keep him another day if you prefer."

"Not at all. We are staying home today, so it would be a good day to do it."

"Okay, I'll bring him up in an hour or so."

"Do I need anything to get him set up?"

"No, I was up and got him acquainted with Sprite the other day. So, we should be good."

"Oh Kid, could you let Nora know we won't be coming today for dinner? We want to take getting acquainted a bit slower than we had planned. We were plagued with nightmares all night."

"I know how that is. No problem." Kid said understandingly, "I will let her know."

While Ruthie cleaned up the kitchen, Ian and Tater walked outside to look around. The little boy was excited to see their cars and the yard. He thought the garden looked pretty. He saw some horses in the pasture across the road and was very excited when Ian told him which horses he and Ruthie had. "My horse is that one. His name is Laramie. Ruthie's is that spotted one and her name is Cheyenne. I suppose after you learn how to ride, we will get you a horse. What would you think about that?"

Tater shrugged, "I don't know how to ride a horse."

"Don't worry, we have a friend named Kid who will teach you how. He is a good teacher."

"I don't go to school."

"I know. He will come over to teach you here. Okay?"

"Okay."

Father and son were just finishing their exercises when there was a knock at the door. Ruthie answered the door and invited Kid inside. He was carrying a cardboard box. He gave Ruthie a kiss on the cheek and then said hi to Ian. When he looked at Tater, he grinned, "You must be just the fellow I was looking for."

"Me?"

"Is your name Tater?"

Tater shrugged, and he put his arm around his daddy's leg. "What is your name?"

"My name is Kid. I have a present here for you from your Mom and Dad."

"Where is it?"

"In this cardboard box. Would you like to see it?"

There was a bit of squeaking and semi-barking from within the box. Tater listened and smiled, nodded eagerly, "Can I?"

Kid set the box down and opened it. He knelt down and handed the puppy to Tater. The little boy could hardly breathe he was so excited, "For me?"

"Yes," Kid said. "Think you will like her? She is all yours."

The little boy's eyes were huge and he hugged the puppy. "Is her name Otis?"

"No. Her name is Widey."

Tater grinned at Kid, "Widey?"

"Yes." Kid said, "I can help you with her because you have to be very careful with her. She is just a baby yet. She has to have someone take her outside to the bathroom and you have to promise not to be mean to her. Can you do that for me?"

"I can if Mommy and Daddy say." He looked at them, "Can I?"

Ian gave him a hug, "You certainly can. That is why we got her for you."

"I can, Kid. I will take care of her good."

"I think you will." Kid and Ian watched them play a minute and Ruthie asked him if he wanted a cup of coffee.

"A quick one, then I have to get ready for church."

The adults sat down and visited for a minute. Ian watched them play, "Kid, the pup is just as sweet as can be. She looks like a wolf pup!"

"She won't get to be much more than a foot and a half tall. I think they are all so cute. Kev's is white and mine is gray and black. Widey is a female, and will need to be spayed. Females are more protective of children, so I think that will be just the ticket for Tater. I just love these pups. They are so vocal. They act like they are talking to you!" Kid had a list of careful instructions all written out for Ian. "Carl and I built a tiny dog pen in your garage. If you are going to be gone, put her in there. I wouldn't trust her running in the house and besides, dogs are cave animals by nature. They like a small, enclosed space. It comforts them. I'm sure it will be okay. Kevin's little Qannik is doing well. After dinner today, I'm bringing Campfire into the house. Then I don't have to sleep in the barn anymore."

"You poor thing!" Ruthie said. "I can't imagine you staying out there with them."

"I didn't want them to forget they were housebroken. Be sure to take her out right after you feed her. She cries when she has to go, so you should be okay. She only has to go out once during the night, usually. She is spoiled, so she will want a human around."

"That's okay." Ian nodded, "I think there is a human that wants her around. He hardly slept at all last night. Nightmares about his bad experience."

"That would do it. I sure hope he gets over that soon."

"We do, too. But this has been a lot of change in a few short weeks."

Kid watched him play with the puppy, "He is sure a good-looking kid and seems to be gentle with the pup. I think he will do okay. I will come up and show him how to train her and work with her. Any problems, just give me a call."

"Thanks," Ian smiled. "I think we just need some time."

"Well, I better go." The young man stood up, "Tater, I left a list of things that you need to know about Widey with your Daddy. He can read them to you later. Okay?"

"Okay. Are you going? Are you going to take Widey home now?"

"No, I thought I would let her live with you, if you want. She has to sleep in your room at night. Would you mind that?"

"No," Tater shook his head, "I would like that. You mean, she can live here?"

"Yes, sir. She is your dog. Treat her right and you will have a friend for life!"

Tater hugged him, "Thank you."

"Your Mommy and Daddy are the ones to thank. They told me to find you a puppy. I have to go now, so see you later."

"Bye," Tater smiled, "My puppy is way cool."

Ian and Tater spent the morning talking about the rules for the puppy and playing with her. After they had a little lunch, Ian and Tater took Widey for a walk until she did her business. When they came in, they decided to all take a nap. The whole family went upstairs and Ian asked, "Do you want to sleep with us or with Widey?"

Tater asked, "Are you going to leave the door open?"

"Yes, sir."

"Okay. I think I should sleep in my bed so Widey knows where her room is. Okay? Unless you are going to be sad if I don't sleep with you."

"I think we will be okay," Ian smiled. "We have each other."

Tater nodded, "Me and Widey have each other, too."

A little later, Ian and Ruthie peeked into Tater's room. The puppy was curled up in the crook of Tater's arm and they were both asleep.

Ruthie whispered to her husband, "I hadn't thought that I wanted the pup to sleep on his bed, but I don't mind at all. I think this will work."

Ian kissed his wife, "I do, too. You know, I think I need a nap with my wife."